Only a warm, sunny glow. One that had faded long, long ago.

She relaxed, snug in police officer Luke Northrup's safe embrace.

This was what she needed, Calli realized. Luke. Witty and compassionate, stubborn yet funny, he knew who and what he was. He had his priorities straight—fatherhood first, law enforcement second—and he didn't require anyone to affirm his convictions.

Yes, Sergeant Luke Northrup was a man of integrity.

Calli sadly backed away from him.

For the last thing *he* needed was a woman with none.

Books by Carol Steward

Love Inspired

There Comes a Season #27
Her Kind of Hero #56

CAROL STEWARD

Carol Steward has always been creative. She says, "When I was sixteen, I bought my first key chain. It said Bloom Where You're Planted, and I've tried to follow that advice ever since." She eventually followed God's leading to write inspirational stories about men and women overcoming insurmountable obstacles to find that special person who, along with Christ, can make their life complete.

Colorado has been home to Carol for more than thirty-two years. She and her husband have also lived in Wyoming and North Dakota. Their three teenagers keep their lives from becoming mundane. Together, their family enjoys sports, camping and discovering Colorado's beauty.

Having volunteered for several organizations, Carol encourages others to strive to learn something from each opportunity. "Raising my family is a very rewarding priority in my life. Their love and encouragement continually inspires my own personal growth."

Carol is a full-time child-care provider, opening her heart and home to six additional preschool children. She finds it very rewarding nurturing God's little miracles. She also enjoys exercising her creativity through tole-painting, sewing, needlework and cake decorating. Refinishing furniture and collecting Noah's Ark pieces are just a few of the extras that keep Carol busy in her "spare" time.

Her Kind of Hero

Carol Steward

Published by Steeple Hill Books

STEEPLE HILL BOOKS

ISBN 0-373-87056-6

HER KIND OF HERO

This edition published by arrangement with Steeple Hill Books.

Printed in U.S.A.

For when we were with you, we told you
beforehand that we were to suffer affliction; just as
it has come to pass, and as you know. For this
reason, when I could bear it no longer, I sent that I
might know your faith, for fear that somehow the
tempter had tempted you and that our labor would
be in vain.

—1 *Thessalonians* 3:4-5

Acknowledgments

To my father, Tom Bohannan, for a lifetime of insight on law enforcement and showing me that there's a hero in each of us. Ken, Todd, Tim, Ed and the Greeley Police Department for their insights and for letting me experience firsthand the excitement and danger of police work.

My husband and kids for their never-ending encouragement. Anne for having faith in my ability to write this story. Helen, Sally, Ellen, LeAnn, Lynn, Margaret, Linda and Bette for motivating me to write through this challenging year. And to the Creator for inspiring me to share these stories.

Chapter One

Calli Giovanni walked through the stained-glass doors praying that she would someday experience the peace of forgiveness.

Why can't I let it go?

''You can't get discouraged,'' her cousin Hanna said, following her through the doors. ''Don't expect healing to happen all at once. It isn't easy. Like tonight's speaker said, it's one miserable step at a time. For tonight, go home. Stop patrolling.''

''I can't, Hanna. I would think *you'd* understand. He was my kid brother. I want justice served. I can't let it go.''

''I do understand, Calandre. More than you think.'' Hanna took Calli by the shoulders. ''Who can't you forgive, Calli? The killer? Or yourself, for not seeing Mike slip out of the house?''

Calli turned and stared into her cousin's moist eyes. ''Neither.'' Her own tears dried up years ago. All that was left was this numbness. She was an emotional zombie.

''Don't you see what this is doing to you?'' Hanna asked.

"It's not worth it. You don't laugh. You don't cry. You barely exist." Hanna paused, then unlocked her car door. "Go home. It's time for you to stop."

Calli never finished her college degree. Her brother had been killed at the beginning of her last semester. She'd set new priorities. Priorities that cost her dearly. Her family, her fiancé, her happiness. All in hopes of finding answers. "That's easier said than done."

Hanna hugged Calli. "You can do it. Just don't give in. Sorry I have to rush off, but I'm expecting a call at nine-thirty. Take care." Her petite cousin slid into her sports car and waved.

"That's my problem, Han. I don't ever give up. I don't know how." Calli took off her down-filled coat and tossed it into the passenger's seat, her voice a whisper into the darkness. She watched Hanna drive away without a care in the world. "It's cost me everyone I loved, and I still can't let it go."

Her mother, father, older brother and even her sister were like distant relatives. They had put the past behind them and moved on. Recovered. Only she was stuck trying to erase the shadows lurking in her mind. Fighting the unknown in a city of dark corners and unlit alleys. Doing the only thing she could to avenge her brother's death.

Thinking of Mike, she closed the door and reached under her seat. Calli pulled out a zippered bag and stared at it, considering giving up on this thankless mission. She zipped the pouch open and emptied the contents into her lap. "Just one patrol before I head home. Maybe tonight's my lucky night." She tugged the long blond wig over her own hair and covered her lips with tropical punch-colored lipstick. Horn-rimmed glasses completed the disguise. *Good grief, I even look like Aunt Calandre.*

It was a quiet night in Palmer, Colorado. Calli spent over an hour cruising without anything to report. Feeling a sudden chill, she reached for the heat control, only to find it was already set on high and pumping hot air into the small compartment. *Calm down, Cal. There's not even any action.*

As she continued down the alleys and streets lined with dilapidated buildings, Calli prayed. "Though I walk through the valley of the shadow of death, I shall fear no evil, for thou art with me."

She perused the business district, then paused to consider what she was doing before turning toward the city's core. It was a neighborhood within a neighborhood. A place where nothing was sacred. Not property, not values and especially not human life.

The only thing flourishing here was the Eastsiders, a gang that preyed on the weak and helpless.

Maybe they would provide her with some clues. After all, that was the gang her brother had allegedly been joining when the "initiation" went too far.

Adrenaline pulsed through her veins as she turned into the parking lot of a dimly lit apartment complex. Her breathing became shallow and ragged. *Why do I keep doing this? Is it even worth it anymore?*

A shiver raced up her spine and Calli quickly glanced left, then right. The rays of the streetlight reflected off of the glistening ground. She dialed "911 send" on her cellular phone just as three figures bolted from the icy parking lot toward the apartments, dodging cars and jumping wobbly handrails. "Gotcha."

One threw a small crowbar at her, hitting the front fender.

"911 Emergency."

"Columbia Boulevard and 15th Street." Calli swallowed, trying to smooth her raspy voice as it scratched through the wires. "The Willows Apartments. There's broken glass everywhere."

One teenager slipped and fell to the ground. Calli skidded to a stop inches from him. He got up and looked at her, his dark eyes filled with fear. He glanced behind him, then stumbled ahead to where his cohorts had disappeared.

"Ma'am, are you there?" the 911 operator repeated.

Calli's heart pounded faster and she dragged in another breath. Shadows wrapped their arms around her. Streetlights flickered. Vines covered apartment windows like victorian lace curtains. Calli shivered. *Where'd they go?*

"Are you okay?"

"Fine. I'm fine. Three kids..." Calli pressed on the accelerator. She searched beyond the tinted glass for any movement as she drove slowly toward the exit to conclude the loop. She wanted desperately to leave before the officers arrived, armed with endless questions and expectations.

"They're wearing dark clothing, bulky coats." She paused, hoping to recall more. "One wore a starter jacket...and a bandanna. A blue bandanna." She turned the last corner before the exit. "They weren't very tall. Around sixteen, maybe younger."

The woman stopped her and repeated the information, then asked for more details.

Calli knew the more she could remember, the better the chance that justice would be served. "One had bleached blond hair, the other two had dark hair. I think one's hurt."

Sirens wailed in the distance, then abruptly stopped. They'd be here any minute. *Time to go.* Calli thought of the gang's leader with a wretched sense of pleasure. Another bust. She may not be able to find the proof she needed to put the gang's leader away, but she could make Tiger's "work" more difficult.

She stepped on the gas pedal but it was too late. A white police car fishtailed as it rounded the curve. It slid on the ice and headed toward her.

Calli pumped the brakes. Time stopped, and the terror seemed to continue in slow motion. It was no use. Her tires couldn't grip.

She pressed the brakes again. Harder. Still nothing. Finally she slammed her foot to the floorboard and gripped the steering wheel, directing her skid away from the police cruiser.

Her four-wheel drive slammed into the curb and jerked to a stop. Seconds later, the officer pulled closer and rolled down his window. The set of his strong, square jaw personified authority. She couldn't look away from the deep-set eyes and rugged features that expressed sincere concern.

Trembling, Calli opened her window. The dark-haired officer leaned out of his car. "Are you okay?"

She nodded stiffly, and they drove on, into the parking lot. *Pull yourself together, Cal. Get going.* She shifted into first and stepped on the gas.

The truck didn't budge.

Depressing the clutch, Calli turned the key. "Come on, start." Without allowing the engine to settle into an even idle, she pulled away.

"That was too close for comfort. I've got to get out of here. Where's the phone?" She found it in the far corner of the floorboard and shut it off, then turned south on Columbia Boulevard. A few minutes later, flashing lights beckoned in her rearview mirror as backup turned into the apartment complex. "They're all yours, guys. I've done as much as I can."

Calli's heart raced in an unsteady rhythm as the motor purred down the street. Four miles later, she pulled into the parking lot of Teodoro's, the Quonset hut-turned restaurant she frequented. She clicked off the ignition and leaned her head against the seat. *Darn it, Calli. You're pushing too hard. You've got to stop.*

Tugging the bristly hair from her head, she stuffed the

blond wig into the bag and let out a deep breath. She gazed into the rearview mirror, removed the glasses and studied herself disapprovingly. After wiping the gauche color from her lips, she applied ointment to help remove the remaining tint. The near-accident replayed in her mind as she yanked a brush through the matted mess of black curls. She had hung around too long, almost long enough to meet the cops in person. That was one complication she didn't need.

Stuffing the sundries and the makeup bag into her purse, she slammed the truck door, then walked to the restaurant entrance. Calli took a deep breath and tugged the glass-and-iron door open, anxious to meet friendly faces.

"May I help you?" the young woman asked.

Calli didn't even consult the menu. "Barbaccoa with black beans instead of pintos, and a large diet cola." She watched as rice and beans were piled onto the tortilla, then salsa and shredded beef. Last was the cheese and sour cream.

Teodoro's owner, "Teddy" Chavez, greeted her with a smile. "Your usual, eh, Calli? What are you doing out this late?"

She let his friendly wink soothe her nerves. A member of her neighborhood watch group, he knew very well what kept her out this late. Yet he always shared her silent celebration at making it through another night safely. She glanced at the staff, and went along with the conversation. "Couldn't wait for one of your burritos. Just thinking of them keeps me awake at night."

"That's no good. Ah, well, eat and enjoy." He turned to his employees and rattled off directions to them while Calli crossed the room and seated herself in the plywood chair. She rested her head in her hands and begged her heart to slow down.

Eating alone beneath the dangling halogen light bulb was much too comfortable. She sliced the giant burrito into two halves and set one aside for tomorrow's lunch. Her kid brother had always teased her about eating when she was upset. If he could only see her now. Listening to alternative music in a dingy restaurant, trying to forget the good-looking cop who'd nearly run her over.

Calli pulled the journal from her purse and turned to today's date.

January 22, 11:05 p.m.

She documented her evening's patrolling events, descriptions and response time of the local law enforcement on the blank pages.

Calli had started journaling in her early teens, as a way to deal with the loneliness of frequent moves, foreign languages and the other drawbacks of being an army brat. But in recent years the pages were filled with fewer emotions, and more details.

She thought through the events of the day, then wrote.

Has no one ever realized the guilt I feel? Surely they have. Over and again, Mom and Dad tell me it wasn't my fault—that Mike had snuck out before, that nothing anyone had tried had helped him. Why can't I move on?

It was not my fault. But maybe if someone had called the cops, maybe he'd be alive today.

She closed her eyes and whispered, "As in David's day, I see violence and strife in our streets, on city walls. Be my shelter and my strength, Father."

How can I stop now? Community involvement is making a difference. The neighborhood's crime rate has dropped. I have to keep trying.

The media tries to convince us that gangs are losing their appeal. They say gang members are frightened off by friends getting hurt and others sent to prisons. Yet, every week, I still see them out there, luring innocent kids into believing that they've found a place to belong. Tempting them with the promise of easy money. Trapping them into a life without hope.

Calli recalled the look in the youth's eyes as he stared at her. Fear, raw and exposed, spoke to her.

What was that kid looking back for? A way out, or someone they left behind?

Police sirens jolted her back to the present. The cruiser sped past the front of the restaurant. The officer she'd nearly collided with reappeared in her mind. His concerned gaze lingered there, like an unwelcome guest. Reflections of light glimmered over his handsome face. She shook her head. *He's just another cop. They all have that look.*

Thankful that she took the time to don her disguise, Calli wondered if they would place her as the caller. Did they get her license number? Hopefully she'd gotten away before they had the chance.

How can I give up now? There has to be a way to help kids like that.

The pen stopped.

Kids like Mike. She never believed that he wanted in to the gang. Never allowed herself to see him as needing something more in his life. Maybe she'd been wrong. About Mike, and the gangs, and thinking she could make a difference—to anybody.

She noticed the employees wiping Formica-topped tables, wrapping stainless-steel food bins and polishing the glass block room divider.

"Calli, we're closing." Teddy set a foil sheet next to her plastic basket. "For your leftovers."

She finished chewing and gulped her soda to wash the bite down her dry throat. After closing her journal, Calli wrapped the extra half. "Thanks, Teddy. Have a good night."

"You be careful out there."

"Always." She left the eatery, climbed into her truck and turned west, toward her apartment. It was after midnight, and morning would come early.

Fog rolled in from the river and a fine mist coated the streets with black ice. Even four-wheel drive wouldn't help in conditions like this. The light ahead turned green and Calli took her foot off the gas pedal. From the side street, a truck spun out of control.

She tried to determine a way to avoid it, but there was no escape. The truck rammed the passenger door, pushing her vehicle into another car parked along the street. Her head slammed into the driver's side window and shattered the glass.

Calli screamed, then covered her eyes with her hands, feeling a cold draft. She tried again to open her eyes, but they hurt too much. She pulled on the door handle, but the door didn't move.

"Help! *Help!* Someone help me." A few minutes later, sirens wailed. Voices commanded that she not try to move. Louder and louder the noise grew, then stopped. The fireman knocked away the remaining glass from the door. After the paramedic took Calli's vitals, he reassured Calli that they would have her out soon.

Calli awoke to pitch black. She tried to blink and found her eyes were covered. Reaching out, she felt a hard rail to her side. Her head hurt and her left arm ached. She vaguely remembered an accident and an ambulance.

Where am I?

The room was silent except for beeping noises in the distance. She licked her parched lips and grimaced. She heard breathing, then footsteps, followed by a warm deep voice.

"Calandre Giovanni? I'm Sergeant Northrup, Palmer Police Department."

The police? What are they doing here? Am I just imagining an accident? Or is this about the break-ins at the apartment complex? For all she knew, he may not even be a cop. "Where am I?"

"University Hospital. You were in an accident."

Calli gasped, then let out a moan as she tried to move. She must have been seated, as her mind was fuzzy. "What's wrong with me?"

"Let me call the nurse for you." He stepped out of the room, and was gone for a few minutes.

His voice sounded familiar. What were the chances that he was the patrolman who'd nearly wiped her off the road? Next to zero, she assured herself. If the officers who'd responded to that call had caught the kids, they were probably still at the juvenile facility booking them at this very moment.

When the cop returned, Calli decided she'd rather ask questions than answer them. She needed time to clear her mind. "Where's the nurse?"

"It'll be a few minutes before anyone can come down. Emergency room's a busy place tonight. You okay?"

"Do I *look* okay?"

He stammered a minute, then apologized. "I meant, you're not going to be sick or anything, are you?"

"I'll live. Were you the officer at my accident?"

"No. That would be Jake Williams. He asked me to take

your statement while I'm here. I came in with an unrelated ambulance call.''

Hysteria threatened to return to her voice. She swallowed, trying to soothe the scratchiness. Absently she ran her dry tongue over her lips.

''Need a drink?'' Without delay she felt the officer lean against the bed. ''Here.'' She lifted her hand, ready for him to place a paper cup in her hand. Instead she felt a strong hand wrapped around a huge insulated-type mug. Pursing her lips to drink, she jumped when she felt the brush of his fingertip against her lower lip as he placed a straw in her mouth.

He chuckled. ''Sorry, I forgot to tell you what to expect.''

Embarrassed that all of her assumptions were wrong, making her feel even more helpless, Calli resented the warmth of the personal contact between them. She jerked her hand away. ''Thanks. That's enough.'' The sooner she got rid of him, the better. The last thing she needed was a cop to keep her company. ''So what do you need from me?''

''Just need to ask a few routine questions. No hurry. I'm here waiting to talk to another patient. My partner's still on the streets. Sheesh, they're a mess tonight. You'd think these drivers had never seen ice before.''

Calli tried to sit up, and failed. She heard him bump into something, then felt a strong hand on her arm.

''Can I help?''

''I want the nurse. Where's the call button?''

His warm hand fumbled with hers and gently guided her fingers toward the side of her bed. His baritone voice was edged with control. ''Here's the call button.''

A calm confidence echoed his voice, and the scent of his aftershave sent a shiver of awareness through her.

Memories from her past tainted the image of this knight

in shining armor. Calli realized that not only did she not have a clue as to what Officer Northrup looked like, but she had no idea if this man was really a cop. *I've been watching too much television. He couldn't be the one I saw earlier.*

"I'm sure it's frightening not to be able to see anything. You may not even believe I'm a police officer. Who could blame you, after the night you've had?"

The fact that he'd read her mind made her more suspicious. "Sorry, I'm not used to..." *trusting people.*

"You're cautious, just as you should be under the circumstances."

"Cautious." Now that *is an understatement.*

Calli struggled to pull herself out of the fuzziness and remember more about the accident.

Shuffling noises followed by a nearby clank dragged her back to the present image of a cop sitting next to her bed, as if he planned to stay a while.

I've managed to avoid the officials for three years, and now, over a simple car accident, I'm trapped. "So, what did you want to ask me?"

"Can you tell me what you remember?"

Chapter Two

Luke finished Miss Giovanni's statement just as his partner radioed from the car that he was ready to call it a night. With all the reports they had to fill out, Luke didn't argue, but silently confessed he wouldn't have minded spending a little more time with Calandre Giovanni.

Back at the station, Luke opened the locker room door; a strange mixture of aftershave and gun metal slapped him in the face. After the night he'd had, a room full of his fellow officers should have been a relief. It wasn't.

He shrugged the blue shirt off and straightened his uniform on the hanger, trading it for his street clothes. The young officer next to him was doing just the opposite. "What a night," Luke said.

"What's wrong, lucky Luke? Tired of leaping tall buildings in a single bound?" Vic Taylor drawled with distinct mockery.

Luke felt the muscles in his jaw tighten when he saw the smirk on the rookie's face. In no mood to confront the kid, Luke attempted to be civil. "Nah, piece of cake, Taylor. One kid in a coma, a woman who narrowly escaped losing her eyesight, and a city full of drivers who act like they've never seen icy roads before. Not to mention the two punks in the slammer for breaking into a dozen cars and nearly beating the life out of a friend. All in a night's work."

"You are so lucky. You always get the excitement." Taylor spat a four-letter word as he poked a finger in Luke's face. "All week I've been called off before I saw any action. You'd think my wife worked in dispatch or something."

Luke laughed before he lost what little self-control he had left. "Don't be so eager, kid. The action's not all it's cracked up to be."

The rookie adjusted his belt and puffed his chest out, as if ignoring Luke's advice.

"And by the way, it has nothing to do with luck." Luke tugged the gray T-shirt over his shoulders and rubbed the ache buried deep in his muscle. He noticed his partner, Tom, coming into the locker room.

When Luke turned around, the rookie was strutting into the briefing room.

Luke flung the leather jacket over his shoulder then slammed the metal locker door closed. "What's Taylor's problem? If he thinks two hours of paperwork and tagging thirty items into the evidence room is fun, he's got a lot to learn."

His partner chuckled and slapped Luke's shoulder sympathetically. "Let it go, Luke." Tom continued. "I've learned the best way to deal with people like Taylor is to let their ignorant comments roll off your back."

The reality of his best friend's comment sobered him. Luke glanced at Tom and shook his head. "I'm sorry, Tom. After all these years, it just isn't right that a person's race still brings such discrimination."

"Nothing for you to apologize for."

An icy draft followed the command sergeant through the

door from the parking lot, his shotgun slung from one shoulder and bag in the other hand. "Good work tonight," he said, nodding toward Luke and Tom. "One by one, we're putting those gangs out of business. Did the kid come out of the coma?"

Luke shook his head. "I'm going to check in on him throughout the day. If he doesn't, we really need that witness. The two suspects won't talk." Luke chugged the last of his cold coffee, watching as Tom moved his duty weapon from his belt to a waist-pack "holster."

After securing his handgun, Tom looked at Luke. "I still think we had a break tonight. I'll lay you odds that our anonymous caller is that blonde you nearly wiped out in the parking lot."

"Just what we need. A woman determined to eliminate Palmer's worst gang single-handedly. Why doesn't A.C. volunteer at one of the after-school programs or something safe?"

"Maybe she already has gang connections."

Luke didn't like that possibility at all.

"We should check out gang members' ex-girlfriends. Could be one trying to settle a personal vendetta."

"Against the whole gang?" Luke shook his head. "No way. But whatever the lady's reasoning, she's playing with fire." An image of the flustered blonde in the white truck flashed into his head. Couldn't be her. After three years, A.C. would be too used to the streets to get that upset over a little skid.

He rinsed his coffee mug and set it in the cupboard to dry, then tossed his taped report to Tom. "Can't believe neither of us got a look at that license plate."

His partner placed both microcassettes in the manila envelope and filed them for transcription. "Nothing more we could've done. It was a bad angle. No light. Backup hadn't arrived. You know as well as I do, she was low priority."

"I should have told her to stay put so we could talk to her," Luke mumbled, continuing down the hall to the parking lot.

"Go home and chill. We're going to find A.C. It's just a matter of time." Tom disappeared from view, leaving only his footsteps echoing on the marble stairs.

"Don't hold your breath. She's as elusive as the Eastsiders' leader himself." Luke knew there were few on the force who believed that the same woman was responsible for the majority of their tips. Thank goodness, his partner happened to share his theory.

Tilting his head from one side to the other, Luke hoped to shrug off the tension in his shoulders and the headache lurking behind his eyes. Tom was right, he needed to loosen up. Twelve years on the force was going to be the end of him if he didn't find some way to enjoy life again.

He recalled the woman's dark eyes and fair skin—recalled the quick recovery she'd made, slipping back into control in those brief seconds of their encounter. Tom's suspicion that she was their informant crossed his mind again. *No way. I'm just not that fortunate.*

"Hey, Northrup. Hear your lady tipped you off again! One of these days, you're going to have to introduce us. Bet she's hot." Laughter followed as the officers from the next shift made their way to the squad cars and loaded their gear.

Luke feigned a good-natured rebuttal, too tired to care if they were being funny or serious. "Better watch it, boys. A.C. is good, and she just may be after your job."

The laughter stopped abruptly. Luke pulled his legs into the sports car and closed the door to the hoots and jeers that would follow his idle banter. Revving the engine, he backed out, then shifted into drive.

"Lord, help me find this lady, before it's too late."

* * *

Mrs. Maloney had already prepared Jon's breakfast and done the dishes when Luke arrived.

"Morning, Dad."

"Hey, sport. I'll take you this morning. Don't forget to return your spelling test today."

"I have it."

"Then let's get going. Traffic is a mess."

After he dropped his son off at school, Luke decided to stop for breakfast, then go by the hospital to check on the kid. And Calandre Giovanni.

Luke wasn't sure what it was about the woman that intrigued him. *Maybe it's that interesting name—Calandre.* He smiled. The name itself sounded strong. Determined. Spunky. And the woman? Well, the name fit. Perfectly.

He tried to justify seeing her again. *Am I crossing the line between personal and professional?* He didn't like the answer, so he looked at the situation from another angle. Deciding the least he could do was make sure she found someone to help her until the doctor allowed her to remove her bandages, Luke proceeded. Even one day without his eyesight would send him up the walls. *Nothing wrong with offering to help.*

Luke stopped at Teodoro's and greeted Teddy warmly.

"Good morning, Luke."

"Make me two breakfasts to go. Say, do you happen to know a blonde who drives a white 4 Runner in your neighborhood watch group?" Luke dug his wallet from his pocket.

"Blonde, 4 Runner," Teddy repeated, frowning. "No. Doesn't sound familiar. Something wrong?"

"We're looking for a witness. Thought she may have been the one. Thanks anyway, Teddy." Luke waited for his food, then paid and left.

Walking into Calli's hospital room, he felt helpless. Before him was a woman who was totally vulnerable. She lay on her side, her left arm propped on a pillow. Her short black hair was a mess, her thin lips pale and dry and her delicate features were mottled with bruises. *What in tarnation am I doing here?* Just as he considered turning and walking away, she moved.

"Mmm...Teddy's breakfast burritos." Her voice was soft.

"That's quite a nose." He wanted to elaborate, but figured he was pushing the boundaries by coming back at all. After all, he had met her in the line of duty. He'd consoled his conscience with the knowledge that he wasn't the primary officer on her case, and, since completing the statement, was now officially "off" the case.

"Sergeant Northrup..."

"Just Luke. I'm off duty." He opened the paper sack and unloaded two foil-wrapped packages.

"Oh," she said, her voice unable to conceal her puzzlement. She fumbled with the pillow, then the bed controls, obviously uncomfortable with his return. "Did you need me to answer more questions?"

He cleared her untouched breakfast tray from the bed table, glad she couldn't see the guilt-laden grin across his face. "No, I uh, wanted to check on the kid, and thought I'd stop in to see how you're feeling.... As long as I'm here. I have an extra burrito if you'd like one. I see you don't think much of the food here."

There was a long pause, then the corner of her mouth lifted. "I plead the Fifth. But I never turn down Teddy's burritos. Thanks. You're off duty, and you're here? Aren't you tired?"

"Takes me a few hours to wind down after a crazy shift like last night's." Luke unwrapped the burrito and placed it in her long fingers. She was enchanting—even in this state. Visiting her was not the best way to unwind, he reflected.

"How *is* your other patient?"

Here she lay uncertain of her own future, and she seemed more concerned about a total stranger's condition. Luke wished he could brush her worries away. "Still in a coma."

"I'm sorry."

She didn't ask for the details, for which he was eternally grateful. He didn't know how he could've politely told her he couldn't discuss an open case. Especially when one witness lay in a coma and the other had left without a trace.

It seemed like forever since there'd been anyone he'd been remotely interested in. Which made it even more difficult that Calandre Giovanni's case had to involve him. "I understand you get to go home today." *Ingenious, Northrup. You'd think this is the first woman you'd talked to.*

"I guess so. The doctor says there's no need to hang around here. The bandages make it look worse than it is. I think they're trying to slow me down." She ran her fingers over her head. Or what little hair was exposed anyway. She tentatively explored the gauze and slipped a finger under the edge and scratched her temple. "My things…from my truck. Are they here?"

"Just your clothes and purse. Whatever else you had, you can pick up at the salvage yard where your car was towed."

"Salvage yard?" She nibbled her lower lip.

"That's where vehicles are taken until the damage has been determined." He wondered if she had someone who could take her to get her belongings. "If you'd like, I could take you to clean it out."

Again, the silence was ominous. Her tone changed from the friendly exchange they'd established to one of total skepticism. "Thank you for offering, but I'll manage. My cousin is on her way with clean clothes."

"Okay. If you need anything, feel free to call me. Here's a card with your case number, the responding officer's name and my number if you have any questions." After visiting for a while longer, he placed his business card in her hand and left.

At home two days later, Calli found the switch to turn on the radio, and rocked in the antique chair. Music was the only thing she could enjoy without her sight. Running her fingers over the card in her hand, Calli wondered why Sergeant Luke Northrup had really returned. She inhaled, flustered as much by the fading aroma as she had been the man.

At first she thought he'd discovered a connection to the apartments when filling out the remainder of the report, but later she began to wonder if the personal interest was mutual. Yet she still couldn't allow herself to call, even to thank him for his kindness. He was a cop.

It didn't matter that he had a soothing voice that made her forget her past. Or manners that her grandmother would applaud. Or enough compassion to rewrite her personal definition of *law enforcement officer*. He was still a cop.

Until she met with the doctor to get the bandages removed, Calli could do little besides rest and wonder if Luke Northrup was really as wonderful as first impressions left her believing. Even if the nurse was exaggerating about Luke's appearance, it wouldn't matter. Looks weren't at the top of her list. But then again, cops weren't, either. In fact, they were no longer anywhere on her list. For more than one reason she reminded herself.

From the little she'd talked with Luke, her instincts said he wasn't a typical police officer. When he left her hospital room, Calli felt a longing to be someone she wasn't. An innocent bystander instead of a silent witness. Suddenly she wished she'd been born to a washer repairman instead of to an army officer. She longed to know Luke better, if only circumstances were different. If only *she* was different.

She'd tried to change. Even her grandmother had tried to help. Tried to teach her to crochet baby blankets and bake angel food cakes. Had tried to instill in her the more "delicate" aspects of women's traditional roles. Calli had almost succeeded in dousing the embers of her fiery temperament. Until that night three years ago.

The shrill ring of the telephone startled her from the unsettling walk down memory lane. She fumbled for the receiver and answered.

"I see from the newspaper that you're still patrolling."

The gruff tone caught her off guard, but it didn't take more than a second to recognize his voice. It had been months since she heard from him, yet she immediately felt herself cowering to his authority. With a blind search for her glass, she took a drink of water to smooth her vocal cords. "Yes."

"I worry about you, Calli." His voice softened.

Her hand moved to the bandages on her head. She couldn't even argue that point with him today. So how could she ever make them understand? Patrolling wasn't something she wanted to do. She had to. Someone *had* to care enough to stand up against the criminals who were tainting the city. Yet she said nothing.

"It's too late to help Mike. It's not too late to help yourself," he added.

Calli took a deep breath, then swallowed. "You taught me to be careful. I know how to protect myself."

"Your best protection is to stop. It's *not* your job," he insisted. "Let the police clean up the streets."

You taught me to care, to stand up for what's right. This may not be two countries fighting, but it's still war. How can you not understand? she wanted to scream at him, but the words caught in her throat.

"We've already lost a son."

"I have to go, Daddy. Give Mother my love." Calli hung

up. She rested her bandaged head in the cradle of her hands. *Oh, Daddy, don't you see? Just because I'm a girl it doesn't mean I can't fight my own battles. I have to do something to protect the helpless.*

She knew the day would come when she would have no choice but to blow her cover, mission accomplished or not. Once she testified on any case, everything would change. She wouldn't be able to keep a job working with the public. She'd have to watch over her shoulder. And, she realized, it could even mean losing her own identity. Each night she asked herself the same question: Is it really worth it?

Chapter Three

Calli zipped the ski parka, adjusted her earmuffs and pulled on the bulky gloves. She checked her gear then felt her pocket to be sure she had remembered lip ointment, tissues and sunglasses.

Everything accounted for, she skied toward the footprints marking the loading zone for the tramway that would carry her away from the pressures of the city. Since the accident two weeks ago, she'd done little besides work the checkout lanes at the grocery store, then go home and struggle with the temptation to patrol again. With any luck at all, she'd be too tired tonight to care if the whole town crumbled at her doorstep.

She wanted this ski trip to revitalize her senses. Wanted it to make her forget the urge to protect the weak and helpless.

Experts said forgiveness was the key to moving on in life after a tragedy. Yet try as she may, Calli found it impossible to forgive—a hit-and-run driver, an unfaithful fiancé or an elusive murderer.

Calli took a deep breath of the crisp clean air and closed

her eyes. *Okay, Father, I'll quit patrolling. But there has to be some way I can help. Show me how. Take my life, my heart, and change it. Starting today, Lord, remind me how to relax and have fun.*

She watched tufts of clouds floating in from the west. "For I know of the plans that I have for you…plans to give you a hope and a future." Today she would be carefree. Happy. Relaxed. *Today I'm starting over.*

She noticed the broad shoulders ahead of her, and again found herself daydreaming about the cop with the resonating voice and tender touch. Though she'd never actually seen Luke Northrup, her mind had created its own image. His business card was still in her purse, with his home number scrawled on the back. She'd read it over and again, too stubborn to succumb to the temptation to actually call him. As kind as he had been, he was still a cop.

"Excuse me, sir."

He didn't respond.

As she waited, another chair passed. She looked at it, then to the man who was now struggling with the binding on his ski.

Calli watched as the next seat approached, then tapped the man's shoulder. "Excuse me. Are you going up?"

"Just a minute." he snapped. He stepped aside and Calli eased forward, her gaze climbing the ski slope.

Calli heard a clamor as the chair rounded the curve of the pulley. She hurried past the man to the loading zone for the lift. When the chair bumped the back of her legs, she instinctively sat down and knew immediately that something was wrong. She wasn't on the chair. She was on *somebody*. "What's going on?"

"Hang on!" a deep voice commanded. Calli grabbed hold of the vertical bar connecting the chair to the cable, then looked down and realized three things. The chair was already twenty feet above the frozen ground. To her right, skis dangled from jean-clad legs, confirming her suspicion that she was sitting on someone. And she didn't dare let go.

"How—how did you get here?" she stammered. As Calli yanked the safety bar down in front of them, she felt his hand grab the back of her parka. "What are you doing?"

"Trying to keep you from falling, ma'am." He shoved her to one side, then kicked his long legs in a final effort to sit upright.

The chair jolted from side to side. "Watch out! The pole." She heard the snap as his skis hit the huge metal post. The chair jerked to a stop, bumping Calli off the seat again. She screamed.

"Don't worry. I have you." He hoisted her back into the chair, then pulled her into the circle of his arms.

Calli whispered a prayer, unable to stop clinging to the man who'd brought her to safety. He held her securely. Tenderly. Sympathetically.

"It's okay now. You'll be fine, miss." The deep timbre of his voice was somewhat disconcerting and the spicy scent of his cologne sent a shiver up her spine.

Slightly perturbed that he did nothing to dissuade her from clinging to him, Calli concentrated on slowing her breathing before she totally collapsed into his arms, further making a fool of herself.

"It's okay. Take a deep breath—let it out." She could feel the rise and fall of his chest as he imitated his instructions.

Her breathing was ragged, and with each gasp the cold air burned her throat. How long they clung to one another, she wasn't sure. Calli could feel his heart pounding against her own, and, with determined control, she pushed herself away from the security of the man's embrace. Looking into his eyes, she felt as if a warm blanket had just been wrapped around her. His rough cheek brushed hers, and she fought the temptation to lean close again. Calli straightened her jacket and took another cleansing breath, the thin air only intensifying the dizziness.

"I...I didn't think you were going up...." she said, her words trailing off as she lost herself in his jade-green eyes. Her gaze strayed to the black stubble framing his smile, and it was suddenly a struggle to think.

A voice bellowed from the ground below. "Everyone okay up there?"

Her companion glanced down, then back to her. His voice held none of the irritation she'd first heard, but was strangely warm and comforting. "Are you okay?"

She swallowed with difficulty and finally a raspy sound emerged. "Fine. But you. Your ski. And..." She raised her body off the seat again, and reached under her. "Oh, no, I bent your ski pole."

He yelled to the ski patrol and confirmed they were both fine. The lift started with a jerk, and both grabbed for each other.

She watched the play of emotions on his rugged face. His eyes searched hers and they broke into laughter. His laugh was warm, deep and fully masculine.

"You couldn't have bent that pole if you'd jumped on it. There's hardly enough of you to—" He abruptly stopped midsentence.

It couldn't be. The laughter ended and she felt her cheeks heating up, despite the cold wind on her face.

Did he feel the same unexplainable bond as she did? It was crazy; they'd just met. Or had they? This wasn't like her at all. Every time he spoke, it sent a ripple of awareness through her.

"I'm very sorry, miss...." When she didn't answer, he continued. "I lost my balance and couldn't stop with these skis on." A smile immediately softened his rugged features and further melted her indignation. He lifted the faded baseball cap covering his unruly short black hair, swiped his brow, then replaced the cap. "I am sorry."

She nodded and looked the other way.

Calli couldn't help but wonder if her attraction to this stubborn, arrogant and attractive man was God's will. Heavens, she thought, He could have broken me into this new plan of His a little easier.

Her mind must be playing tricks on her, she decided. Not only did this man sound familiar, if she really used her imagination, he almost looked like the police officer who nearly ran into her that last night she patrolled. *Couldn't be.*

She wished she could think of something clever to say. Anything. She hesitantly admired his strong square jaw and thick brows which arched over the deep-set green eyes. *I am not ready for this, God.* She shivered, then felt a warm sensation relax her body.

Already she'd seen a gentle side of this man replace the severity of his earlier arrogance. He measured her with an unnerving silence.

He extended his hand, firmly grasping hers. "I'm Luke Northrup."

Her heart stopped beating. She'd just convinced herself that her mind was playing tricks on her. Convinced herself that the nurse exaggerated. She was stunned—Luke was as handsome as the hero conjured up by her crazy imagination. Searching her pockets, she found what she needed and slipped behind the screen of mirrored sunglasses. "Calli," she said simply. No need for more.

It didn't matter that she'd thought of him on a daily basis. Or that she'd promised God she'd give up patrolling, Teddy's burritos...anything, if she could just resist falling in love with another police officer. What did matter was she couldn't see him again. *This isn't fair, God. And I showed such restraint not calling him.*

Luke obviously didn't recognize her without her bandages and she quickly decided it would be safest to play dumb. "You must see stupid things like this all the time up here."

"Up here?" Luke's brows furrowed, with a glint of wonder in his eyes.

"On the slopes," she added, relieved that he'd not made the connection between her given name and her nickname.

He chuckled. "You think I'm a ski bum? I'm flattered."

Just like a cop—arrogant. Calli straightened her back and handed his bent pole to him. "I'll be glad to pay for the damage."

"Don't think a thing of it. If this binding had been working properly, none of this would have happened. They could be more careful about training employees, too. I'm not sure that guy even knew how to stop the lift."

"Are you security?" The rasp in her voice was getting worse. She had to calm down. The crisis was over. Everything was fine. He wasn't making the connection.

"No, but I'm sure the folks who run this place will trust my credentials."

An uncomfortable silence was avoided as she cleared her throat and nodded. If Luke Northrup didn't want to admit to being a law officer, she wouldn't push.

They bounced along in silence. Minutes later, Calli looked up at the signs telling them to prepare to unload. Reminded of his accident, she assessed the situation. "So how are you going to get down off this mountain with a broken ski?"

"We'll just ride the lift back down. That ought to get their attention."

Calli yanked her sunglasses from her face and turned to him. "We?"

"I'll need you to file a statement...to verify what happened."

"I thought you said they would trust your credentials. It took me... Well, you can't imagine what I've gone through to arrange *this* ski trip!"

"Better safe than sorry. And we'd better have your arm checked. You gave it a pretty good yank. I don't think either of us will be safe on this slope today." He smiled, then added, "And, I think I at least owe you a cup of coffee for ruining your morning."

Her arm *was* sore, but she knew it wasn't broken. As she considered Luke's logic, the dismount ramp approached. He wasn't thinking of himself, but of her safety, as well as the other skiers. She, of all people, should understand his protective nature.

He waited for her answer. "Consider it a peace offering."

She looked at the glint in Luke's eyes and felt that crazy magnetism between them. *Just one cup of coffee couldn't hurt. He doesn't even remember me.* "If you insist. But I'll warn you, I'm not the forgiving type." *A cup of coffee. What could happen over a cup of coffee?*

Chapter Four

Luke unlocked the apartment door and hobbled inside, greeted by his son and an overwhelming garlic aroma. Jon must be toasting hoagie buns for his favorite after-school snack.

"Sorry I'm late. How was school?"

"Okay. We're out of garlic salt, but I added it to the grocery list." He walked around the corner, carrying a plate overflowing with bread. One glance at Luke and the thirteen-year-old stopped short. He brushed the dark bangs from his eyes. "Wow! What happened to you?"

"Nothing out of the ordinary. A little investigating. Some crisis intervention. Rescuing damsels in distress. Filling out paperwork." Luke collapsed in the brown recliner nearest the door and took off his boots. During the fifty-minute drive down the mountain, his sprained ankle had swelled and stiffened.

"I thought you were going to use the ski pass I gave you for Christmas today."

Luke released the footrest and pushed the chair back. "I did." After asking his son to bring him an ice bag and something for the pain, Luke told him about the excitement, minus the part where he'd struck out with the damsel. He could have sworn that beneath Calli's cautious exterior, she was interested.

When he awoke two hours later the television was blaring. Jon, seemingly oblivious to the racket, surfed the channels until he found a college basketball game. His son tossed a fringed pillow from the sofa at him. "How're ya doing?"

Luke stretched, yawning aloud as he folded the chair under him. "Ask me after I shower." He stood and limped across the room without the pain he'd had earlier. "Your grandma left a casserole in the fridge yesterday. Would you put it in the oven? I'll be out in a few minutes to finish making dinner."

Jon was slow to respond. "It's not that potpie thing, is it?"

"Yeah. Why?" Luke placed his hands on his hips and stopped. "You didn't throw it out, did you?"

"Not exactly." His son remained slouched on the sofa, peering at the TV from under the curtain of hair.

Luke waited for a further explanation. "Well?"

Jon raked his hand through his long bangs. "I ate it."

"You ate the whole thing?" Luke couldn't believe he bothered to ask such a stupid question. Of course he did. Jon was thirteen. He was supposed to eat them out of house and home.

"Well, I didn't know it was supper."

"Do me a favor. Don't tell me how great it was." Turning back to the kitchen, Luke rummaged through the freezer, hoping to find a replacement. There was none.

Kneeling in the middle of the kitchen, a pain shot up his leg and into his hip. From the cupboard, he pulled two empty peanut-butter jars and a few nearly empty boxes of crackers. His son was obviously going through a growing spurt. Jon only needed another six inches to reach Luke's height of six foot three, but the way the boy was eating, that would take less than a couple of months.

Luke settled for an overripe banana on the way to the shower. Between bites, he told Jon to clean up so they could grab dinner on the way to the grocery store.

After showering, Luke and Jon ate, then went to buy groceries. Luke bought double what he figured they needed, hoping there'd be a few crumbs left for his own meals after Jon finished eating.

Halfway through the store Luke found himself thinking of Calli. She'd mentioned that she'd almost completed her teaching degree, but was working at one of the downtown grocery store chains. He paid special attention to the employees as he browsed, certain that she also said she usually worked evenings. When he didn't see her, he made a note to start shopping in the evenings so he could run into her. *A few phone calls should turn up a "Calli" at one of them. It's not that common a name.*

As they were driving home, Jon was unusually quiet. They discussed another Nuggets loss and their tickets to the upcoming Avalanche game against the Red Wings. All the while, Jon barely uttered two words that wasn't an answer to a direct question. It was twice as tough to keep the conversation going, when all Luke could think about was the gorgeous woman he'd spent two hours trying to charm, only to be ignored when he asked if he could call her sometime. Before he had a chance to ask any more questions, Calli had slipped back into her cautious camouflage and politely excused herself. He drove home, replaying their conversation, trying to figure exactly what they'd been talking about when he'd blown it.

"Dad...did you hear me?"

"I was thinking of something else. Sorry. What did you say?"

"Nate wants me to stay with him Friday night. He's kind of bummed since his dad left. Can I go?"

"Friday, as in tomorrow?"

"Yeah. I know we were going to the hockey game, but... Well, it's important."

Nate lived upstairs, and the two had been friends since preschool. Only a few months earlier, Nate's dad had left his mother for another woman. The family was devastated. Especially Nate.

Luke thought of Friday's Avalanche game and how long they'd waited for these tickets. "Sure. Go ahead. Nate's more important right now."

"Really? Thanks, Dad. You're all right."

Hang on to that thought. It won't last long. Luke stuffed the disappointment away. He wasn't ready for his son to choose friends over him. Yet here it was. They unloaded the groceries, Jon finished his homework, then went to bed as Luke got ready for a night at the station. With his leg hurting like this, he knew he wouldn't be able to handle full duty.

Mrs. Maloney knocked quietly and came in.

"Hi, Marge. Jon has finished his homework and is already in bed. I should be home early tonight." He limped to the table and loaded his notes in his briefcase. Motioning to his foot, Luke offered an explanation. "Officially I'm off until I see a doctor, but I need to catch up on some paperwork. Shouldn't take more than a few hours."

"That's fine, Luke. I'll just watch the late shows."

"Feel free to go to bed. I can wake you when I get home."

He went to tell Jon good-night, but the room was dark and silent. Luke closed the door, remembering when Jon was a baby and his mother had just walked out on them.

Jon had gone to child care when Luke worked the day shift, and had gone to Luke's parents at night. It became more difficult as Jon got older. Luke and Jon had argued about the neighbor coming to "baby-sit," but in the end, his son didn't give either of them any problems. It was a teenager's obligation to argue, but inside, Luke suspected his son was as relieved as he was that their favorite neighbor was here.

The command sergeant watched Luke try to walk without a limp. "Face it, Northrup, you're going to be at the front window for a month with that bum leg."

"Not a chance. A week, maybe two at the most. I'll do anything, Sarge, but not the front."

The front window was known as the department "Miracle Cure," known to heal any ailment twice as quickly when an officer was assigned there. Unlike dispatch's duties, working the front meant answering the phone, dealing with stupid questions, handling complaints due to "cold calls" that were filed at the bottom of the priority list.

The sergeant tossed a file on his desk. "For now, see if Angel and Dunn need help with their case."

Luke reviewed the file, looking for anything to tie a white 4 Runner to the case. They too needed their witness to come forward. Angel had asked Luke to listen to the tapes to confirm that it was the anonymous caller.

Luke pressed Play and again listened to the female caller on previous 911 tapes, including the calls from the night of the auto prowls two weeks ago.

He compared the voices one more time.

Tom shrugged. "You must know this by heart, Luke. Let it go. She'll call again soon."

Her voice was soft. "Is she whispering, or scared to death?" Luke asked Tom. Sirens wailed and Luke held up a hand, quieting his partner. There was a gasp, a rattle, then a clunk, like the receiver had fallen. The voice was quiet, but urgent. ''Turn it up. She said something.''

Tom rewound the recording and pushed Play and raised the volume. The transcription was full of static. ''Come on. Start.'' He heard more static. Then, ''Too close. Get out of here.'' Static and her voice saying, ''Phone?'' The line went dead.

After a quick drive back to the scene to reenact the call, Luke shook his head. ''The lady in the 4 Runner was the anonymous caller. We could have had her.'' His frustration became more evident as they returned to the station. Tom left the room, seemingly aware that Luke needed time alone. The man knew him too well.

Luke rubbed his rough jaw. This anonymous caller case was getting to him. Of that, there was no doubt. After several minutes, he decided there wasn't much he could do besides turn it over to a higher power, one with more insight than his.

Tom passed by the desk for the fourth time in ten minutes.

''Would you stop pacing. My ankle hurts just watching you. What is it?''

''You okay?''

The bite of anger subsided. ''I'll be fine. Just checking in with the Boss.'' Luke pointed up.

Tom nodded. ''We're going to need it. Captain was just telling me Tiger came to the jail to visit Marlow yesterday. The guard says it looked like there was plenty of tension between them. Money must be getting tight.''

Luke understood Tom's silent implication. It was time for the Eastsiders ''to put in some work.'' They were bound to be getting edgy. Luke twirled his pencil, ''walking'' it from one finger to the next, then back again. ''You said it yourself—there's nothing we can do besides wait for her to call.''

Tom sat down and leaned back, folding his hands behind his head. "She's digging herself in deep, Luke. If we're looking for her, you can bet *they're* even closer to finding her."

Friday night Jon and Nate finished supper and went to Nate's bedroom. Nate's little brother ran into the room, screeching about not getting to watch his favorite show. The eight-year-old wouldn't be quiet.

"Mom! Tell James to leave us alone."

"I sent him to his room. He won't leave your sister alone, and I can't take any more of their fighting."

"And what're we supposed to do?" Nate argued with his mother as if she had the power to mend all of their problems. Jon felt sorry for her, but he couldn't tell Nate that. As far as his friend was concerned, he was the only one hurting. Nate felt like no one understood. Jon was trying.

"We're going to Jon's."

Jon didn't argue, though he knew he should have. His dad had gone ahead to the hockey game with Tom and they wouldn't be home for hours. He knew his dad didn't like him having friends over when he wasn't home. It wasn't that his dad didn't trust him, but he knew other kids sometimes didn't think before doing stupid things. For a dad, his was okay.

"C'mon, Jon. Let's get outta here."

Nate led the way down the stairs and out the front door of the building.

"Where are you going?"

"Out. I'm sick of this place."

"Let's just go to my apartment like you told your mom, Nate. What if she comes looking for you?"

"She never checks up on me—she's too tired to think of it. You coming or not?" Nate's language turned foul more often these days, and nothing anyone did was worthy of his attention. Jon didn't know what to do to help. But he had to try.

They headed down the street, meeting a couple of kids Jon recognized from school. From the way Nate greeted them, Jon realized this wasn't the first time his friend had escaped to the streets.

He looked around uncomfortably.

"Daddy on duty tonight, Northrup?"

He shook his head. That didn't matter. Everyone in the precinct knew him.

"Come on, Nate, let's split."

"In a minute."

Nate continued to talk with the group, which had doubled in size since they arrived. The gang headed down an alley. Jon lagged behind, unsure what was going on, but he knew he didn't want to be here.

They walked to a park, meeting up with a couple of older guys. After a few minutes, Jon got up the courage to tell Nate he was going home.

"You can't. Your dad'll ask questions, and if you go to my house, my mom'll get all uptight."

He pulled Nate away from the gang. "This is stupid, Nate. Let's go to my apartment. We can play video games, order a pizza, whatever."

"Time for business." The guy they called "Tiger" looked at them. "You in or out?"

Jon watched as everyone looked at him, expecting him to chicken out. Daring him. He'd heard what happened when they suspected a snitch. If he ditched out now, he'd be in deep trouble. And if his dad found out, it would be even worse.

Chapter Five

Calli picked up her paycheck and rushed past the checkout lanes. She tucked the paper and two videos into her backpack, waving to her boss on the way out.

Ten minutes behind schedule already, she parked the rental car and ran into the recreation center. Hanna met her in the lobby and they rushed to the women's locker room where Calli changed into her sweats and a T-shirt.

"It's a class of women." Calli said, watching Hanna brush her hair then freshen her makeup. "We're practicing self-defense, Hanna," she said with a laugh. "There's no need to primp."

Her fair-haired cousin was an easy target for muggers. Precise schedule, expensive car, drop-dead attractive. Over the years, Calli had tried telling Hanna to vary her routine, as well as other safety precautions. It wasn't until a woman had been attacked a block from Hanna's office that she'd been persuaded to pay attention to Calli's advice.

"I don't know, Bart's kinda cute."

"And kinda married." Calli laughed. "Not your type."

Hanna tossed the brush down. "I didn't see a wedding

ring.'' Then as if there'd been no interest at all, she changed the subject. ''Do we have to do anything 'real' tonight? Like flips or anything?''

''Probably a few moves. You'll do fine. Let's go.''

Hanna pulled her hair into a ponytail at the top of her head and they rushed out the door. ''Easy for you to say. You've been tossing men over your shoulder since you were a kid.''

''I was merely defending myself. If you had brothers you'd know how to take care of yourself, too.'' Calli had carefully locked those memories away, and yet with that innocent reminder, they returned. Calli would never forget the first time she successfully flipped her older brother. Her dad took her for an ice-cream cone right before dinner, ignoring her mother's protests. To this day, Calli never figured out why her mom had been protesting; had it been the nature of the celebration, or the fact that the ice cream would ruin her dinner?

''Did you know that your dad tried to convince my mother to let him teach me self-defense once?'' Hanna acted as if this was entertainment.

Calli stared ahead, afraid to open the door to the past any further than a tiny crack. Few people could overlook her father's tough militaristic exterior, and even fewer saw the loving emotional side that he reserved for his family. She slipped back through that door and slammed it closed. ''Dad was a good instructor, but so is Bart. He knows what he's doing.''

Hanna told her about her latest date, and the two started laughing. Calli didn't enjoy the dating game like her cousin did. For Hanna, meeting new people was fun, but Calli rarely went out, and only with men she knew well. Calli and Hanna joined the rest of the class on the mats and they began stretching.

Suddenly, hushed voices buzzed around her. She turned

just as Luke Northrup introduced himself as their new instructor. Calli's smile disappeared.

"Bart broke his leg and asked me to take his place. I'm a certified instructor, and have taught personal safety with him before."

The other women seemed to have the same reaction to the handsome man as she had. Tonight he wore a black tank top and sweats, and as before, his hair looked as if he'd just used his fingers as a comb. His five o'clock shadow wasn't as pronounced as it had been at the ski resort, but he still had that air of authority which commanded instant attention.

Okay, God, what are you up to? I thought we agreed, no cops. Then she recalled Luke's gentler side. The care and concern he had shown at the hospital. The way he comforted her when she clung to him after the skiing accident. His tenderness was as startling as an ice cube on a hot summer day.

As they visited over coffee, she had relaxed and temporarily put the past behind her. Luke had never recognized her from their meeting at the hospital. But once again, he teased and tormented the emotions she'd long locked away. Then suddenly she caught herself entertaining the notion of seeing him once more. Before he could ask her for her phone number, she politely thanked him for the coffee and ran.

There wasn't room for a man in her life. Especially not this one. Not one who made her forget her past, her mission, her mistakes. Not even for a minute.

Luke's steady gaze bored into hers in silent expectation. Their eyes met—dueling, dancing, laughing. There was that maddening hint of arrogance again.

She found herself studying him as he turned his attention back to the class. Was she imagining it, or had his back straightened, his shoulders become broader and his determination grown stronger?

"We're going to start with a defensive move. I'm going to need a volunteer to help me demonstrate." Hands flew into the air, yet he looked right at Calli, as if waiting for her objection. "Miss...?" he teased.

Begrudgingly she stepped forward. "Calli."

Luke explained the move, then demonstrated the steps in slow motion. He wore the same spicy aftershave as that night in the hospital. She silently searched for a plausible explanation to the shiver that went up her arm as he held her wrist. His hold was firm, challenging her to break loose. Her move was quick and instinctive.

She expected him to call on another volunteer for the next demonstration, but he stepped behind her as she turned to leave and wrapped his arm around her neck, as a mugger would.

Calli braced herself on her left leg. She tugged at his arm, leaned forward, and "swept" at Luke's legs with her foot. The move was enough to knock him to the floor so she could escape.

The class watched wide-eyed as Luke lay sprawled across the mat, laughing. He rose to one elbow. "A perfect example of the benefits of the element of surprise. Great job...Calli."

Her heart raced. "Glad to help." She returned his smile, careful to hide her pleasure at seeing him again. Class resumed, and Calli fought the constant temptation to join in his gentle sparring. He'd explain a move, then the class would pair up to practice. As he made his way to her group, Hanna seemed to enjoy seeing Calli's discomfort escalate with each step Luke took.

"How's it going here?" His voice seemed deeper than before.

Hanna spoke first. "I don't quite understand." Calli

watched Luke go through the steps again, this time, wrapping his arm around Hanna's neck. She couldn't explain the crazy longing she had to trade places with her cousin at that moment.

"You kind of elbow the attacker in the stomach as you reach up...." Calli's eyes met his, and she stopped. "Sorry. I didn't mean to interrupt."

"We're here to learn, from one another or from me, it really doesn't matter. Care to try it again? I'm ready this time."

"I'll give you a break."

Luke smiled, then turned to the class. "I'll be the first to say that one can never underestimate the opponent. That in itself could be a woman's best defense." Luke looked at his watch. "That's it for tonight. Have a good week."

Several women thanked Luke, then Calli for her "help." A wave of giggles followed, and he shook his head.

"Calli, I'd be willing to forgive you, if you'd agree to help with the class. We seem to make a good team."

Despite her laugh, Calli felt an unwelcome reaction to his innuendo. "Think the third time's a charm, huh?"

"Third time? Unless I'm mistaken, we've only met twice." He crossed his arms and put his back to the wall.

Great, Calli. How're you going to get out of this one?

When she didn't answer, he added, "Unless you consider tonight memorable enough to count as twice, which I happen to agree. Can't remember being knocked off my feet by a more beautiful woman."

Calli stepped aside, struggling to find an answer to his question before his flirting turned her brains to jelly. "No way," she said, realizing she was way behind in the conversation. *Forget it, Luke Northrup. No way am I going through this blessed torment every week! Enough is enough.*

"Hanna, does your friend always back down from a challenge?"

"Cousin," Hanna corrected.

His eyebrows arched and his mouth fell open. "Cousin?"

Calli watched as he eyed the two of them. Hanna and her long blond hair, blue eyes and robust figure, then Calli's classic Italian coloring and willowy body.

"Plead the Fifth, Hanna, or you'll be walking home." She turned to leave, feeling Luke's challenging stare.

Hanna leaned close and whispered. "What's going on here, Calli?"

She couldn't answer. Couldn't admit the truth—that she was falling for another police officer.

"Just think about it. It's one thing to have an instructor who can tell them what to do, but it's something else altogether to see one of their own succeed. These women could learn a lot from you. I'll call *you* this time."

"Don't bother. The answer's no...*Officer* Northrup."

Hanna looked at her, then to Luke and began laughing. "You're kidding. Not again."

Jon tried phoning Nate after dinner, but according to his five-year-old sister, Nate was supposedly at Jon's. Jon had become his best friend's alibi more than ever before. He wouldn't have minded at one time, but fact was, he rarely saw Nate at all anymore, and Jon didn't like his friend's new pals.

He finished his algebra and threw his reading book aside. "I'm going to take the trash outside, Mrs. Maloney."

She looked up from her knitting and seemed to know he had something on his mind. "Don't take long. You haven't finished the dishes, and I assume you still have reading to do."

"It's a stupid book," he muttered.

"That may be your opinion, but I don't think that will

answer the questions on your test. Take a break, then get back to your homework, young man."

Jon grumbled, then walked out of the apartment. He checked the stairway, then headed outside.

Nate's recent hangout seemed to be the park. Without hesitation, Jon rounded the corner and sauntered to the end of the block. He saw Nate and his new friends near the picnic table, laughing. Jon paused, then backed behind a budding lilac bush and watched. The huddle tightened, then Nate backed away from the group and looked around.

A few more minutes passed, and the group broke up. Jon stepped into the alley and ran home. He rode the elevator to the third floor, waiting for his breathing to slow before going into the apartment. It was about ten minutes later that he heard the sirens, and wondered if they'd caught Nate this time.

The next morning, Jon went to school alone. Nate finally showed up third hour, unprepared for the reading test. After another of Nate's outbursts of profanity, the teacher ordered him to finish the class period in the office. Wearing a smirk, Nate turned to Jon as he left the classroom. It was all Jon could do to meet his friend's gaze.

In the lunchroom, Nate approached Jon. "So what's up, Jonny boy?"

"What's with you, Nate?" Jon kept eating.

His friend ignored the question. "Saw you at the park last night."

Their eyes met. "You're asking for trouble with them, Nate."

"They're my friends."

"Whatever."

Nate pushed his tray closer to Jon's. "You the one who called the cops on us last night?"

"I wouldn't do that to you. Besides, I'm not stupid enough to cross the Eastsiders."

"They're not so bad," Nate insisted. "Give 'em a break."

Jon looked at his empty tray. "Nate, don't tell your mom that you're at my house next time you ditch out." He stood and backed away from the table. "I'll see you around."

Chapter Six

"How soon's that cellular tracking system supposed to be active? That may be our best chance to find the anonymous caller."

"A few weeks." Tom took a swig of pop. "Typical glitches in the system. Tested it the other night. The call was made right outside the station. Showed in the system near Golden Acres."

"A lot of good that does us." Luke turned on the alley lights, looking for anything out of the ordinary.

"Let's hope she can stay out of trouble until it's ready." Tom cleared his throat. "Say, you never finished telling me about Bart's class last night."

Luke proceeded to tell his friend about Calli. Tom laughed, making a few good-natured comments. "You haven't had that look in a long time, bro."

"Don't get any ideas." Luke shone the spotlight behind a trash can, then up a dilapidated fire escape.

"Doesn't look like I need to. Vanessa's been nagging me to plan that night out. Thought I got away from dating when I said 'I do.' Did you ask Calli?"

"Who said anything about a date?" Though Luke would like nothing more than to ask Calli to dinner, he wasn't fond of beating his head against brick walls.

"Last week I told you to find a date for dinner and a movie. You did ask her, didn't you?"

Thinking of Calli's reaction, he shook his head. "I need to spend some time with Jon. Sorry. Maybe next time."

"You didn't get her number, did you?" Tom tossed his head back and began laughing. "You are out of touch with women, Luke. No wonder you're still single."

"I have her number. For your information, she's going to help me teach Bart's class. Then I'm going to convince her to help with the classes at the high schools."

"She agreed to work with you, but she won't go out with you? Did you even get her name?"

His partner knew all of his downfalls. "What do you think I am, a rookie?"

"I don't have to think, I *know.* You're so out of touch with women, you'd have fallen for any lame alibi."

He thought of the way she'd avoided telling him her name, and hated to admit his friend could be right. Though he didn't blame Calli—or whatever her name was. He continued the thought aloud. "A single woman can't be too careful nowadays. There's a whole lot of kooks in the world. I'm not going to push her."

"A man of integrity. One of these days, I'll teach you everything you need to know to find the *right* woman."

Throughout their patrol, Luke thought about Calli. He was ready to call the registrar for the self-defense classes, when he remembered where else he had seen her. *Why didn't I see it before? Sassy, short dark hair. Tall and thin. Calli—Calandre. Calli Giovanni. That's it.*

Luke radioed dispatch to end their patrol as Tom shifted the cruiser into park. He was still razzing Luke about letting Calli slip away. Hoping to get Tom off his back, Luke mentioned the blonde in the 4 Runner. Contrary to what he wanted Tom to believe, Luke had just made his own plans, with Calandre, a.k.a. Calli Giovanni. "You have plans for tomorrow?"

Taking the bait, Tom nixed his idea of researching the anonymous caller. "Get a life, Luke. You can't be married to the job. It'll kill you."

"Thanks for the vote of confidence, partner."

A shrill ring woke Luke before he'd even had a chance to fall into a deep sleep. He moved the phone from one ear to the other and flopped onto his back, listening to his ex-wife's whining. At one time he'd have sympathized with her, but not any longer. She'd changed her mind too many times. This time she thought she wanted to take Jon for the summer.

"If you want to see Jon, I don't have any problem with you coming to visit."

Along with a few remarks meant to upset him, she threatened to contact a lawyer. Now, in addition to the summer, she wanted to petition the courts to let Jon decide whom to live with.

"Nancy, have you forgotten that you signed away your maternal rights twelve years ago? I never had to let you see him at all. It's been at least six months since you've even called. You missed his birthday, Christmas..."

She hung up. Without even asking how her son was doing. Nothing had changed. Luke set the receiver in the cradle and let out a deep breath. *Kids do stupid things, Jon. I was a kid once, I know.*

An hour later the apartment door clicked closed. Luke heard his son open the fridge, take a glass from the cupboard and close the refrigerator. Luke could imagine Jon chugging down his usual quart of orange juice. Footsteps approached the bedroom and his door creaked open.

"I'm home, Dad. I'm going to shower and go back to bed for a while."

"You're home awfully early. Things go okay with Nate?"

Jon grumbled a response and disappeared.

The phone conversation left him wide-awake. Luke got out of bed and pulled his sweats on. Before his son went to sleep, he ran the vacuum, then straightened the rest of the apartment. His mind returned to Nancy's phone call. At least a million times in the last fourteen years Luke had regretted his carelessness that night. They'd been dating for several months, and with stars in their eyes, one thing had led to another. And before they'd stopped to think about repercussions, they'd become parents.

He walked to the door of Jon's room and leaned against the doorjamb, watching his son's peaceful slumber. Luke would always regret his irresponsibility that night, but he had never once regretted having a son or being a father. Not even when his seventeen-year-old wife had walked out of their short-lived marriage, dropping their baby off at Luke's parents' house while he was at school. He gave up dreams of the military in order to give Nancy time to grow, adjust and change her mind about leaving the two of them. Two days after Jon's first birthday, she returned, just long enough to hand Luke the papers giving up her son.

That had been a dark, difficult time in his life, but Luke had found that, as his faith had grown stronger, so had his ability to cope as a single parent.

He wouldn't back down now, either. He had to think of what Jon had been through. Consider his son's feelings. His mother's rejection hurt, though Jon would never admit it.

Luke remembered the day about a month before Jon's fifth birthday when he first realized his family was different. Sure, they knew other single-parent families, but those kids went back and forth between Mom's house and Dad's house. Jon didn't.

"I want a brother for my birthday."

Luke had never believed in lying, especially to a child. In fourteen years he'd faced some doozies, but he'd never lied.

Luke stared at the anger and confusion in the five-year-old's eyes. His own emotions were mirrored on his child's face. "I can't give you a brother. I can buy you a present at the store. Would you like a bicycle?"

"No. I told you what I want," Jon growled. "I want a brother."

"Come on, Jon, you've never seen a brother for sale at the store, have you?" Luke chuckled, groping for some levity. "Do you want a doll? Is that what you mean?"

"*No!* I want a baby, just like Nate's mom had a baby."

"I see." He paused to swallow the lump in his throat. "Babies need a mom and a dad." He wasn't ready to go into this discussion, but he felt the questions coming. "I'm not married, and it's best to be married to have a baby. Babies look like a lot of fun, but they're lots of work, too."

After Luke told Jon a simplified version of how babies are made, the two embraced. As if he finally understood, Jon's smile faded. "But *I* don't have a mom."

It hurt to tell his own son that he had a mother who didn't want to be one. "So we can't have another baby without someone to be a mom. Someone who wants to be a mom as much as I want to be a dad and you want to be a big brother."

Even now, Luke still noticed Jon's interest in babies. Tom and Vanessa and their new twins were great fun for Jon. Every few days, Jon stopped by after school to visit the Davises. It was painfully obvious. His son still wanted the one thing Luke couldn't give him: a family.

* * *

Calli watched the leader of the gang walk past as she checked Mrs. Polanski's basket of groceries. Every Saturday afternoon, her neighbor came to check out in her lane.

"How are your eyes doing, Calli?"

"They still tire easily, but other than that, just fine, Mrs. Polanski. The doctor says there doesn't seem to be any permanent damage."

"Is there any loss of vision?"

Calli smiled and shook her head in lieu of an answer. She ran the boxes past the scanner, thinking about Luke Northrup's request for her to help him teach the self-defense classes. She did little but think about it since their class. On one hand, she firmly believed in the cause. But on the other, she had to be crazy to consider spending even one evening a week with the very man she should be avoiding.

She glanced nervously at the kids wearing gang colors, and totaled her neighbor's order. "Twenty-five dollars, fifty-three cents, Mrs. Polanski." While the elderly woman dug through her tapestry bag for money to pay her bill, Calli turned to the bagger and whispered, "Jake, help Mrs. Polanski into her car, and be sure it's locked before she leaves." He nodded. Feeling a bit easier, Calli watched Jake and her neighbor walk out the door.

The manager tapped Calli on the shoulder. "It's time for your break."

"Thanks." She turned her light out, signed off her money drawer and strode to the back of the store for some fresh air. It had been a long day already. She stepped outside and headed for the abandoned loading docks. Taking a deep breath, Calli leaned to one side, the other, then forward, stretching her tired back.

She took a sip of soda, admiring the clear sky. The brisk wind tousled her hair and refreshed her senses. Finding a clean spot on the cold cement, Calli sat down. The breeze and drastic drop from the dock reminded her of the day she'd met Luke at the ski slope.

Don't get any ideas, Calli. That man is off-limits. Her watch beeped, alerting her that it was time to get back to work. She went down the steps and around the corner, surprised to find three kids spray painting graffiti on the wall of the store in broad daylight.

"Hey, guys. You need to clear out of here."

They laughed. "You going to make us?" the kid with the blue bandanna around his head taunted.

Calli took a deep breath and quickly dispelled the notion of doing just that. The odds were stacked on their side. Tiger glared at her. "Just a bit of advice. Take it or leave it. It's your choice." She hurried past them and turned the corner to the front of the store, relieved to see the flurry of activity.

Knowing they had followed her inside, she went straight back to her lane and entered her number into the register. For the next half hour, they lurked nearby, she supposed to make sure she didn't call the police. One picked up a candy bar and started eating it. She pretended not to notice, until he opened the second one. Calli was ready to confront him, when he stepped up to the register and handed her two one-dollar bills.

"Remember this, lady, you talk, you pay."

She snatched the bills from his hand and waited for him to take the change from the automatic dispenser at the end of the counter. "Your bill is paid, now leave."

Another customer stepped into her lane, and she decided to ignore the boys. *Why me, God? Why did I have to find them out there? I'm trying to convince myself that these kids aren't all bad, and this happens. I'm not convinced. If you don't want me to get involved, why do you keep bringing trouble to my door?*

"Good afternoon. Would you like plastic or paper?"

Calli addressed the customer absently, pulling the cart forward until it rested against the stainless-steel counter.

"What a coincidence meeting you here, *Miss Giovanni,*" a smooth voice answered.

Calli looked up, stunned to see Luke. He looked over her shoulder, also surveying the boys she'd been watching. She looked nervously at him, then at the teens. "How did you find me?"

"What, you don't believe in coincidences?" Then he lowered his voice, still smiling. "Just keep checking, Calli. I'm watching them. Why are they bothering you?"

He reached under his leather jacket.

When she saw him release the snap of his holster, her shoulders tightened. Then her neck. She could feel her throat constrict. "Call me a skeptic, but no, I don't believe in coincidences," she said, squeezing each word out. In no time at all, she'd sound like a child with croup.

Calli turned toward the gang. Tiger was gone, and the remaining kids acted as if they'd never seen her. "Nothing. They're just loitering," Calli added.

Luke's rigid profile exemplified power and control. "Loitering?" Smiling, he leaned over the counter and whispered, as if he was flirting. "You're lying through your teeth, Calli Giovanni. They have you terrified. Now what's up?"

She looked at him wide-eyed, stunned at the sparkle in his eyes, despite the seriousness of his words. "That is quite a performance, Sergeant. You should get an Oscar."

"All in a day's work. Now are you going to tell me why they are harassing you and none of the other clerks?"

She thought of the kid's threats and backed away. "I can handle it myself, but thank you anyway."

Luke paid for his groceries in silence and took them just outside the door. He asked an employee to watch his basket and stepped back inside and behind the pop display. Easing his way closer, he listened as the two remaining gang members grilled Calli about their conversation. After hearing implications that threats had already been made, Luke addressed the suspects, obviously surprising Calli as well as the kids by his return. "Afternoon, boys. I don't know what this is about, but it's obvious that you're not shopping. Why don't you get on your way?"

"What you talkin' about, Sarge?"

"Well, Pete, maybe you'd like to tell me what the lady here won't."

The two looked at Calli, then back to Luke. She recognized the steely look in Luke's eyes. A cop's eyes.

"Nothing. We didn't do nothing."

"Then I suggest you leave before I haul you all downtown to get answers."

The two left the store without any more "encouragement."

Unable to deny her relief that he'd returned, Calli struggled to maintain her composure. They had shaken her. There was no doubt about that.

Luke touched her shoulder. "You okay?"

She nodded, knowing her scratchy voice would again give her away.

"How long until you're off?"

She'd walked to work this morning, not concerned with walking home alone midafternoon. Now she couldn't deny the fear. Calli wanted company, even if it was Luke. "About an hour."

"I want to make sure you get home okay. Will you wait so I can get these groceries home and let my son know I'll be out for a while longer? He was still asleep when I called."

Calli assessed him openly, her doubts softened by the silver cross dangling from the chain around his neck, and the surprising news that Sergeant Luke Northrup was a father. ''I'll wait. I don't want to walk home alone after this.''

The hard-edged cop again faded, replaced with a caring, gentle man. ''I'll hurry back.''

Surprisingly enough, she wanted him to do just that.

Chapter Seven

Before she had time to consider leaving without Luke, he appeared in the employees' locker room. When he gazed at her, she fought to conquer the involuntary nervousness that overcame her.

"The manager told me where I could find you."

She smiled weakly. "Hi. I really don't need a police escort."

"Good, because this isn't official." He tilted his head to one side. "To be honest, it wasn't a coincidence that I came here."

She'd been unable to take her mind off Luke Northrup since he stepped into her checkout lane. This guilty feeling was due to the joy of his return. "Oh, really? Isn't it a little unethical to use police records for personal interests?"

Luke leaned against the wall and folded his arms across his chest. "It certainly would be. It is not, however, unethical to ask your cousin which store you work at." He stepped closer, a grin of amusement softening the stubborn set of his jaw.

Calli shook her head and pulled the miniature backpack-style purse from her locker and tossed it over her shoulder. "I should have figured."

"She said to tell you she won't argue with you this time. Considering the grilling she gave me before giving me any information, I'll deduce that comment has to do with your usual choice of men?"

Calli slammed the locker door closed and collapsed against it. She felt her flesh color. "I'll…I'll get even…"

"Ah, Calli, don't forget, I'm a cop. I take all threats seriously, even toward obnoxious cousins." He smiled suggestively, then laughed.

She twisted her mouth, then smiled. "It's not considered a threat if I didn't finish the sentence."

Shaking his head, he said, "Considering the afternoon you've had, I'll forget I heard anything. Let's start over." He paused, then extended his hand. "Good afternoon, Miss Giovanni. May I see that you make it home safely?"

Calli crossed her arms over her chest. Luke reached past her and turned the combination on her lock, then followed her through the warehouse and down the stairs. They walked in silence through the produce section and past the customer-service counter. When they turned to go outside, she took his hand for support.

Figuring out why Calli had looked so familiar at the ski area wasn't any relief. After the car accident, he'd come to the conclusion that it was for the best that she hadn't called. All of that was immaterial now, he decided. He'd met her twice outside the line of duty. It couldn't be a coincidence. There was a reason the two of them kept running into each other.

Luke saw the strain in her face return as she remembered the violent afternoon. He had told her the truth—he planned to come back after she got off work, even before everything had happened. But now it was even more obvious that she needed someone. And he prayed that he was the right person.

She remained silent, her lips pressed tightly closed, her eyes dry.

He opened the passenger door and closed it behind her, scanning the parking lot for any unwanted company. There was none. He got in and started the engine. "You'd better let it out. Cry. Scream. Yell. Something."

"I'm fine."

He gave her a sideways glance before laughing. "Considering your response to Hanna leading me here, I find it hard to believe you have no reaction to what happened this afternoon. Have you forgotten, I've seen you under trying conditions before?"

"Well, this is different. I'm not falling off a chairlift." Calli's gaze skipped along the street, as if she were looking for someone. Or maybe watching to see who had seen her. "Did you see the other kid?"

"No, but I can guess who it was. This kid is trouble, Calli."

"I can handle myself, Sergeant."

He was tired of sugar-coating the truth. "Let me put it this way, Calli, if I had been trying to push you off that ski lift, I wouldn't have failed."

"Would that be anything like the self-defense class?"

He wanted to kiss that smirk right off her face.

"Like I said, if I'd been trying..."

Calli's retort was sassy, quick and on target. "Face it, Officer Northrup, I got you."

In more ways than one, Calli. Trouble is, what in the world am I going to do about it? "Lucky break." He grimaced as the words slipped from his mouth. "Now, about this afternoon..."

"I don't want to talk about it. Tell me about your son. How old is he?"

He'd seen people break down after experiencing less than she had been through today. Even those trained to deal with those situations.

"I've been a single dad for over thirteen years. Jon's a good kid." He saw the way her blink faltered, hiding her beautiful eyes. The fringe of her long lashes formed shadows on her cheeks. "What about you?"

"No family, just me." He didn't miss the wistful inflection in her voice.

"And what about Hanna's comment?"

Calli looked out the window, yet remained silent. He pulled into an old-fashioned drive-in restaurant and turned off the car. "Would you like something?"

She shook her head. "Thanks anyway."

He ordered, then waited for her to answer his question.

"Hanna and I have a long-standing disagreement about men."

"All men? Or just yours?"

She looked at him quickly, then turned away. "If it matters, mine. I seem to be attracted to men who are completely wrong for me."

He put their few conversations together and decided to test his only theory. "Because I'm a cop?"

"Yes."

"So if I was a banker, or a mechanic, you'd go out with me?" Not that that mattered much. He was a cop. Had no intentions of changing that for anyone. "Is that why you introduced yourself as Calli instead of Calandre on the ski lift?"

"My name *is* Calli. If your parents had named you Calandre, wouldn't you go by another name? I didn't even think about it."

The food came, interrupting the conversation. He paid, and pulled his bacon double cheeseburger and fries off the metal tray hanging on the car window. As soon as the young waitress left, Calli went into some analogy of cops seeing things in black and white, trying to make him understand her reasons for not wanting to get involved with a police officer. Unfortunately he didn't.

"So, because I'm a cop, you wouldn't consider going out with me?"

She remained silent, shook her head, then nibbled on her lower lip. Calli looked like a fragile porcelain doll. Her ivory skin was smooth, her eyelashes feathered over those incredibly dark brown eyes and her full lips made a beautiful pout.

"Look at me, Calli. Please."

She hesitated, then turned to face him. "Luke, it's not the right time in my life. We're just too different, okay?"

"I don't buy that. Is there someone else?" He didn't want to know, but he had to ask. If there was, Hanna didn't approve, or she wouldn't have led him to Calli.

Calli's gaze met his, then she looked down. Wisps of hair fell around her face, and she pushed them away. There was a tangible bond between them, if only she'd let him tap into it. "Leave it alone, Luke. Please."

"Fine." He took an oversize bite of his hamburger, too mad at his own foolishness to say much else. He wasn't looking for anything serious anyway. So why was he acting like she'd just ripped his heart out?

He hadn't heard a word she just said, but she looked as low as he felt. It was as clear as daylight that she was lying. "If I was a gambling man, I'd say you're a loner, Calandre Giovanni."

She glared at him, then laughed nervously. She didn't answer. Didn't deny it, either.

"I don't know who's responsible for your unhappiness, but I do know someone who could help you deal with it."

Her eyes widened. Then she glanced quickly to the cross around his neck. Luke reached up to touch it.

He nodded. "God can handle anything."

"Sometimes I truly believe He's stopped listening."

"He's stopped listening? Sounds pretty serious. Why do you think that?"

As if she realized someone finally heard what she was feeling, she let out a quick gasp. "It's nothing," she insisted.

He lowered his head, saying a silent prayer for Calli. "It's not nothing when you think God doesn't care about you anymore. Whatever happened, it must have been pretty painful."

"Yeah, well, 'A purpose for everything' as my mother says. You deal with it and move on."

"That's what they say. Supposed to make us feel better, but it never worked for me." He held out his box of fries and offered her another chance to have a bite when he heard her stomach growl.

"Isn't there some regulation about officers fraternizing?"

"Yeah, we're right up there with priests," he grumbled, feeling guilty again. "But thankfully I'm not on your case."

She laughed aloud. "You have an answer for everything, don't you, Officer?"

She was pushing him. It was time to do a little pushing himself. "All but one. Have you decided to teach the class with me?"

"Why should I do that?"

"I understand you've kept after your cousin to take the class for years. You're just the kind of partner I need. One who really believes in the program. Need I say more, Miss Giovanni?"

"Oh, and I suppose the wise move would be to throw myself at your mercy before you learn *all* of my secrets, right?"

"Yup. And while we're at it, I'm taking a group of kids from our church in-line skating tomorrow. Why don't you come along? No strings. Just a chance to see that all kids aren't the same."

"I offered to fill in at work."

"After what just happened?"

"I was given the choice. I *offered* to work."

She is stubborn. "I'll pick you up after work, then. Make sure you get home okay."

"Luke."

He grinned. It was the tender way she'd said his name, and hiding his satisfaction was useless. "I don't want you to have to use that self-defense on anyone else. Okay?"

A smile peeked through her mask of uncertainty. "You're impossible."

"I guess that makes two of us. Give me your hours for the week." He pulled out his notepad and pen, ready to copy them down.

"Is that an order, Sergeant?"

He wanted to say yes. He didn't dare. "I wouldn't think of ordering you around."

Chapter Eight

The questions niggling Luke's conscience surfaced again as he drove away from Calli's apartment. He was puzzled by his sudden interest—not just the attraction to Calli, but the feeling that this wasn't about a date. He wanted...more. He didn't know how else to say it. He wanted... understanding...companionship...friendship.

Trying to talk to Tom was useless. Every time Luke mentioned Calli, Tom's answer was "Love at first sight." That *wasn't* it; she had been bandaged and bruised, her hair tangled and taped, and she was as feisty as a six-month-old puppy. Yet he definitely felt a bond with her from the first time he met her.

Am I crossing that fine line between personal and professional?

Luke rubbed the tension in his shoulder, as if he could swipe the difficult question away. "If I knew, I wouldn't keep asking."

What will the squad say about my seeing a woman involved with a case? "She's not a suspect. It's not a problem."

But you wouldn't have met her if it hadn't been for your job, his conscience probed. "Give me a break. That'd take away half the available population! Besides, we met skiing before I knew who she really was."

You gave her your card at the hospital with your phone number on it. She never called. What makes you think she's interested now? Luke revved the engine and turned the corner. "Who asked for your opinion?"

Since that morning in the hospital, he'd tried to understand this longing to ask a woman he'd barely met out to dinner. And each time he sees her, that unexplainable sense of purpose only grew stronger.

Reasoning through the circumstantial evidence wasn't enough to justify his yearning to know her better, and the battle waged on. After wasting his time on relationships that had gone nowhere, Luke didn't want to make the same mistakes again. Contrary to his partner's philosophy of love at first sight, Luke planned to approach women differently. Simple as having a relationship once seemed, he was beginning to have his doubts that God ever planned for him to be happily married.

He and Calli may have gotten started on the wrong foot, but it wasn't too late to set things straight. Friendship. That left plenty of room for growth and change.

There was a lot more to think about in a relationship now. He had a teenage son, a stressful career and no room for some woman who couldn't deal with either. At this point in his life any woman he'd consider a relationship with had to accept both.

He and Nancy had never really been in love, something he once thought could change. They'd made a baby together, and he was convinced that he'd done the right thing by marrying her. He did admire the fact that Nancy never tried to lie about her feelings. She didn't want to be married, didn't want children and didn't want to be tied down.

It took years to accept that both he and Jon were better off without the additional stress of the rocky relationship.

The next relationship was the total opposite. Jessica was agreeable with everything he said and did. Beautiful—and spineless. Then Gretchen, who was strong yet boring. And Dana, who was fun, but possessive. He discovered there were as many combinations as there were flavors of ice cream.

Through Jon's childhood, Luke continued his search for the elusive match, until he'd recently come to the conclusion that *he* wasn't relationship material. And despite Tom's constant attempts to find Luke the right woman, he'd become content with being a father and then a cop.

Until Calli came along.

Calandre Giovanni. Spunky and...impetuous.

"Hmmph. Just what I need—a headstrong, impulsive, unpredictable woman in my life." *Is there really any other kind?*

This thing with Calli—who knew for sure? Beauty and excitement? Beauty and youth? Beauty and trouble? Whatever the combination, it would pass. Friendship... Now that was a new angle. So what was he doing complicating the equation with thoughts of being a husband?

Luke pulled into the underground garage and shoved the gearshift into park. *Father, I'm struggling here. I've worked so hard to understand why I'm not meant to be married, and just when I think I've got it figured out, you send Calli Giovanni into the picture. What's going on?*

Walking past the elevator, he sprinted up the seven flights of stairs hoping to exhaust some of the energy he was wasting creating reasons why he shouldn't see Calli. He paused at the top of the stairs.

You promise peace and understanding to those who ask. I don't even know what I'm asking for, Father, but some-

thing tells me, You have a reason for bringing this fireball into my life. So I guess I'll leave it to You to lead the way.

Luke unlocked the apartment door, shocked with the surprise greeting him.

"Nancy." He froze in the doorway. Jon's mother was sitting in his recliner. "You didn't tell me you were in town."

"I wanted to surprise both of you." She glanced at Jon, who was sitting on the sofa, looking less than thrilled.

Luke looked from one to the other. One was working hard to look confident, the other trying to look totally ambivalent, neither succeeding.

"I'd like to take you both to dinner tonight."

One look at his son told him to decline whatever the cost. "Sorry, Nan. We're busy. If you would have let me know you were coming, we could have made other arrangements."

She blinked, an uncertain expression flashing across her face. "It was a spur-of-the-moment decision."

"From California? Is everything okay? Nothing's happened to your folks, has it?"

"No, they're fine. They send greetings." Her voice turned sticky sweet.

"I'll bet." He watched as she tipped her nose in the air and flicked her hair over her shoulder. From the look on his son's face, the last hour hadn't been easy. "Jon, why don't you let Nancy and I have a few minutes to talk?"

Jon sent him a look of gratitude that would be etched in Luke's mind forever. Launching himself off the sofa, Jon headed for the front door. "I'll see if Nate's home." He turned to leave, then paused. "Oh. Bye…Nancy."

"Goodbye, son. I'll see you soon."

Jon eagerly dashed out the door, slamming it behind him.

The look of confidence on Nancy's face disappeared and Luke was feeling less than cordial. He placed his hands in his pockets, trying to ignore the floral scent of her expensive perfume. ''So, tell me what's really going on, Nancy.''

''I needed to see my son.''

Luke propped himself on the edge of the desk, trying to appear more nonchalant than he felt. ''And?''

Nancy shifted in the chair and crossed her legs. ''I'm not some suspect you're interrogating, Luke.''

He lifted his hands, simultaneously shrugging his shoulders. ''Didn't realize I was out of line. You haven't contacted Jon in months, you hang up on me when you finally call, then I find you sitting in my living room that very afternoon. I can't turn off my instincts, Nan. Especially when Jon's involved.'' Luke moved to the antique chair facing Nancy.

''Don't call me Nan.''

''Sorry. Thought you liked it.'' He waited, anticipating an argument.

''I'm getting married.'' She ran her hand down the leg of her jeans. An obnoxiously large diamond blinded him clear across the room.

Luke was mildly surprised. Shouldn't have been, but he was. Nancy lived a fast-paced life. If the diamond was real, she had finally hit easy street. If not, she had hit bottom and hadn't figured it out yet. Either way, he didn't care. He knew just enough about her current life to know that there was no more room in it for his son now than there had been in the past thirteen years. ''I hope you'll finally be happy.''

''I want Jon to spend the summer with us. See how it goes.''

He stiffened, as though she had just punched him in the gut. ''See how it goes?''

''You've had Jon for twelve years, Luke. It's my turn to have him now.''

In thirteen years she'd taken her son no farther than

across town to visit her parents. And even that had never been for more than an obligatory "showing." Her parents had made it clear that Luke wasn't good enough for Nancy. They had plans for her, and he didn't fit into that mold—neither did a child. Now she wanted to play mommy. "I didn't think you were into sharing. You gave him up. Call a lawyer, Nancy. I've been more than fair."

"I'm pregnant." Her voice cracked and she looked at her hands. "I want Jon and this baby to know one another. I want them to be a family."

Luke stood up and walked into the kitchen. He needed a glass of water before he choked on his own words.

All this time he'd been both father and mother. Struggled to raise his son alone. To make a family from just the two of them. And now, after walking out of their lives, she wanted to offer Jon the one thing Luke couldn't.

She followed him. "I'm sorry to break it to you this way, Luke."

"What did you tell Jon?"

"That I want a chance to know him."

"Does he want to go?"

"No," she said bitterly.

"Then I'd suggest you listen to him." Luke took a deep breath, struggling to remain calm. "No offense, Nancy, but Jon hasn't spent more than a couple hours with you every other year." He felt little more than pity for the spoiled woman he'd once married. "I'm no lawyer, but I think you'd have a stronger case if you'd shown a little more consistent interest. If you really want to be part of his life, take it one step at a time."

"Still giving orders, aren't you, Luke? You seem to think you can decide what's right for everyone. I think it's up to Jon to decide if he wants to see me. I think he will, too, if you'd let me have some time alone with him," she demanded just as Jon walked in the door.

Jon stared at his mother, disgust in his eyes. "I don't want to have anything to do with you!"

"Jonny," Nancy whispered, looking at Luke, her eyes pleading for help. "Please don't do this. I'm sorry."

"I'm never going with you. My family is here. You don't care about me."

"I'm your mother."

"You're nobody's mom, especially not mine. I don't want your stupid family. *Dad* and I are a family."

Luke sensed his son's pain. He embraced the young boy who was trying to stand up for him. "Settle down, Jon. Nothing is going to be forced upon you."

Tears brimmed in Jon's eyes. "I won't go!"

"We're not going to talk about that now." Luke lifted Jon's chin. "I'm going to walk Nancy to her car. Just try to calm down. We'll handle this together."

Luke took Nancy by the arm and led her to the door.

She paused momentarily. "I'll see you soon, Jon."

In the elevator, Luke backed against the wall, arms crossed in front of him. "Anything else you want to say?"

"I can't believe you let him talk to me that way!"

"Under the circumstances, I think he has every right to voice his feelings."

"And where were you today? Is he always left alone like that?"

"Before you start, I think you'd better face the facts. Number one—before I'd even consider letting Jon go to *visit* you, he'd have to agree to it. Number two—you *have* no maternal rights where Jon is concerned. And number three—just to set your mind at ease, he's of legal age to be left alone for a few hours." Having unconsciously worked his way toward Nancy, Luke backed away. "I'm sorry—always have been—that you made the choice to give him up. But then, you never asked me, did you?"

"You'd really deny your son the chance to have a complete family?"

"How can you think that you can make a family by throwing a few people into a house together? A family is a huge investment, Nancy. And being a parent means one hundred percent investment. Is that really what you have in mind?"

When the elevator door opened, Nancy ran past Luke and through the lobby door. He followed her, and blocked the car door when she tried to open it. "I've *never* tried to stop you from seeing him. All I'm asking is that you take this slow. He needs a mother, more than two hours a year."

"You don't have to throw my mistakes in my face, Luke."

"You're the one who's threatening me with legal action. I'm merely stating the facts." Luke stepped back and opened the door. "Keep in touch."

Luke went back upstairs. Facing his son was agony. Defending his ex-wife was worse.

"I won't go with her. She's never cared about me."

"That's not true. She was only four years older than you are now when she had you, Jon. She had tough decisions to make."

"Lots of kids keep their babies."

"I don't know what to tell you, Jon. It may have been the best decision for her—for all of us. I can't say. You and I moved on and did the best we could."

"What did you *ever* like about her?"

Luke thought, then blew out a deep breath. This kid knew how to go for the jugular. "I guess all the usual things a teenage boy likes about a teenage girl. She was pretty and fun, and paid attention to me. What we did wasn't right, or even very smart. We made a poor choice, and faced the consequences."

"But you kept me, and she ran."

"Our priorities were different, but that doesn't make her a bad person."

"Do you still love her?"

Luke shook his head. "She gave me you, Jon. I don't love her, but I do care about her. I would never change the way things turned out. I wouldn't trade being a father for anything."

Jon remained silent. Luke knew it was a lot for a kid to think about. There was nothing he could have done that would have prepared him for this day.

Luke again thought about the time Jon asked for a baby brother for his birthday. Year after year, they had the same discussion, with the same end result. No. And now Nancy was giving Jon the opportunity to have what he'd asked for.

Chapter Nine

Calli closed the door to her apartment and groaned, upset with herself for giving Luke her phone number.

Not only was she upset at that, but also because she had agreed to help him teach the self-defense class. He was right—she did believe in the cause. Anyone who knew Calli knew she preached personal safety. It had nothing to do with the fact that Luke would be the instructor, she silently insisted. If Bart had asked, she'd have done it, as well. *But not with such anticipation.*

She dropped onto the checkered couch, hugging her well-loved rag doll with the incriminating smile. "Don't look at me that way, Bessie. He may *not* be the cop from the apartments. And even if he is, I didn't see anything that would help his case." Running a hand through her hair, Calli immediately stifled the smile that resulted from thinking of Luke Northrup. In three years, no one had broken through the cold shell of hostility she had wrapped around herself. Until Luke.

Could she ever completely let go of the anger that had

become so comfortable? Would she ever feel the peace of forgiveness? Or the satisfaction of seeing justice served?

She reminded herself that Luke Northrup was a sergeant for the Palmer Police Department. For all she knew, Luke could be one of the many officers who loathed the mere idea of citizens joining the fight against crime. There could be nothing personal between them.

Calli fixed herself a sandwich and salad. Sitting at the table, she automatically pulled the journal from her purse. Calli paused, then tossed the book aside. She hunched over and rubbed the tension tightly strung between her eyebrows and her shoulders. *Why me? Why Mike?* Why *God?* Then in a faintness she didn't dare acknowledge—*Out of all the possible men in this city,* Why *a cop?*

The ache traveled from her stomach to her heart as the anger overwhelmed her fragile emotions. In desperation, she took a bite, choking it down with determination. *I cannot cry.* She guzzled milk, then took another bite, willing this guilt to quit eating at her from inside out.

Calli recalled the pain of her brother's untimely death. The torment of losing the man she'd loved to the system of justice. So determined was her fiancé to impress superiors with his ability to disassociate himself from a case that Brad had watched the family bury her brother—then closed the case, stating there was not enough evidence to go for a conviction. As the months had passed, her entire family moved on with their lives, leaving Calli alone, hiding in the shadows.

Love and betrayal. They went together like fire and ice. And she knew better than to play with fire.

Calli opened a bag of chocolate sandwich cookies and took a handful with a glass of milk. Dipping a cookie, she thought of Luke's suggestion that she "let it out." She'd caught the concern in his eyes. He cared that she didn't react; he worried about her anger.

She didn't want to feel again. Not for Luke. Not for anyone. With a deep breath of resolve, Calli opened the journal and started writing about the afternoon's events. Reading back through the entry, she was startled by her own words and the feelings expressed.

Her fiancé had never been able to handle emotions. He constantly badgered her to forget the past. The more she tried, the more she failed. Even as a cop, Brad couldn't understand her need to do what little she could to protect the innocent. In his opinion, that was up to the police. She tried to change for him, but in the end, lost everything anyway. Lost the love and support of her fiancé and her family.

Where are you, God? All around me the enemy strikes, and each day I see a little less of You.

"They can't get away with this! Tiger can't elude justice forever." Memories of Mike came to mind, and tears blurred her vision. "Don't go turning to mush, Calli. Get back out there and patrol."

"Refrain from anger and turn from wrath." The verse brought peace, loosening the hold guilt had on her conscience.

She rinsed her dishes then splashed water on her tired face. Calli snuggled into the sofa and pulled out the tea towels she was embroidering for her grandmother's birthday.

The phone rang, and Calli was surprised to hear Luke's deep voice. "I wanted see if you gave me a working phone number."

"Don't trust me, Officer?" She realized that her smile was growing wider; her grip on the receiver tightened and a spark ignited in her chest.

"Let's just say I'm in the hard evidence line of business."

Her heart sank. "Everything in black and white."

"So to speak."

The reality of the situation was returning. She'd been this route before and wasn't ready to repeat it. Luke Northrup, like all the other significant men in her life, seemed to look at life logically; he was used to being in control, and would never understand her life in the shadows. Why did she let herself hope he would be any different?

"You there?"

She blinked, and realized she'd tuned him out. "Sorry. I was thinking of something else. What did you say?"

"I was saying that this isn't like me."

She giggled softly. "What? You're not usually arrogant and pushy?"

"Afraid that goes with the job. No, I don't..."

Calli found herself worrying her bottom lip between her teeth. She was sinking fast. If he asked her out one more time, she wouldn't be able to decline. Mission or no mission. "Go on, I'm listening."

"Great. *Now* I have your attention. I'm not doing something right here, am I? What I'm trying to say, Calli, is that I don't date much, and I'm not usually this...direct in my personal life. I want to apologize if I've come on like a bulldozer."

She laughed. Calli couldn't believe her ears. He was humble and honest. And she'd just laughed with Luke. Again. There was something warm and captivating about his humor.

"I don't usually go to such lengths to find someone, I mean personally...off duty." His voice echoed her unspoken longings.

"I'm glad you did," she whispered before thinking. *I shouldn't have admitted that. I can't help but hurt him.* "Luke, I...I was en..." She tried repeatedly to tell him about Brad, but the pain went too deep. How could she ever trust another cop? *No, I can't do this.* "Luke, I have to be honest with you...." *Slow down, Calli. He's obviously not like Brad. Think about this before you do something you'll regret.* "I'd like to be friends, but that's all I'm interested in right now."

On the other end of the line, she heard Luke exhale. "That's exactly what I wanted to say."

Calli and Luke met before class the next week to review the course objectives. Luke looked across the table, old fears and uncertainties dousing him in constant showers of reality. Nancy's visit served as a bitter reminder that he wasn't the marrying kind.

Teaching the first class with Calli was awkward, but uneventful. They both rushed off afterward, as if equally hesitant to give anyone the impression there was any sort of attraction between them.

Annoyed with himself for letting Nancy's return interfere with a possible relationship with Calli, Luke found himself reassessing every nuance of the time they'd just spent together.

Patrolling that night would have been impossible alone. Tom didn't say much, except that Luke "had it bad." Then Tom dropped the subject, knowing the silence would torture Luke all night. They had three routine speeding contacts and followed a lead on the case they were working on, but nothing panned out.

Luke found himself cruising Calli's neighborhood more often the next week. And as promised, he met her at the store each evening to make sure she made it home safely. In hindsight, he was kicking himself for insisting to do so. The agony of seeing her every day was like buying candy when you couldn't eat it.

Calli seemed annoyed with the arrangement, as well, and before class that Thursday finally told him about it.

"I'm perfectly capable of seeing myself home after

work, Luke. You don't need to bother.'' Calli unzipped her bright pink-and-navy jacket and tossed it onto a chair.

It had already been a long day, and Luke was anxious to get through the class and away from the sweet temptation of Calandre Giovanni. ''Just trying to do my job.''

''Then do your job! I don't need a personal bodyguard.''

He shook his head and chuckled. ''Fine, Calli. Take care of yourself.''

As if she was prepared for him to play the possessive fool, she stared at him for a brief moment before satisfaction lit her coal-black eyes.

''Happy now?'' He yanked the sweatshirt over his head and tossed it into his bag, ready for class in his tank top and shorts.

Calli stepped back. With her eyelids lowered, she looked coy and more alluring than ever. ''Thank you. It's just that I know what a bother it is, and there's really no reason for it.'' A softness lingered in her voice.

''Nope, no reason at all.'' Luke spread mats across the small gym floor, taking advantage of the few minutes to let out his irritation.

''Shouldn't I move these chairs?''

''They're fine.''

''But when we break into groups, there won't be enough room. Will there?''

''We're not doing much role-playing tonight,'' Luke snapped.

''Well, you could have told me earlier.''

''If you want to do something, get those canisters out of my bag. We're going to review some optional weapons tonight.''

Calli hesitated, then looked in his bag, and held one up for his approval. ''This?''

''Yeah, slide the one off my belt, too.''

Hanna nudged Calli when she came into the classroom. "So, how's it going with the cop?" she whispered.

Calli turned to her cousin and saw the laughter in Hanna's eyes. "Where have you been? I've been trying to call you for two weeks. What in the world were you thinking when you told Luke how to get hold of me?"

"I was on a business trip." Hanna said innocently. "I was thinking he's just your type."

"Says *who?*" she growled.

"Ladies—let's save the combat for class. Calli..."

"Would you quit telling me what to do!" she snapped, accentuating the annoyance within herself.

Luke walked toward her, his mouth clenched tighter with every step. Calli felt her heart beating faster as she backed herself into the wall. "In case you forgot, *I'm* the instructor. When I tell you to do something, I don't need a debate! Now, would you *please* quit arguing with *everything* I tell you?"

Looking into his jade-green eyes, Calli fought her attraction to the dynamic vitality and control Luke exuded. Realizing she'd taken her frustration out on him, she bit her lip to stifle a defensive outcry while Luke pivoted and strode to the front of the room.

Hanna smiled as if to say "I told you so!" Calli straightened her back, vowing not to reveal his effect on her. She couldn't fall in love with another cop, and she had no intention of permitting herself to be snared in his trap. Girding herself with resolve, she rushed past her cousin and to Luke's side. Women filtered into the room, and Calli met his accusing eyes without flinching. "So, what is on tonight's agenda?"

"Just follow my lead," he said, leaving no room for discussion.

She stiffened at the challenge. "No problem. You're the boss."

Calli watched Luke "perform," using his sense of humor to make everyone more comfortable with the frightening topic that could make a difference between life or death. She admired his ability to laugh and poke fun at human nature while leaving no doubt of his intolerance for violence.

"Another mode of protection we highly recommend women carry is pepper Mace. You can find it at most sporting-goods stores."

Calli held up the canister that Luke had set on the desk.

"Pepper Mace is an oil-based spray which is as effective on dogs as it is on humans. That's why the postal carriers use pepper Mace instead of the older version of chemical Mace. It's also more intense."

Without looking, Luke added, "The canister Calli has is what we call an inert, which is used for training." He walked across the room. "You spray it in a zigzag pattern to form a 'wall' between you and the assailant. Go ahead."

"But Luke..."

He backed up, the humor disappearing from his voice. "Come on, Calli. Just spray it."

The class was laughing.

Calli looked up from the hairspray-type can, surprised to see Luke barreling toward her.

She pointed the nozzle and pressed the trigger, madly waving her arm.

Luke ran straight into the foggy "wall."

"Don't stop until... A-a-a-ugh." Luke coughed and dropped to the floor.

Calli ran toward him. "Luke..."

"Stay back. It's Mace."

She stepped away, eyes wide. Instantaneously the class stopped laughing.

Unable to open his eyes, Luke stood up and reached for Calli. "Help me to the rest room. I have to wash this off."

Grabbing his arm to lead him, she felt her eyes sting. "I'm so sorry, Luke."

"Water. Quick. This stuff is killing me," he complained.

Calli's eyes began to water from the residual spray. "Oh, I'm sorry. But you told me to..."

"I know what I said," he growled.

Rounding the corner, Calli paused in front of the two locker room doors.

Men's. I can't go in there.

Women's. He can't go in there.

"What're we waiting for?"

"Nothing." She pushed through the door, rushing him past the dressing room and to the showers. She turned on the water, and guided Luke into the spray of water.

"Soap." He rasped, gulping water and spitting it out.

"There isn't any. Hang on." Calli spun around. "Is there *any* soap in here?"

"Check the sink," a man in a business suit suggested. Luckily, he was the only other occupant in the locker room at the time.

At the sink, Calli pulled the lever to dispense the soap and ran back to the shower.

"It's liquid soap. Hold out your hands."

Luke lathered his face and arms. "What do you think you're doing in the men's locker room?"

"Where did you want me to take you? Into the women's?"

"It's not like *I* could see anything!"

Calli grinned, beginning to see the humor in the situation, now that he was out of intense pain. "Don't worry. There's no one else in here but a guy in a suit. Actually, his tie is so bad, I think my eyes hurt a little, too," she added in a hushed tone.

Luke laughed. He finished rinsing, opening his eyes under the flow before turning off the water. Then he sloshed to the bin for a towel.

Calli labored to keep a straight face as Luke marched out the door, sopping wet and straight into a crowd of wide-eyed women.

"Class dismissed." Luke squished down the hall to the gym.

No one moved.

"I think Luke would appreciate some privacy right now. I hope he has dry clothes in that bag of supplies." Calli watched him in silence.

Hanna was the first to laugh. "I can see it now. Grandma Giovanni is going to ask, 'How did you meet Luke, Calli?' 'Oh, I sprayed him with Mace.'"

A round of laughter shot from Calli's mouth before she regained her control.

Most of the women had already gathered their belongings from the room and were leaving. Hanna and Calli visited in the lobby until Luke joined them. "This bag was still in the room." He tossed Calli's jacket to her.

"It's mine," Hanna admitted. "Hope you get feeling better, Luke. I'll talk to you tomorrow, Calli."

Calli faced Luke. "Are you okay?"

"Other than my pride, you mean?"

"I've never seen a better demonstration of the effectiveness of Mace. Everyone was totally impressed." She bit her lip, trying to keep the corners from turning up.

"I'll bet."

"I don't know what you're worried about, Luke. I'm serious. They were speechless."

"After my spiel, it's a good thing someone could stay speechless."

She smiled sympathetically. "It was nothing to beat yourself up over, under the circumstances. One day you're going to laugh at this."

"You can tell which side of the demonstration you were on."

"Do you have time for a cup of coffee—as a peace offering?"

His eyes sparkled with the love of combat. "I wish I did, but I have to go back home to get dry clothes before work. How about Sunday afternoon?"

She could hardly say no after tonight. Neither of them had acknowledged the friendship had moved past the platonic level. Not aloud anyway.

Chapter Ten

Calli pulled the Indian blanket jacket over her turtleneck sweater. She'd spent the past two days practicing her apology for being so rude before the incident with the Mace.

Luke had left a message on her answering machine with the time and Tom's address. She'd played the message over and again just to listen to his voice. Still, Calli had to remind herself that this wasn't a romantic dinner. Unsure she was ready to take this step to a closer friendship, Calli had tried to back out, but finally consented when Luke admitted it was dinner with him and Jon at his partner's house. It couldn't even be considered a date.

Calli picked up her keys and the piece of paper with the Davises' address. Somehow, she thought, this should be less intimidating than a date. But it wasn't. She was not only meeting Luke's best friends, but his teenage son, as well. Not that anything had changed between them. There wasn't any point trying to kid herself. Calli had vowed that she would never fall in love with another arrogant, egotistical law enforcement officer.

Immediately recognizing Luke's cherry-red sports car,

she parked behind it. Before she had a chance to look for the house, Luke stepped from the arched doorway. Calli watched him cross the street, his stride long and easygoing. The faded denim hugged his lean legs and the gray T-shirt made his shoulders look even broader than usual. His arresting smile and wink made her glad she'd come, despite her plans for later.

His friendship was as tempting as a healing dose of Colorado sunshine, yet dangerous as the scorching heat that accompanied it.

"There aren't any numbers on the house, so I've been watching for you."

Calli opened the hatchback of the rental car and removed a platter of layered dip and a bag of tortilla chips. "Hope I didn't keep you waiting."

"Why was I afraid you were going to stand me up?" he whispered, standing behind her.

Trying to ignore her hammering heart, Calli took a deep breath and let it out slowly. "Instinct. You're a cop. You've learned not to expect anything from anyone."

Luke chuckled. "You're only half-right, I am a cop. But I've learned to expect the worst, from everyone. And you, Calli Giovanni, have proven how wrong that is. I'm very glad you came." Luke held the door as Calli admonished herself for being so frank with him.

She had to be crazy to think she could go into a friendship, putting her own motives against those of one more man whose legal, moral and ethical obligations were to protect and serve. Tonight she'd explain to Luke that she couldn't see him again. There was no need complicating her life any more than it already was. She'd tell him everything, and it would be over. Surely the truth would convince him that they weren't meant to be together.

All she had to do was stay in control. *Easier said than done!*

Luke introduced her to his son, Jon, Tom's wife, Vanessa, and their twins. Calli was surprised to see how captivated Jon was with the babies.

The group played a round of table tennis and ate snacks, taking turns entertaining the newborns. She hadn't held a baby in years, and was enthralled with the warmth of such a tiny child. When the baby cried, Jon rescued her, and Joseph quieted instantly.

Calli could see immediately that Tom and Luke were much closer than just partners. They joked around and shared family tales. Jon was polite and comfortable with his father's repetition of his baby stories, and even joined in, ribbing Luke in return.

While the two men played a tie-breaking round, Vanessa, Jon and Calli talked about Jon's school. Then Jon excused himself to go to Youth Group with a friend.

Luke wrapped his arm around his son's shoulder and discreetly hugged the boy. "I'll pick you up at eight."

Jon nodded, grabbing his coat from the rack. "It was nice to meet you, Calli."

"You too, Jon."

He stopped to say a special goodbye to each baby, then ran out the door and down the street.

Calli looked admiringly at Luke. "Jon reminds me of my younger brother." As soon as Calli said the words, she froze.

"I hope that's good. I know how younger brothers can be."

A lump in Calli's throat prevented her from responding immediately. She blinked away the temptation to let her emotions take over. This wasn't the time. "You've done a fine job raising him, Luke."

He smiled, a soft smile that confirmed what that job had meant to him. Calli looked away, unable to meet his gaze. Baby Joseph wailed from the corner of the room. Vanessa was upstairs checking dinner, and Tom was changing Jordan's diaper.

Luke turned and rescued the fussy infant from the swing and walked back to Calli. She marveled at the sight of Luke's long fingers cradling the baby and declined his silent offer to let her hold Joseph. The man was a natural with babies. Luke was a father first, she noted, then a cop. *Just like Daddy.*

Calli cooed at Joseph as he whimpered in Luke's arms, uncomfortably aware that Luke's gaze was nowhere near the baby, but on her instead. The child quieted momentarily, then began to fuss again.

Tom returned, seeming flustered by his frantic twins. "So I'm not Superdad."

Luke made a lame attempt to sympathize. "One was tough. I can't imagine two at a time. But if anyone deserves this, it's you, bro." He chuckled mischievously and snuggled the baby next to his shoulder, undaunted by the noise.

Calli smiled. Jordan started screaming in Tom's arms. "Ah, Vanessa, I think your son needs something we can't give him."

Vanessa joined them in the basement and cradled the baby. "We'll be back in a while. Excuse us. Tom, would you mind helping me." She jerked her head to the side, motioning for Tom to follow.

Ducking under the low ceiling light, Tom backed away. "I'll go change Joseph. I'd tell you to make yourself at home, Luke, but you already do."

Luke shook his head, and tipped his head down, seemingly to hide his embarrassment. Calli felt his discomfort at being so obviously left alone.

"How long have you two been partners?"

"Too long." He motioned toward the Ping-Pong table, and suggested another game.

Getting ready to serve, Calli picked up the white ball and lifted her paddle.

"This time, cut the act."

"Act?" He'd figured it out. Somehow he'd placed her at the scene. It was over. She wanted to cry. Why? If she wanted to bring an end to this before it got more complicated, why did she suddenly feel an ache of loss?

"You are one dreadful actress, by the way, if you don't mind me saying so."

"What do you mean?"

"Pretending you don't know how to play this game. If my ego needed boosting, you'd be the last person I'd hire for the job, Miss Giovanni."

Calli felt as if a huge weight had been lifted from her shoulders. *He's not talking about the anonymous calls.* Wondering if she should feel guilty for the relief she felt, Calli turned toward the table, glancing over her shoulder to Luke. "There you go insulting me again. And I was about to apologize for being so rude in class the other night."

"It's not an insult at all. Thankfully my ego is more than capable of handling a fireball like you. In fact, it's growing *very* fond of the challenge."

He stepped closer, first setting his paddle aside, then hers. Their eyes searched each other's, until his gaze settled on her lips.

She couldn't move. Couldn't think. His nearness made her senses spin. Without a touch, he'd brought her back to life. "You're arrogant."

"Yup." The intimacy of his smile soothed her.

"And relentless."

"I suppose so."

"You're..."

"Calli, don't talk." His lips brushed against hers as he spoke. It was a silent challenge, and she was determined to meet it. After a series of slow, shivery kisses, Calli succumbed to his sweetness, giving up her own agenda. Her knees weakened as Luke coaxed her lips into unison with his.

When the kiss ended, Calli relaxed, snug in his embrace. For the moment, there were no shadows across her heart. Only a warm sunny glow. One that had faded long, long ago. Too long, she decided. This was what she needed. Someone to care about.

Not just anyone, she realized, but Luke. He was exactly the type of man she wanted. Witty and compassionate. Exactly the type of man she needed. Stubborn, yet funny. He knew who—and *what*—he was. He had his priorities figured out and didn't need anyone to affirm his convictions.

Luke Northrup was a man of integrity, and the last thing he needed was a woman with none.

With that realization, Calli backed away, letting her hands drop to her sides. She tried to speak, but couldn't form the words.

Luke smiled. "You were getting ready to throw another insult at me."

She laughed, too stunned by her own reaction to argue. Tears burned beneath her eyelids, and she blinked away this foreign urge to cry. "You're incorrigible."

"You're slipping, Calandre. Surely you can do better than that."

During dinner Luke and Tom began discussing a current case. They were careful to avoid using names, and if Calli hadn't been on the scene, she'd have never figured out what they were talking about. The hospitalized kid Luke had been waiting for the night they'd met *was* the boy who'd fallen in front of her four-wheel drive.

Luke took a bite of enchilada immediately followed by a swallow of milk. "We have to find out what A.C. saw."

Calli furrowed her brows. "Who's A.C.?"

"Stands for anonymous caller. She's been calling in for years. We can't seem to catch up with her."

They gave me a nickname, she thought.

Trying to look genuinely innocent, yet curious, she pressed for information. "And what do you think she saw?"

"Maybe she saw the Eastsiders beating up the poor kid. Maybe just the break-ins. That's what we need to find out."

Calli nodded in silence. She didn't dare ask anything more for fear of giving herself away. She listened as the two discussed other cases, wondering when and how she could tell Luke.

After dinner, Calli and Vanessa took the twins for a walk while Luke and Tom did dishes. Calli instinctively held the baby's bottom through the denim of the carrier.

"Luke looks happier than I've seen him in years, Calli."

Calli swallowed a lump of guilt. "He's easy to be with."

"He and Tom are quite a pair. Little did I know they were preparing me for twins. What one doesn't think of, the other does. I think that's why they are such a good team at work."

Calli laughed, more at the irony of this entire mess than Vanessa's comment. Here she was falling for the cop that happened to be looking for her. *Hide in plain sight.*

"I can see that in them." Calli longed to know more about the man who made her laugh, and cry and live again. "How do you deal with being a police officer's wife?"

Vanessa raised one eyebrow and looked Calli square in the eye. "It's like living for God. You live each day as if He would come back for you any time. With Tom, I don't leave things unsaid. I don't go to bed angry. We just don't know what tomorrow brings."

"Do you ever worry about him?"

"Every day. Some wives don't, but I think most of us worry more than we let on. Tom doesn't tell me everything, but I can tell when something is bothering him." They walked in silence, then finally Vanessa continued. "It's worth the risk. Loving Tom, I mean. I just can't imagine who I'd be without his love."

Calli rubbed her hand over the curly-haired infant cuddled against her.

What would it feel like to have another human being love her unconditionally? To have someone know everything about her and love her anyway? Right or wrong, to accept who she was and what she did? She wasn't sure she believed it possible.

Would Luke understand her silence? She thought of her brother and her long-lost mission, and losing Luke.

She once thought there would never be a man who could chip through this bulletproof vest she wore to protect her heart. But here he was. And just her luck, he was a cop.

Chapter Eleven

Calli and Hanna met at the park for lunch and a walk to enjoy the first day of spring. After listening to her cousin's complaints about recent dates, Calli told her about joining Luke for dinner at Tom's the previous Sunday. "The man is arrogant."

Hanna laughed. "Arrogant? Luke?"

"Of course Luke. You saw him before class last week, ordering me around, playing 'macho man,' in control..." Calli felt the warm Colorado sunshine on her face and looked at the tall skyscrapers surrounding the park.

"What I saw was a man with the patience of a saint. It's you who's painted that arrogant image of Brad on every uniformed officer you meet, Calandre. Luke is *nothing* like Brad. And as for class last week, *you* were every bit as responsible for that squabbling."

She couldn't argue that point. "Okay, enough. Luke and I already settled that."

Halfway around the path, Calli heard her name.

"Calli? Is that you?"

She spun around. "Hi, Vanessa. How are all of you?"

Calli knelt next to the stroller to say hello to the two fuzzy-haired boys. The twins appeared to be enjoying the beautiful day, intently watching the ducks and geese as they passed. Their mother's rosy glow made Calli wish for a family and that same happiness. "Looks like Jordan and Joseph are having fun. Vanessa, this is my cousin, Hanna Giovanni. Hanna, this is Vanessa Davis, Luke's partner's wife."

"Oh, yes, Luke has told us about you, Hanna. It's nice to meet you. We sure enjoyed having you over, Calli. I'd like to do it again. You and Luke interested?" The sparkle in her dark eyes made Calli wonder what Luke had told his friends.

"I'd like that. With all of our crazy schedules, it's tough to find time, isn't it?"

The three women chatted a bit, and laughed again when Vanessa mentioned the incident with the Mace. "They stopped by that next night for a cup of coffee and Luke actually blushed when Tom told me."

Hanna lifted her eyebrows. "Luke blushed? Ooh-eee. Love is in the air."

Calli laughed nervously, afraid to admit that she wanted more than anything for the words to be true.

Vanessa turned toward home, and Hanna and Calli continued around the lake. "I spent a lot of time thinking about what you said, Hanna. I wasn't after revenge when I started this mission. I simply wanted to find enough evidence to let justice be served."

"I know. It's a fine line to draw."

"And I think I crossed it. I lost sight of my goal. After Brad destroyed what little evidence there was against Tiger, I... Well, it doesn't really matter now. What does matter is I'm through patrolling."

Hanna let out a little squeal. "Really? Completely through?"

Trying to free herself from her cousin's suffocating hug, Calli laughed. "Don't get excited yet. That's not all."

Hanna's arms dropped and she held Calli at arm's length. "And?"

"I'm through patrolling, but I'm not through with my mission. I'm still looking for a way to prevent gang problems. I'm going to go back to school and finish my degree. I'm going to change my major to counseling."

Her cousin's face lit up. "That's my cousin!"

"It's not as easy as it sounds. I still find my resentment taking over at times. But I am trying to let it go." She told Hanna about the graffiti incident at the store and the anger the gang member's threats renewed.

"Remember Philippians 4:13 says, 'I can do all things through God who strengthens me.' Don't forget where your source of strength comes from, Calli. He won't let you down."

"How could I forget with you here to remind me?" *You and hopefully Luke. Maybe that's why we keep meeting. He's as stubborn as you, Hanna. Neither of you seems to give up on me.*

Later that evening, she shifted in her seat as the speaker's monotone drifted to mere background noise. The lecture hall had been filled with community leaders, law enforcement personnel and social services workers. Calli was among the few "interested citizens" who wanted to understand more about the gang culture and what could be done to help.

She looked around the room, wondering what others were doing to change the situation. Since she was no longer actively patrolling, Calli was particularly interested in information on programs that worked to prevent the problems gangs represented. Throughout the workshop several of the speakers referred to gangs as a "single-parent syndrome," claiming that there was a severe lack of role models for youths to reach out to when trouble strikes.

Calli had felt the repercussions of the single-parent household, and guessed that it had been even tougher for her brother. At least she had had her mother. But her mother had been totally exasperated by Mike's strong personality. And with her father away so much…it made sense now.

She didn't want to agree with one of the opinions expressed that members of gangs were also "victims" in their own rite. Yet, she realized, sometimes the truth was a double-edged sword.

Clapping startled her from her daze and concluded the program. When she realized the speaker had finished, the room was quickly emptying. Calli had no idea how long she'd been in her trance. Gathering her bags from beneath the chair, Calli saw Luke walking across the lecture hall, toward her. His badge glistened against the dark blue shirt—a glaring reminder of what stood between them. He looked even more handsome and confident in uniform.

All week long Luke Northrup had occupied her thoughts. She'd tried to come up with a way to stop her feelings for him from growing. She didn't want either of them to be hurt. They were going to be. More than she wanted to admit. He hadn't a clue who she really was.

Not only that, but Luke could very well have been one of the officers involved. One of the officers who'd dismissed her claims that Mike had not been interested in gangs. If Luke was one of them… No, she didn't want to know. After tonight, the foundation of her argument was on shaky ground, even in her own eyes.

Her parents had tried to convince her that there was no way she could have prevented what had happened. Yet to her, it was she who was responsible for Mike that night. She'd never forget the phone call from the hospital asking if her brother was home, and the horror that had followed when she'd discovered he'd snuck out of the house through his bedroom window.

For three years she'd tried to prove her brother's innocence. To find the gang member responsible for taking Mike's life. She'd struggled to move on. She had done what little she could to prevent the same thing happening to someone else's brother, or son or nephew. For three years she'd put her own life on the line. Spent her time, money, her very soul chasing the ever-elusive justice. What else could she do?

"Commit your way to the Lord." The words came to Calli from nowhere and a calm washed over her. *God? Is that you? Or the enemy trying to make me feel guilty about staying home?* Calli could no longer deny that everything that happened the night of her accident still frightened her.

Her decision didn't come without a struggle. She had promised Mike she would find his killer. A promise was a promise. Yet her mission had already cost her plenty. And if she didn't do something, her friendship with Luke would be the next casualty.

She avoided his gaze, knowing she couldn't avoid him.

"I didn't realize you were interested in gang intervention. What did you think of the program?"

"The officer's talk was...very informative." And a bit idealistic, she reflected. There are a lot of facts they conveniently left out. She couldn't look him in the eye. Not when all she could think of was telling him the truth, and then telling him goodbye, forever.

"You okay?" Luke asked, as if she looked ill. He folded the burgundy theater chairs, clearing a path for Calli.

Calli stood and backed away, trying to forget the peace she'd felt when wrapped in Luke's arms. There was no use wishing for something she couldn't have. "I'm fine." She stepped past Luke and headed for the stairs of the antiquated college building, hoping to steer clear of the chatty stragglers who were also making their exit.

"Let me walk you to your car. It's dark out there."

Calli deduced it wasn't really a question, but a statement. Arrogant or not, Luke had a protective nature. She couldn't believe he'd like the extent of her involvement in amateur crime fighting. To a cop, interest didn't directly translate to action. She knew that from past experience.

Pulling the radio from his belt, Luke informed Tom that he'd be escorting a citizen through the parking lot. A macho confirmation reverberated through the walkie-talkie.

"Unfortunately, Tom and I officially went back on duty when the class ended. Three officers called in with the flu tonight." Luke held the outside door as Calli fished her keys from her purse. Within a few yards of the building they were enveloped into the shadows.

Calli subconsciously wove a key between each finger.

"Think you could join me for lunch tomorrow?"

The courage she'd felt a minute ago waned. "We agreed to keep this platonic, Northrup."

He crossed his arms over his chest. "You agreed, and 'platonic' doesn't exclude eating. We need to discuss this week's class."

Calli pushed her shoulders back and glanced at him. Even in the dark, she could see something sparkling far back in his eyes. Confidence. Determination. Interest. She may be able to avoid the attraction between them temporarily, but she knew that Luke Northrup wouldn't give in easily. Nor did she want him to. This time though, she wouldn't get what she wanted, and neither would Luke.

She knew that she couldn't start a relationship this way. Without the truth, she would eventually have to choose—her mission, or Luke. Even with the truth, Calli was on shaky ground. As much as she wanted to think Luke was different than the other men she knew, she doubted it. He'd taken the same oath as her ex-fiancé. He, too, saw things in black and white.

Luke reached down and took her hand in his, wrapping his fingers around her fist. Calli tried to move the keys before they gouged his hand, but didn't have time.

"What's this?" He took hold of her wrist and raised her hand to look. "You don't trust me to protect you?"

Pulling her hand from his grasp was no easy feat. "It's a habit. Doesn't mean anything."

"It does to me. You're scared of something—or someone. Me?"

"Of course not! How did you come up with that?" Annoyed by the contempt in his voice, Calli sidestepped when Luke reached for her arm. The radio on his belt squawked and Luke turned it down. At the same time his pace increased.

A patrol car zoomed up to them and stopped.

His partner lowered the electric window and leaned across the seat. "Luke, we've got a hot one. Evening, Calli."

"Hi, Tom."

A muscle flicked angrily at Luke's jaw. "I'll talk to you in the morning."

Calli recognized the look in his eyes. She didn't want to get on the wrong side of the law with Sergeant Northrup on the case. "Be careful out there."

Luke winked, and she smiled back.

She thought of the first time her and Luke's "paths" had crossed—the night she'd witnessed and reported the auto thefts. She recalled that it had been that night that the support group had talked about letting go of the past. After all this time, was she finally going to succeed?

After Luke's kiss, the mission was losing its appeal. She wanted love, and happiness and a family.

Chapter Twelve

When Luke and Tom and their patrol car were out of sight, Calli crawled into her sport utility vehicle, relieved that the repairs were finally complete and that she had thought to have it painted a different color. That gave her some comfort—anonymity from Luke and the gangs.

She closed her eyes and whispered. "What do I do, God? I really care for Luke. I know I can't keep going like this."

Anxiety crept through her. Calli lifted her cellular phone and dialed Hanna. "Are you busy?"

"Not too busy to listen." Calli heard the television in the background.

"I'm already out. Would you mind if I came over?" The traffic was heavy but it still wouldn't take long to make the trip to her cousin's new house in the suburbs.

"Come on over. I'll make some popcorn."

Calli headed west and turned the stereo up. Listeners were calling the radio station, requesting love songs to dedicate to lovers, ex-loved ones and special friends. She wondered if Luke listened to music, if he was the type to cuddle up and watch movies or if she would ever have a chance to learn all about what he liked and disliked.

Hanna's house was bright with landscaping lights edging the sidewalk. The crab apple tree stood stark against the deep azure sky, and bright yellow crocuses peeking through the dried leaves in the flower beds glowed in the moonlight.

Calli rang the doorbell and Hanna answered immediately. "So what's up?"

"My life is such a mess!"

Leaning out the door, Hanna said, "I thought you got your sport utility vehicle back, but this one's black! What happened?"

"It's hunter green. They offered the color change at a price I couldn't refuse." Shrugging, Calli continued. "I thought it would make everything with Luke easier, but it doesn't—that's half the problem."

"How's that?" Her cousin turned on the stereo and the two sat on the sofa with an enormous bowl of fluffy white popcorn between them.

"I told you about dinner with Luke at Vanessa and Tom's house Sunday." She continued to tell Hanna about learning that Luke was the cop that had nearly run her off the road. "So now, even though I haven't patrolled since that night, I know Luke needs to ask me questions." She brushed her hair off her face.

"I didn't see anything that will help Luke on the case, but he doesn't know that. Every time I look at the truck, I think of how I'm lying to everyone, myself included...."

Hanna shook her head, as if it was a lost cause. "I hate to state the obvious, but maybe the truth would be best. Either way, Luke probably won't be happy that you've waited this long to tell him."

"I don't want to lose him." Calli's voice cracked with the blatant admission.

"If you don't tell him, you're going to make yourself

sick worrying about when he's going to learn the truth." Hanna took Calli's hand. "Besides, once you answer his questions, it'll be over."

"Do you really believe that?"

Hanna shrugged. "Well, that part will be over."

"And the relationship will be over." Her mind wandered to the night he questioned her in the hospital. She couldn't believe that he'd never asked nor noticed the make of her vehicle and convinced herself that it wasn't lying if he never asked for the information.

The two cousins talked for hours among the plush sofa pillows and soft music. Through a yawn, Hanna finally said, "Calli, I don't have the answer you want."

"No one does."

"You sure about that? When was the last time you bothered to ask?" Her cousin never was one to mince words.

It was after midnight when Calli went home, still thinking about the symposium, and the voice she heard, and Luke. She walked into the apartment, finding it difficult not to compare her tiny apartment to Hanna's new house. They were dusk and sunrise, a warrior and a princess, simplicity and elegance.

She thought of Hanna's disturbing question, unable to put it aside and fall asleep. She recalled the calming voice she'd heard at the end of the symposium. "What did it say? Something about returning..." Calli went to her bookshelf and pulled her dusty Bible from the shelf. Calli closed her eyes and hugged the book to her heart. "What are you trying to tell me, God?"

"Commit your way to the Lord."

Calli had attended church with her family as a child, and explained the voice with having memorized verses and now His words of comfort were subconsciously returning.

The words echoed in her mind. "In quietness and trust, shall be your strength."

What is that supposed to mean? Calli looked up the verse listed in the back of her Bible and read silently, "In returning and rest you shall be saved; in quietness and trust, shall be your strength."

Punching the numbers almost as she took the phone from the receiver, Calli trembled. "Come on, Hanna."

Her cousin's greeting was garbled, as if she was still asleep.

"Hanna, the strangest thing has happened. You have to help me. Wake up." Calli waited, then repeated the plea.

After a few minutes, Hanna woke, dismayed to learn it was four in the morning. "Couldn't this have waited?"

"No." Calli had no idea how to explain.

"Are you okay?" The question was followed by a breathy yawn.

"I'm not sure. Something weird is happening, Hanna. I don't know what to do." Calli told her cousin about the voices and how the Scriptures seemed to speak to the events in Calli's life.

"Wow."

"Wow what? What is God saying to me? Or is it me imagining things?" She gasped for another breath, then babbled on.

"Calli. You do have to be careful when looking at a single Scripture. Just a minute. Let me get my study Bible and we can look the verses up. I'm no theologian, but maybe I can help you find them."

Calli heard noises in the background and shivered as she wrote in her journal what the voices said. She turned to a clean page so she'd have room to write.

Hanna's voice was calm. "Okay, tell me again what happened. I was half-asleep before. We'll start with the verses you heard, then read the whole chapter to see if it still fits the circumstances." When Calli finished, Hanna claimed that she had goose bumps on her arms, as well. "This is stuff you read about."

Together, with the miles of cable connecting them, Hanna led Calli on her search. Hanna looked up key words, then gave Calli a few verses to look for, and she looked for the others.

While the two raced on to the next reference, Calli added, "It doesn't seem that long ago that I was reading this, Hanna. How could I have strayed so far away so quickly?"

"You've been through a lot, Cal. Between the stress and grief, it's understandable."

"Not everyone understands."

"I do."

"You try, but..."

"I do, Calli. There are things you have to let time heal. I couldn't change what you were going through, as much as I wanted to. I knew that God was always with you. He was just waiting for the right time to let you realize it, I guess." There was a long pause. "Or maybe He's been talking to you all along, and you couldn't hear Him. Oh, listen, here's the one! 'Commit your way to the Lord; trust in him and he will do this: He will make your righteousness shine like the dawn, the justice of your causes like the noonday sun.'" She paused, then gasped. "Here it is, Calli—the clincher. 'Be still before the Lord and wait patiently for him; do not fret when men succeed in their ways, when they carry out their wicked schemes. Refrain from anger and turn from wrath: do not fret—it only leads to evil."

Tears welled in Calli's eyes, and she read the last verse on their scavenger hunt through the Bible. A chill shook her body as she spoke. "'And after you have suffered a little while, the God of all grace, who has called you to His eternal glory in Christ will himself restore, establish and strengthen you.'''

The silence of the night was a gentle breeze that warmed her soul. "I think He's telling me it's time to stop patrolling. You think so?"

Hanna's voice was soft, as if she too had been greatly affected by their journey of discernment. "Yes, I think so."

Calli thanked Hanna and crawled into the soft warm bed, laying the Bible on the other side while she closed her eyes to pray. In exhaustion, His words helped her to relax. "Come to me, all who labor and are heavy laden, and I will give you rest." Calli drifted off to sleep.

The phone rang before eight, and Calli pulled herself from the bed, as emotionally exhausted as she was physically.

"Did I wake you up?"

Calli dropped her head into the pillow, images of Luke still in his uniform from the night before. Her world had turned one hundred eighty degrees since he'd reached for her hand and had been insulted that she didn't trust him.

"Calli?"

"Yes, I was asleep." *And having the most wonderful dream.*

"Sorry. Do you want me to call back later?"

"No. I have something I want to say." For some strange reason, she wanted to tell him about last night. She wasn't sure yet about coming forward as the anonymous caller. They had all the information she could give anyway. Telling Luke would mean rehashing three years in the dungeons. She wanted to put that part of her life behind her.

Calli's voice was deep and husky. His own was loaded with ridicule, ready for another battle with the spunky woman he was beginning to have very strong feelings for. "Good, because I'm ready for some answers."

"To what?"

"Questions. Do you want to go first, or shall I?"

There was a long pause, then in a velvety voice she said, "I had an incredible talk with God this morning."

She had no idea how her news affected him. He'd been praying for her to trust again, but had to admit he'd selfishly asked that God would let her learn to trust him. "Do you want to tell me about it?" Luke poured a glass of juice, waiting for her to continue. "What did you talk about?" he prompted.

"Putting my trust in God." The statement revealed no hesitancy.

God's eternal wisdom brought a smile to Luke's careworn face. "That's great, Calli," he said in a soothing voice, prompting her to continue.

As she told him about her and Hanna looking up verses and the way they fit circumstances in her life, there was a calm he'd never detected in her voice before.

Breathlessly she added, "I have a long way to go."

Luke struggled to control his voice. "You aren't alone. Don't ever forget that. We all struggle to remember who is truly in charge."

A tired laugh tickled his ear through the wires. "That's comforting."

"It's true. I should let you go back to bed. I just have one question I have to ask before I can go to sleep."

"Shoot." He could almost see the sleepy smile in her eyes.

"Was the man who hurt you a cop?"

She spoke in a broken whisper. "Yes."

He didn't like being right, especially when the truth hurt. He wished he were with Calli, to hold her and reassure her that he would do anything to erase the painful memories from her heart. "Trust me, Calli. I won't hurt you."

"That isn't the issue, Luke. It goes much deeper, and I'm working on answers to those questions, too."

"Would you come to church with me tomorrow?"

"That's two questions, Northrup. I thought cops dealt in details. You're walking a fine line here." Calli giggled.

"Answer the question, smarty."

"What time?"

"Is that a yes?"

"That's three. You're losing it."

His mouth twitched with amusement, glad to have his sparring partner back. "I'll pick you up at nine o'clock sharp."

"I get the 'point.'" Her sleepy giggle was a deep and rampant river.

Luke laughed. "Get some sleep, Calandre."

"See you tomorrow."

After nearly dressing Jon himself, Luke decided that teenagers had no sense of urgency. He tossed Jon's pants and shirt onto his son's bed.

"Why are we leaving so early?" Jon groaned.

"I'm picking up a friend."

"Calli? It has to be her, or you wouldn't be so uptight." Imitating their favorite sitcom star, Jon's razzing reassured Luke that his son liked Calli.

"She's a mighty fine lady, Jon. And I'm already walking a fine line here. Don't blow it for me, okay?"

"Don't worry about a thing."

"Famous last words. Go comb your hair. And I think it's past time for a haircut." Ignoring Jon's protest, Luke went to his bedroom and got his Bible from the shelf.

Jon wet his hair down and met Luke at the door.

Calli was waiting out front of the apartment when Luke pulled up. She was wearing a beige skirt and two-tone wool blazer with matching shoes and purse. As soon as Luke parked, Jon jumped out of the two-door and climbed into the back seat. "You look really awesome, Calli."

Luke and Calli looked at each other, then into the back seat and smiled. "Thank you, Jon. I'm not overdressed, am I? It's been a while since I've been to church. Have things changed that much?"

"You look great, Calli. Your outfit is fine."

She smiled impishly, and Luke knew he was in trouble. "Just fine? Not really *awesome?*"

Luke turned away and shook his head. *No wonder I'm still single.* He glanced at Calli; her smile was sympathetic and warm. *Could Calli be the woman to change that, God? Keep my eyes open, Father. I can't let my own dreams blind me.*

The church parking lot was full, so Luke parked across the street. Calli's hand felt cold as ice when he helped her from the low-slung car. In her heels, she lacked but an inch of six feet. Luke was grateful when Jon ran ahead to join some friends, leaving them with a minute to visit.

"I hope you didn't mind the teasing. I was afraid Jon would be offended if I treated him in any other way than I would any young man. He *is* quite a young man, you know."

"He's a teenager. He wouldn't know how to feel offended. I, on the other hand, do. After ten hours on the beat, I'll be doing good to keep my eyes open. And you want me to see my mouthy son as a young man."

"Don't worry, I know how to wake you up. A little Mace does the trick every time."

He groaned, squeezing her hand. "You have a very warped sense of humor."

Calli enjoyed teasing him. "Levity, Northrup, levity."

Luke's deep voice carried a tune with the same strength and vibrancy that he exemplified in the rest of his life. When another couple stepped into the pew next to Jon,

Luke moved closer and she could feel him tapping his toe to the rhythm of the music.

She smiled, the combination of the words of the song and his powerful voice served as nourishment to her starved soul. In the years she had strayed, even the music had changed. She was drawn into the enthusiasm of the repetitious verses. Words of encouragement and praise lifted her heart.

The music ended, and they sat down. She glanced at Luke, surprised by the contentedness of his smile.

He leaned close, whispering into her ear. "Are you okay?"

Calli felt the radiance spread through her as if God was healing her inner hurts one by one. She nodded. Tears stung her eyes, and she was powerless to stop them. She pulled a tissue from her purse and dabbed at the cleansing droplets.

Luke discreetly took her hand and held it tenderly. When the pastor closed in prayer, she added her own thanks for His grace, and for the gift of Luke's friendship.

Chapter Thirteen

Calli plopped down onto the couch and twirled the cord around her finger. "I don't know, Hanna." She wanted to put the past behind her. All of it. Mike's death, her mission, the patrolling—everything. Since the church service Sunday morning, Calli felt a peace she hadn't experienced in a long time. She wanted to see where this relationship with Luke would lead.

"You've said it for yourself. Luke is different. What purpose would telling him serve? It's not an issue anymore. Don't make it one."

Maybe Hanna was right. Telling him wasn't necessary.

"Think of all the people you've helped, not the ones you're not. If it's that important, maybe you should..."

"I do *not* want to be a cop, Hanna. Believe me, there's no pleasure in patrolling. It scares me more than anything. Every night I was out there, and even more since my accident."

"Well it's about time you've come to your senses." As if everything was settled, Hanna started talking about plans for her spring vacation. "You need to learn to enjoy life.

Be carefree once in a while. Do something absolutely crazy, just for the fun of it."

"Yeah, right. That's why Luke's already nicknamed me 'Cautious Calli.'"

"That man has you figured out, girl. *Platonic,* my foot!"

"I promise you, there's nothing going on."

"There's a whole lot going on, cousin. You're just blinded by love, is all."

It was a warm spring Friday, and Luke's day off. His parents were taking Jon to the mountains after school for the week of spring break. He'd worked the rookie's shift yesterday so he could join the family for three days at the cabin later in the week.

He and Calli had seen one another three of the last five days. It had been a challenge, but then, everything about her was a challenge. She was full of spirit. Stubborn and elusive. And one of these days, she was going to give in to the pressure of his charm. And he hoped that day would be today.

Luke pulled up on his motorcycle just as she stepped onto the balcony of her third-floor apartment and sprayed the glass with cleaner. He leaned his forearms onto the handlebars and removed his helmet, then peered over his sunglasses. "Hey there, gorgeous!"

Calli pretended to look up, then to both sides. "I think the sun's in your eyes, mister."

"I think it's your blinding beauty."

Leaning against the rail, she looked at him, obviously amused at something. He was sure it was more than what he'd said. Because his comment wasn't that funny.

"What are you doing here? I didn't think we had any classes today."

"We don't. I just missed your fiery personality." If he ever had doubts about his attraction to Calli, he couldn't remember one reason why. She had a natural rapport with teenagers. She didn't flinch when he talked about work. She had the uncanny ability to take him right past the stress of his job and back into life.

"You're in sad shape, Northrup. Miss your morning coffee and doughnut or something?"

"Or something. Come to think of it, I haven't had my coffee."

She smiled. "Come on up. I'll make you a pot."

"I'm okay, don't bother. But I will join you."

"Good. I'll buzz you in the main lobby. Come up to the third floor. I'm in apartment 3E."

A door opened and Calli peeked out, obviously looking for him. Her smile instantly made him glad that he'd come today. Out of habit, he'd stepped to the left of the doorway and she looked surprised to find him there. "Why are you hiding? Think I might have a guard dog back here?"

She was just as dangerous, standing there in faded denim jeans and a formfitting top.

"Luke?" She waved her hands in front of his face.

"Morning." He swallowed, uncomfortable with his sudden loss of concentration.

"Come in."

Luke walked past her, trying to ignore the overwhelming temptation to kiss her. He tried to remind himself of how good an idea this appeared to be an hour ago. Tried to remind himself of Calli's skeptical nature. Tried to tell himself it was going to take time to win her over.

"So what's going on?"

"Can't a friend stop by?"

"Of course you can. I'm just surprised." Calli stepped into the living room, inviting him to follow. "Pleasantly surprised. I was trying to figure a way out of cleaning today."

Pleasantly surprised? You're serious? Was Calli hinting

that she wanted to do something together? Or was his hopeful optimism leading him into a blind alley? Luke thought of sitting on the sofa, and eyed the variety of dolls inhabiting the room. He reached down to move a floppy rag doll that had seen better days.

"I collect dolls. Excuse Bessie." She tucked the baby into a full-size wooden cradle that had also been around a while.

"Dolls, huh? Was that yours?" He motioned to the baby bed and smiled.

She nodded, seeming oddly uncomfortable with the admission.

"It's beautiful. And I bet you looked adorable in it." Envisioning her as a child was easy—she'd have have had big brown eyes, so dark they looked black, like they most often did now, and wild curls tumbling around her face, and one of those angelic smiles that wrapped her daddy around her little finger. Not much had changed. She was doing the same to him at this very moment with that subtle glow on her cheeks and tight-lipped grin.

She deserved to be carefree as the little girl who'd once held these dolls and sat in the security of her parent's lap. Could Luke offer her that? Could he show her how to be carefree again? Or was he a lost cause himself?

"Are you sure you don't want some coffee?"

"No thanks. I wondered if you'd like to head to the hills with me for the day. I need to buy my parents an anniversary present."

The expression in her brown eyes seemed to plead for friendship, yet caution clouded the way. "To the mountains, shopping, on a motorcycle?"

"Unless you're afraid of bikes."

Trust Me. Calli licked her lips nervously and thought of pointing out the dangers involved. Some of which had nothing to do with the highway *or* traffic. *Okay, God. I'm trying. Really I am. But a motorcycle?* Despite her fears, she needed to learn to give up control. *Well, Hanna, is this crazy enough for you?* "Okay."

"Okay?" He furrowed his brows, then leaned forward, resting his elbows onto his knees and intertwined his fingers. "You're afraid, aren't you?"

She shook her head.

"It's okay. We can take the car."

"No," she argued, then remembered the night he'd asked her to trust him, and inside she knew she had failed. She breathed deep, and exhaled. "I want—need to take your cycle."

As if he realized the significance behind her statement, he simply nodded. "Fine. Let's go. We'll stop for brunch along the way. If you have hiking boots, they'd be best. I brought Jon's leather jacket for you to wear. It's warmer and cuts the wind."

Luke waited as she layered a blouse over the top. When they reached the street, he opened the saddlebag and took out the jacket and helped her put it on. She snapped it up while he detached the extra helmet from the backrest.

"I don't picture you as a cyclist." Calli noted the mischievous look in his eyes.

"Ditto with the dolls. We all have our secrets, don't we?"

He had no idea.

"Jon and I take off every summer. Take time to get back in touch—with each other, and God. Everything's so much clearer on a bike." Luke proceeded to fit his son's helmet to her head, then put his own on and spoke. She jumped when sound echoed into her ears.

"There are speakers in the helmet, so we can talk while we drive."

"Oh, how convenient," she said, wondering if the nearness of her voice would leave him as unsettled as his did her. Luke helped her onto the seat and showed her the footrests. He cautioned her not to tilt the cycle off the automatic kickstand. His long legs straddled the machine easily. Muscled thighs stretched against the thin denim. His brown leather jacket fit his broad shoulders as if it were a second skin.

He kick started the engine and slid back in the seat. "Hang on."

"To what?"

"Me. Wrap your arms around my waist." He twisted the handle and the engine roared. "Put your visor down."

Calli reached up and pulled the dark glass over her face. She tentatively placed her hands on his waist and heard him chuckle. He revved the engine again, and they surged forward. She screamed and clung to his entire torso. She felt a hard lump along his left rib, and realized that he was wearing his gun.

He laughed aloud, that soft laugh that had an uncanny way of soothing her nerves. Or at least it would have, had they been anywhere but on this glorified mode of "transportation." "That's better, but it would help if you let my lungs have room to breathe. I hope the gun doesn't bother you."

"Not at all. No more than my keys bothered you."

"Okay, so I overreacted. I'm not used to... Never mind."

"Women who can take care of themselves?"

"I didn't say that."

"May as well have."

"I know plenty of women who can take care of themselves. What I didn't say was that I'm not used to *dating* women who can."

"Thank you. I'll take that as a compliment."

She loosened her grip until he turned the first corner. He

and the cycle dipped to the right, and Calli jerked left in hopes of keeping them upright. "Relax, Cal. Just follow me. When I lean you follow, stay with me."

"I'm no motorcycle babe."

He mumbled something, but when she insisted he repeat himself, Luke said, "I'm not about to let anything hurt you."

Once on the turnpike, headed out of town, the traffic thinned and Calli finally felt herself relax. His deep voice was reassuring. "You're getting the hang of it. What do you think?"

"I'm thinking God has an awfully strange sense of humor."

"Oh, yeah? You mean watching you squirm back there, learning to trust me?"

Calli hoped he couldn't hear her swallow the gasp. "*No.* That He thinks you and I have *anything* in common."

"You have a lot to learn, Calli. And in spite of your bullheadedness, He's going to see that you do."

Luke turned on a tape of men singing praise songs, some of which she'd heard months ago, some last Sunday in church. The road narrowed, winding among the rock cliffs and ponderosa pines, crossing back and forth over the gushing river below.

The words of the song reverberated in her mind over and again, with every twist of this path she followed. Her path was far from clean, far from free.

Luke pulled into a parking space and shut off the engine. They went inside the lodge and climbed the log steps. Calli studied the historical photographs and antique keys hanging from the log support beams. Once seated, they could overlook the moraine valley.

They'd visited very little on the drive up the mountain. Calli had listened intently to the music and let Luke's wide shoulders block the wind.

"How did you like the ride?"

She met his smile and the hand that was offered. "I don't remember feeling anything quite as wonderful. I guess I don't like taking risks."

With a slight squeeze of her hand, his smile broadened. "You don't say. What do you want to eat?"

"The muffins and fruit look good."

"No eggs and bacon?"

"The muffins are my splurge."

"You could splurge more often."

"You have a lot of room to talk." Hugging his body for the last hour, she could assure the pickiest of dietitians that there wasn't a wasted gram of fat on Luke Northrup. He was solid. Emotionally, physically and spiritually.

A very pretty young waitress took their order. Calli expected some kind of reaction from Luke when the girl complimented him on how *good* he looked in his leather jacket. But he ignored her flirting and politely thanked her, then placed his order.

"Did you like Pastor Don's sermon?"

"I thought about it all day. At first I thought it was talking about street violence, but when he said it was written about a friend's betrayal, I was surprised."

They discussed the scripture, and how not much had changed in the two thousand years since King David's day. "Isn't it sad that after all these years, humans still make the same stupid mistakes?"

With all of her own mistakes, Calli found it difficult to criticize anyone else's, and she decided to change the subject. "With all of the violence you see every day, how can you stay so optimistic?"

"It's all part of His plan. There's nothing to fear."

"You mean you're not afraid to go to work each day?"

"To go to work, no. But there's a keen edge of fear that has to be there constantly. It keeps me alive. A cop ignores that, and he's dead. So yeah, I'm cautious of who could be waiting around the next corner, but afraid of my own end, no. What's waiting for us is absolutely awesome."

Calli remembered her father's reassuring voice before he'd leave on each tour of duty.... *If I don't come back one day, honey, I'll be waiting for you in heaven. We'll have eternity together.* She looked at Luke and forced a smile.

"You okay?"

"It's a lot to absorb, but I'm beginning to see how it all comes together." The sermon scripture had been from the fifty-fifth Psalm, and had spoken directly to Calli. She saw herself patrolling the city, saw Tiger and Mike. When the pastor explained the betrayal aspect, and the pain of the betrayed, Calli had choked back tears of remembrance. Of the love that had once betrayed her. "My dad was a commander in the military. He had a dog tag engraved with a verse on it. It was something like 'Be merciful, O God, for in thee my soul takes refuge.'" Calli paused and Luke finished the verse. "'In the shadow of thy wings I will take refuge, till the storms of destruction pass by.' That's a good one to remember, especially in law enforcement."

"You already knew it."

"I have a whole list in here." He pointed to his head. "Best armor we have against the enemy."

Chapter Fourteen

"Why don't you just go to the mall for a gift?" Calli asked as they went from one tiny, craft-filled gift shop to the next. They'd been browsing the touristy mountain town for half the day, and hadn't found "just the right gift" yet.

"Too much work. Here it isn't crowded, everyone's friendly. And it's fun. I'm having a great time, aren't you?"

Without thinking, she took hold of his arm and pulled him close. "I'm having a wonderful time. Thank you."

Luke tipped his head and kissed her cheek. "This is nice, Calli."

She backed away and pressed her hand against the spot on her cheek where the warmth of his kiss was making a beeline to her heart.

He stared at her, his gaze a mixture of anger and desire. "I get the message. Friends it is. You're probably right. Why ruin a good thing?" Luke turned away, pretending to look in the window.

"That's not what I meant at all, Luke," she whispered. Unsure if he'd heard her, she repeated it again, louder this time.

"I heard you," he answered. "I just wanted to hear it again. To make sure you meant it." His eyes met hers and her heart raced.

"Do you work tonight?"

"Not until Monday." She was so stunned by the absurdness of the conversation, she didn't consider the wisdom of her honesty.

"What luck. Neither do I. You want to do something together?"

"That depends."

Luke grumbled in her ear. "You should know me better than that by now."

Calli felt the tension in his voice and laughed. "I was teasing, Northrup."

"Right. What I was leading into is that Mom and Dad are bringing Jon up here to their cabin for the week. I thought we could deliver their present and have dinner before we head back."

"You want me to meet your parents? Like this?"

"Like what?"

Calli motioned to her faded jeans and the conglomeration of shirts. "I look horrible. I don't want to make a bad impression. I mean, even as *just* a friend, I care what people think about me."

"Don't worry, Mom and Dad love 'biking babes.' And besides, you look awesome in everything you wear." His devastating smile turned to a mischievous chuckle, then he dragged her past the candy store and into another quaint shop.

Luke found his parents a set of ceramic coasters and a matching pine tree candle holder. They drove down the canyon, arriving at the cabin before Luke's parents and Jon. Luke unlocked the door and started a fire. It was already dark when the three Northrups walked in the door, obviously surprised to find Luke and Calli waiting.

"What took you so long?" Luke joked, totally missing the panicked glances exchanged between his parents.

"Gramps had some business he needed to take care of. Hi, Calli."

"Hi, Jon. How's it going?"

"It's cool. *Vacation!*" He ran out the door to get another load of gear from the pickup.

"Mom, Dad, this is a friend of mine. Calli Giovanni. Calli, meet Joan and Ted Northrup."

Mrs. Northrup's smile crinkled the corners of her eyes. She was a petite woman with Luke's coloring. "Good evening, Calli. Jon was telling us about you. He's quite impressed."

Luke's father was stocky and slightly shorter than his son. He nodded quickly then said, "It's nice to meet you, Miss Giovanni. If you'll excuse us, I need to talk to Luke privately. Family matters."

Luke shrugged, raising his eyebrows.

Calli smiled, feeling like an intruder.

"I'm sorry about his gruffness, Calli. It isn't you. This problem has him on the defensive." Mrs. Northrup touched Calli's arm. "And as you probably know by now, a cop on the defensive isn't in any shape to socialize." Ted pulled his son into the next room. Calli heard the deep, hushed voices, mixed with an occasional harsh word.

"I understand, Mrs. Northrup. My father is a retired military man. They're a special breed, aren't they?"

His mother laughed. "Well, well, there may be an answer to my prayers yet."

Jon came in, dropped a load of bags, then dashed out the door again. It was clear that he looked forward to spending time with his grandparents.

With a grim expression, Luke nodded to his father and walked toward her. "Calli, I'm afraid we'd better head back right away. Sorry. I'm going to talk to Jon for a few minutes, then we'll leave.'' He disappeared, leaving an awkward silence in the room. Even Mrs. Northrup's chatter stopped as she turned toward her husband. ''He's going to tell Jon?'' she asked incredulously.

''That's not our decision, Joan. He's Luke's son.''

Calli smiled uncomfortably, anxious to know what was going on. When Luke and Jon came back into the cabin, Jon looked at his grandparents. ''You don't have to worry, Grammy, I'm not going anywhere.''

''I'll call you tomorrow and see what you've decided, Jon.''

The teen's chin jutted forward, just like Luke's when he was mad. ''I don't want to see her.''

''Just think about what I said.'' Luke wrapped his arm around Jon's shoulder and kissed his forehead.

''I won't change my mind.'' Jon picked up a duffel bag and headed for the ladder to the loft.

''I'll be back tomorrow. We'll talk more about it then.'' Luke straightened his shoulders and hugged his parents. When Jon was out of sight, Luke gave his mother a stern look. ''Don't push him, Mom. He has to make his own decision.''

Luke helped Calli into Jon's jacket and helmet. Jon ran down the stairs.

''You still look awesome, Calli, even in *my* stuff.''

She laughed and patted him on the shoulder. ''Thanks for sharing, Jon. Have a fun week.''

''We will. See you later.''

Luke hustled her out the door and helped her onto the bike. Calli waited uncomfortably for Luke to start the conversation. If he wanted her to know what the big emergency was, he'd tell her in his own time. They were out of the foothills before either said a word. ''Jon's mother was in a serious automobile accident today. Nancy's father called while Dad was at the apartment picking up Jon's bag. I guess he demanded that Jon go to California with them tonight.'' Even through the mikes she could hear the turmoil in Luke's voice.

Not sure if Luke wanted to talk about it, she hesitated before delving further. ''Jon doesn't want to see her?''

''Nancy was only seventeen when we were briefly married and had Jon. Her parents didn't like me much, and talked her into walking away from both Jon and I. One day, she dropped Jon at Mom and Dad's while I was at school, and never came back. A few months later she showed up with papers giving up her son. I've had full custody since.''

She hugged Luke from behind, and he patted her hand, as if she was the one who needed consoling. ''How old were you?'' Calli was surprised at how easily he opened up to her, and longed for the same courage.

''Eighteen.''

''And you've raised him alone?''

''We lived with Mom and Dad for a while, but as soon as I found a decent job, we found our own place. I wanted my space to raise Jon, and let my folks be grandparents. They'd already raised their family, though they still have a good time together.''

''That's the way it should be, and it's clear that your parents and Jon have a great relationship.''

''That's for sure. Of course, they spoil him rotten.''

Calli chuckled. ''Spoken like a true father. So if Jon's mother doesn't see him, why the big issue tonight?''

''Nancy made a surprise visit recently. She threatened to take us to court to get her custody rights back. Of course, that's been almost a month ago now, and we haven't heard a word since. Jon doesn't want anything to do with her.''

''She doesn't understand how he feels?''

''Nancy's pregnant, getting married and wants Jon to join the cozy family. She always wanted what she couldn't have. I suggested she get to know her son first, let things grow from there.''

His bitterness was subtle, much less obvious than her own opinion of Brad. Calli wondered if that was why Luke had never married again, because he was still in love with Jon's mother.

Luke turned off the interstate.

''Where are we going?''

''To talk to Nancy's father. I'm sorry you have to go with me, but he and Gayle leave in two hours. I don't want to miss them.''

A few minutes later, Luke drove through the open iron gates.

He pulled to a stop in front of an elegant rambling ranch-style home. Luke turned the key of the cycle and climbed off, pausing to help Calli. He tucked the helmet under his arm and mumbled. ''I'm probably wasting my time. Newt and I haven't spoken in years.''

From the rigid set of his jaw, she sensed his determination to do the right thing for Jon and Nancy, even if it meant facing his former father-in-law. She admired Luke's willingness to work with Jon's mother at all.

Taking Calli's icy hand in his own, Luke led her up the steps. ''We won't stay long.''

There was no answer when he rang the doorbell. He pushed the button again. Finally a middle-aged woman answered.

Luke explained who he was and asked for Nancy's parents.

''I'm sorry, sir, they were able to get an earlier flight. It doesn't look good for Miss Nancy.''

''Do you know where I can reach them?''

She retrieved the phone number and handed it to Luke. ''Mr. Newt told me to give this to you when you called.''

"Thank you." Luke placed the paper in his shirt pocket and they left.

The silence was broken only by the rush of traffic. Though Calli knew what a special man Luke was already, this added to her admiration. He could let bitterness stand in the way, yet he didn't. He was ready to offer people who had caused him and his son years of pain and loneliness support when they were hurting.

A few minutes later, Luke turned off the freeway. She gazed at the familiar landmarks as they passed through her neighborhood. Why did the dilapidated buildings look brighter from the seat of a motorcycle?

Luke pulled up to the curb and swung his long leg over the cycle, then helped her off. "Come in for a while?" Calli asked.

"I should get home," he said with staid calmness.

Removing the leather jacket, she felt as if she were peeling off another layer of the shield around her heart. Wondering if Luke regretted opening up to her, she wanted to share her own pain with him. Wanted him to see that she, too, had a past that she'd rather not face. But tonight he was the one who needed to talk. "Go if you want. I just thought you could call the hospital from here. We could order a pizza and visit. An empty house isn't very comforting when you're miserable."

Luke listened to her steady voice of reason. Going home held no appeal, yet was it fair to dump this mess on Calli? *God, I need someone to listen and share this load. You know I want a wife to go home to and hold. I can't hash through everything with someone who isn't willing to stick around and help me pick up the pieces afterward. So if Calli isn't the one you have in mind, God, don't let me be tempted.*

"Luke?" Calli's hair tumbled from the restraint of the helmet. Her eyes looked like onyx and twinkled in the moonlight, reflecting her tears. "I know there isn't much I can do, but I can listen."

He waited to speak, emotion constraining his throat. "You sure you're up to it? It isn't pretty."

"We all have shadows to deal with. Maybe one day I'll share mine." The wind gently fluffed her hair and she pushed a lock behind one ear. Her smile was tender and compassionate.

Once in her apartment, Calli handed him the phone. "Go ahead."

He sighed heavily as he landed in the oak chair. He felt the color drain from his face as the conversation concluded. Luke hunched over, resting his elbows on his thighs. *Dear God, be with Nancy. And help me to say the right words to Jon.*

He looked up to find Calli leaning against the wall. She possessed strength and stamina at odds with the slenderness of her body. Her smooth cheeks glowed from the cold ride home. Her beauty was exquisite and fragile, and he wanted nothing more than to escape in her arms and hide from what he needed to do.

"How is she?"

"In stable condition. She lost the baby."

Calli could see the pain Luke felt and couldn't bear the sight of him without breaking down herself. Biting her lower lip as a reminder to let him do the talking, she simply touched his shoulder.

"I shouldn't have been so stubborn. I wouldn't have been, had I known." His shoulders shook.

Calli knelt in front of Luke. "This afternoon you told me that we all make choices, good or bad, based on our life experiences. Based on your past with Nancy, you did what you thought was best. Now there are other factors."

"I don't know whether I should take Jon. She may not even know us. They can't even say she'll make it."

Calli nodded. She took Luke's hand in both her own and waited for him to speak again. After a long silence, he lifted his head.

"I'd rather err on the side of trying. This may be the last chance Jon has to talk to her. Someday he'll understand."

"I hope so."

They sat together for a few more minutes before she ordered a stuffed pepperoni pizza and salad. She set the table while Luke called the station, then Tom.

When he was through, she sat next to him and wrapped an arm around him. He buried his face in the crook of her neck and silently snuggled against her. He smelled like the fresh mountain air.

Calli's emotions whirled and skidded, coming to a sudden halt when Luke turned toward her. She felt his bearded chin prickling the sensitive skin beneath her jaw. Torn between jealousy that Luke was crying over Nancy, and happiness that he was with her, Calli prayed. *God, be with Luke and Jon, and Nancy. And help me to do the right thing, for all of them.*

One hand supported her back and the fingers of his other hand played with her earlobe and the tangled curls she'd tucked behind her ear. "Calli?"

"Yeah?" she rasped.

"Did you hear a buzzer?" The doorbell rang again, and Calli jumped to her feet.

Calli pushed the intercom, releasing the door. "The pizza!"

He looked at her uncomfortably. "Saved by the bell."

When Luke and Jon returned from California three days later, Luke stopped by Calli's. She invited him in and they sat at the table with a glass of lemonade.

His voice was deceptively calm as he broke the news. "She's improving."

Luke sat across from Calli, drumming his fingers on the table. He told her about the awkward time spent with her family and Jon's apathy about the situation. "Jon's upset, and he won't talk about it. He's mad that I ruined his spring break. His attitude didn't help matters with her parents."

"You can't blame him, Luke. Hospitals are frightening places for kids. Throw in the factor that he's expected to be upset about someone who walked out on him, well, I just think her family should be more understanding."

"Jon doesn't understand what he's walking away from."

"How could he understand something he's never had? They're the ones who walked away. You didn't have to go, but you did."

He looked at her blankly. "This is frightening, but I'm starting to understand the way you think."

Calli slapped his shoulder playfully. "Gee, thanks a lot."

Luke grabbed her hand and held it firm, studying it. "That isn't the main reason I came today."

Calli felt her throat constricting.

"I don't know how to say this, Calli. You've made it clear that a cop doesn't fit into your plans. After what happened the other night, I'm not sure we're both ready to move on."

She considered arguing his point, wanting to remind him that less than a week ago they had been communicating quite well, before the pizza had arrived. Yet she sensed it was more than her fears in the way, that after seeing the effects Nancy's accident had on Jon, *Luke* wanted more space.

He picked up a quarter from the dish on her table and walked it from finger to finger. "I don't want to mess things up between us."

Puzzled, Calli stared at him.

"You asked to keep it platonic, and I blew it. I promise it won't happen again."

"Fine, Northrup."

"It's what you wanted. I should have listened."

She concentrated on the table. It wasn't what she wanted at all, but she knew it was best. They should have gone their separate ways long ago.

Luke stood and rested a hand on Calli's shoulder. "I'll see you Thursday, then."

She brushed the hand away. "You're right, Luke. It's best for us to keep it platonic."

Chapter Fifteen

Calli sat on the step of Luke's apartment building. Waiting. She heard the news on the radio as she headed home from work. A rookie had been killed in the line of duty.

What am I doing here? Luke made it clear last week. He doesn't want to get involved right now.

She looked up to the stars and wondered what she could say to Luke when he did show up. How could she ever explain running to stay with Vanessa until she'd heard who the downed officer was. Or more importantly, who he wasn't.

It had been Vanessa that suggested she'd feel better after seeing Luke in person. The two women had talked about God, and about why Luke was backing away from Calli. Vanessa concluded that Calli was crazy to agree with Luke. The yearning to explain everything to Vanessa grew stronger as they visited, but Calli simply couldn't reveal why *she* should stay away.

Calli went home, even crawled into bed, then proceeded to soak the pillow as she struggled with her feelings for a man she could not have. She closed her eyes, remembering

Vanessa's praise for the protection God had provided for Tom and Luke. Sleep still had not come.

Wondering if he'd get off early because of the shooting, she dressed and drove to Luke's. An hour and a half later, and she was still waiting for him to arrive. *We're just friends. I shouldn't be sitting here like some lovesick schoolgirl.* She looked again at her watch, then stood up to leave. Just then Luke pulled around the corner.

Well, it's too late to chicken out now.

Luke took his time getting out of the car. His rangy body unfolded from the low-slung vehicle and towered above it when he stood. He looked tormented.

When he spoke, his voice was raw. "Morning, Calli."

"Hi. I heard the news. I thought you might need a friend."

His disapproving look sent chills up her spine. *Then again, maybe I was wrong.*

Without a word, he sat on the cold cement next to her and stared into the predawn sky. In the dim light, his bearded chin and eyes were even darker, more intriguing. And the more she thought of what he'd experienced earlier, the more she wanted to know Luke Northrup. How did he cope? Surely in a city this size, he dealt with death and loss often. From his appearance, it bothered him. A lot.

Luke twisted his head, leaning it toward one shoulder, then the other. "What I need right now, you can't give me."

Calli slid up one step and rested her hands on his shoulders. Her thumbs began to make small circles, kneading his tight muscles. "And what's that?" She pressed harder, unsure that touching him was at all wise.

He remained silent. She could feel his pain, the emptiness of loss. With each rotation, Calli acknowledged that her feelings for Luke went far deeper than friendship. "I'm here, Luke." *Don't ask or expect more.*

"For how long, Calli? An hour? A day? A lifetime?"

Unaware that she'd stopped rubbing his shoulders, Luke took her hands and turned to face her.

"Why not?" he demanded as if they'd been through this a thousand times.

Puzzled, Calli searched his face, hoping for a way to avoid the ugly truth. She was here to make him feel better, and the truth wouldn't help. Not today. "You know why."

"Lots of men are cops." Luke muttered a curse. "Am I anything like the jerk that hurt you?"

Calli was totally taken aback by this interrogation.

"Then why are you here?" He studied her, then stood and unlocked the building door. "You shouldn't have come, Calli. Because Jon and I need someone who'll be around tomorrow."

"*You* can't promise *me* tomorrow, Officer Northrup!" She watched as the door closed behind him. Calli felt all of her dreams fading into the light. The more risks she took, the more she lost.

Luke climbed the stairs and unlocked the apartment door. Mrs. Maloney rose from the sofa. "I tried to run interference, but Jon already heard it on the radio. He took forever to fall asleep. How are you?"

"I feel a whole lot more vulnerable this morning."

"Fix yourself a cup of tea and spend the day with your loved ones. Every day is a precious gift. It'll do you good, both of you." She patted his arm as she walked past him.

Luke considered Mrs. Maloney's advice, immediately recalling the way he'd yelled at Calli. Regret waged a war within him. He didn't want her to be hurt. He couldn't promise he'd make it home at the end of his shift. He knew that.

Yet he couldn't let her go.

He followed Marge out the apartment door and rushed

to the stairs. She turned for the elevator and looked at him, puzzled. "I forgot something downstairs. Go on home, Marge. I'll be right back."

"Good day to you, then."

He reached the street just as Calli was pulling away. He ran to catch up with her, and knocked on the window of her vehicle. Calli braked and rolled the window down.

Out of breath from the sprint down the stairs and chasing her down the street, Luke gasped, "I'm sorry, Calli." He offered her a sudden, arresting smile.

She smiled. "You're forgiven."

They stayed there in the middle of the street, saying nothing, but gazing into each other's eyes. It was a day to be with those he cared for—his son, and Calli. Life was too short.

"Would you join Jon and I for breakfast? I could use the company."

"Jon won't mind?"

"Are you kidding? He's crazy about you."

"If you were my dad, I wouldn't want to share you today."

The tip of his tongue touched his lower lip just before he grinned. "Since I'm *not* your dad, how *do* you feel?"

"It's part of being a cop—taking risks. I understand that." Her eyes grew moist and she quickly blinked the tear away.

"That's not what I was talking about, and you know it, Cal."

She swallowed, afraid to take another chance.

Trust me.

Nervously Calli bit her lip. "I was worried about you."

A car honked from behind them and Calli pulled ahead to the curb. Luke followed, thinking of the courage it took for this woman to come to him today. In the two weeks since he and Jon returned from California, he'd made no attempt to call her. And after the self-defense class ended, he doubted he'd see her again. Yet here she was.

She'd obviously not slept a wink, been waiting in the cool morning air, and from the puffiness of her eyes, she'd spent a good while crying, as well.

According to Tom, she'd kept Vanessa company while the two of them waited for the official announcement of the officer's name. A day like this was typically followed by the majority of cop's girlfriends breaking off relationships.

Luke crawled into the passenger's side and took hold of her cold fingers. "You didn't have to come. Why did you?"

"I may be a lot of things, Luke, but I'm *not* a fair-weather friend."

For better or worse, through good times and bad. Luke fought the hope building inside. He'd been hurt too many times by women who tried to convince themselves—and him—that they could handle the stress of his career. That, combined with full custody of his son, had marked the end of his few relationships.

Yet here was a woman who claimed to want nothing more than a friendship and was ready to stand beside him and his son after one of the worst months of his life. "I could use a friend today, and maybe if tomorrow works out, that'd be okay, too. We can take it one day at a time."

"It's a deal."

Calli flipped a U-turn and headed back to his apartment, and Luke covered his eyes. "I didn't see that."

"Good. It's been a long day. I'd hate to make you write up another ticket."

"Gee, thanks." He laughed, relieved that she was with him. "You like waffles?" Calli parked and they walked inside.

"Only homemade ones with my grandmother's secret syrup."

He pushed the button for the elevator. "Okay, I'll make the waffles, you make the syrup."

The elevator opened, and electricity seemed to arc between them as the doors closed them off from the rest of the world. Luke moved close. The mere touch of his hand holding hers sent a warming shiver through her.

The light conversation from a moment ago was suddenly jolted by Calli's intense feelings and the awareness that Luke was silently demanding such an admission from her.

Neither of them had tomorrow to promise, she repeated, desperately trying to convince herself that Luke's friendship would be enough. Calli knew the value of appreciating what she did have—each other—today. One day at a time.

Since the elevator was barely quicker than a snail, she assessed that the tingle in the pit of her stomach was the result of Luke's blatant appraisal of her.

"I know I agreed to keep this platonic, Calli, but I'm going to have to renege on that promise."

"Really?" *It's about time.*

"I can't help but wonder what it would take to fluster Calli Giovanni."

Calli laughed, silently daring him to try.

"Tell you what, if I succeed, you agree to fix dinner for me. If I don't, I make dinner."

She put her hands on her hips in defiance. "Wait a minute. Either way, you..."

"Win. And what's wrong with that?" He stepped closer, his intense gaze ripping her willpower to shreds.

Calli's eyes widened as Luke pulled her against him and whispered, "I'm falling for you, Calli."

She gasped. Her eyes drifted closed as his hand rested against the small of her back. He kissed her, deeper than ever, the instant warmth sending another shiver up Calli's back.

"Luke..." she rasped.

"What?" he murmured into the tender skin below her chin.

"You win."

He laughed, and she felt his chest relax. "You're slacking off, Miss Giovanni. I at least expected some resistance."

"I'm too tired to argue with you today. Anyway. You flustered me." The elevator stopped, and Calli backed away, afraid of making another mistake. "You coming, Northrup? You did promise me breakfast."

"Wait just a minute."

Calli stopped and looked into his green eyes. There was a need there that she wasn't sure she could deny—a commitment. A hope for tomorrow.

Could she give it to him?

His gaze held her tenderly.

How could she not?

"This isn't much of a life to offer you. Sitting at home worrying about whether I'll make it home from work each day. And you waiting with Vanessa last night tells me you want more than friendship, too."

"I asked her not to tell you."

"She didn't." His expression stilled and grew serious. "Tom told me."

"What happened to black and white? That's a definite gray area, Officer Northrup."

Luke's expression was one of pleading. "Look at it this way. With me you'll always know where you stand. If you want to leave, do it now."

Calli knew what he was saying. If she turned and walked away, it was forever. She tried to push her confused emotions into some sense of order. "Then I guess we'd better do some serious talking."

Luke pressed the Close Door button, then sent the elevator toward the parking garage. "So talk. We have plenty of time."

After weeks of testing, her willpower was dissipating in front of her. "I've already tried to walk away, Luke. I've even asked God not to let me care. But tonight terrified me. I've never worried about anyone like this."

"What is it, Calli? Is it my job that worries you?"

She shook her head. "No, I know you're careful and well trained." She took a deep breath, then let it out. "I was engaged to a *very* domineering man."

"Mmm-hmm." he nodded, his arms crossed in front of him.

"I don't want to make that mistake again."

"Good."

She looked at him, startled. "What do you mean, good?"

"I mean good. No one should live with someone else pushing them around, telling them what to do. And I, for one, don't plan to let you marry the wrong man."

"And you don't think that's domineering? Or conceited? Or..."

"I call it love. I'm not saying that I'm perfect, Calli. Yet I'd like to think I have just enough confidence to keep me alive. Too much, a cop begins to think he's invincible. Too little, he just isn't able to do the job. And in case that balance gets out of whack, I think you're perfectly capable of setting me straight." Luke leaned against the carpeted wall inside the tiny cubicle.

"You don't know me, Luke."

"Is there something you think I *won't* like?"

"Yes." She breathed deep, silently asking God for strength to tell him everything. The words wouldn't come. *Not today. He has enough to handle right now.*

"I'm in no rush, Calli. If it's that upsetting to you, wait until you feel more comfortable."

The door opened, and an older gentleman carried his groceries into the elevator. The silence stretched thinner with each floor that passed. When they reached the third floor, Luke led Calli into his apartment.

"When you're ready. Not until then." He kissed her cheek, then walked away.

Luke left Calli in the living room while he went to tell Jon that he was home. She overheard the relief in the two masculine voices, a cold reminder of the tragedy that Luke had been through earlier. Today wasn't the time to tell him. She wasn't ready, and Luke and Jon needed today to heal.

Calli studied the pictures on his walls. Wooden frames held photographs of himself and Jon, hiking and canoeing. There were some pictures of waterfalls and mountains, and one snapshot of his parents' cabin, with Luke and Jon and several other people standing in front of it.

Wrapping her arms around herself to fend off the sudden chill, Calli was startled when Luke leaned over her shoulder and pointed to each person, "introducing" her to each sister, brother, in-law and "out-law" as he affectionately referred to the nonfamily members. His rough cheek grazed hers, and she smelled the faint remains of his cologne mixed with that fully masculine scent of a long stressful night. Strangely, just knowing he'd come home unhurt made the pungent aroma soothing.

"It sounds like you have a very close family."

Luke led her to the kitchen. "Yup. You don't have time for meaningless squabbles in this line of work. Dad is a retired street cop. Mom was a teacher. We learned young not to take family for granted."

Pulling the waffle mix from the cupboard, he paused, then turned to Calli. "What do you need for the syrup?"

"Sugar and water."

''White sugar?''

Calli nodded. ''Oh, and vanilla.'' She saw the disbelief in his eyes. ''You just caramelize the sugar, add the water, let it boil, then add the vanilla extract and serve it. It's wonderful.''

''Mmm... Sounds interesting. So what do your folks do?''

''Dad's retired from the military. Mom raised us kids.'' She waited for the ''military brat'' comments to start.

''Where are they now?''

Calli wanted to change the subject. She did not have the energy to go into detail about what had driven them apart. ''In Glenwood Springs.''

''Ah. Do I hear, 'Close enough, yet far enough away' in your tone?''

''Exactly.''

Breakfast was a welcome break, working side by side. Jon set the table and made conversation. After breakfast, Calli yawned, then Luke did, and the circles under Jon's eyes confirmed that none of them had slept. ''I don't think any amount of coffee is going to take this fatigue away, guys. I'm going home so you can get some rest.''

Luke took her hand, and Calli found it hard to avoid his gaze. She felt Jon's eyes on them. Father and son needed time together, time alone to share their relief, their fear. They didn't need a stranger around.

Jon crossed in front of them and hugged his dad. ''I'm really glad you're okay, Dad, but I'm going back to bed. I'm glad you came today, too, Calli.''

Calli looked into Luke's eyes and felt the heat rush to her cheeks. Every time his gaze met hers, her heart beat a little quicker.

''I'm not going to be far behind. Go ahead, Jon Jon.''

''See you guys later.'' Jon closed his bedroom door behind him. Luke took Calli's hands in his.

''I want you here today, Calli.''

Chapter Sixteen

Calli heard footsteps and rolled over, rubbing the sleep from her eyes. Mrs. Maloney had left her belongings on the bed, and Luke insisted she take a nap on his. The furnishings were totally masculine. Totally Luke. The comforter was navy with white snowflakes and twinkling stars and elk running through pine trees. On the walls were old wooden snowshoes and more collages of photos. A poster of the Longs Peak in the springtime faced the bed.

It was nearly noon. Calli sat up in the bed and pulled her legs to her chest. She peered down the hall to the living room where Luke slept. He was still sprawled in the recliner like a guard dog protecting his domain. Jon tiptoed past the doorway on the way to the bathroom.

I should leave while Luke's asleep. He doesn't have a clue what odds are against us. She continued to think while putting her tennis shoes on and folding the blanket that she'd used to cover herself. She wasn't patrolling any longer, but that didn't take away from the facts. Luke was looking for a witness who he suspected was the anonymous caller, and unfortunately, it happened to be her.

"Afternoon, Calli."

She turned, surprised to see Jon come into the room. "Hi, Jon. How did you sleep?"

He shrugged, looking more his age than she'd seen him before.

"That probably makes three of us who didn't get much rest." *And probably all for different reasons.* She couldn't help but wonder how Luke had managed as a single father for all these years—and how both father and son would adjust to having a woman in the house.

The boy was nearly as tall as she was, yet he was already developing his father's broad shoulders. His hair wasn't as dark as Luke's, but his facial expressions were obviously copies of his dad.

And looking at the teen, she wondered how he felt about the danger of his father's job. Without really thinking, her thoughts were spoken aloud. "When I was growing up, my dad was in the military. I sometimes wished someone else's dad would save the world. I wanted *my* dad to stay home and teach me to play softball."

"Yeah, it stinks sometimes, but most of the time it's okay." He smiled tentatively, raising his already bushy eyebrows. "It could be worse. At least my dad isn't gone for long stretches of time like your dad must have been."

Calli smiled. Jon was a cop's son for certain. He didn't talk about the possibility that the day could come when Luke may not come home at all.

As a young child, she never realized the danger of her father's career or the pressure it must have put on her mother to create such normalcy for herself and her family. There was always plenty of love and security. Home was wherever they were, and each day spent together was what her mother called "a precious gift from God." Calli smiled. Today she understood what her mother's saying really meant. Her mother's claims that her faith had carried her through finally made sense. Calli wondered who that "buffer" was in Jon's life.

Was it Luke's parents who played the role of mother, protecting Jon from the harsh reality of law enforcement? Days like today couldn't make it easy on an officer's child, when everyone looked at you with unspoken fear—and heaven help the person who spoke the words aloud.

You can't promise me tomorrow, Luke.... All we have is today. One precious day at a time. She clung to the hope that she could live with that. She couldn't deny that her own fear had taken over as she'd watched Luke turn and walk away. She knew in that moment that life with Luke was an all-or-nothing proposition. And walking away was no longer an option.

"My ears are burning." Luke's voice relayed between Calli and Jon as the two exchanged glances.

"Afternoon, Dad. I'm going to shower." Luke pivoted to let Jon squeeze through the doorway.

"What's your hurry? You two planning some sort of conspiracy?"

"Nothing. Just talking."

Luke looked suspiciously at Calli. "Trying to figure out how to convince me to spring for dinner after all?"

Calli felt her insides warm and her fear dissolve. "That goes without saying. After all, you won the bet."

He smiled. "Excuse me, but I did win the bet, which means you fix dinner. So if that wasn't it, what *were* you two talking about?"

"What's wrong? Afraid I might be finding out some of *your* secrets for a change?"

"No way. Jon's been well trained."

The blanket was bunched in her hands as she paused midway through folding it. She quirked her eyebrows, gently teasing him. "Had a lot of practice at new girlfriends, has he?"

"Depends on who you talk to. According to Tom—not enough. According to me—too many."

Calli finished folding the blanket and set it at the foot of the bed and took two tentative steps toward Luke. "What does Jon think?"

"He doesn't get attached. Self-preservation."

"I don't know if that's good or bad. Did he get attached to someone?" Calli saw his expression soften as he watched her with a keenly observant eye. The magnetism of his gaze drew her closer.

He paused, tipping his head as he shrugged. "He was pretty young, seems to have come through it okay. Maybe you'd like to take care of that, once and for all."

This time, when Luke invited her into his heart, she took that perilous leap of faith. She lifted her trembling hands to take his. Luke pulled her close and wrapped his arms around Calli.

The water turned on, and Jon started singing obnoxiously loud.

Tucked comfortably in Luke's embrace, Calli felt Luke's smile against her cheek and the rumble of his laughter as he drew her closer. Their lips met and his kiss sang through her veins.

Later that day, Luke slammed his fist on the captain's desk.

"Settle down, Luke." Captain MacIntosh handed Luke a printed report. "It started with some spray paint incident. Rizzo was arrested last night, claims you had some connection to his arrest. I don't take kindly to threats toward my officers. I want you off the streets for a few days."

"You've got to be kidding me. You're not going to let that scum run the precinct."

"Come on, Northrup, you know me better than that. A couple of days of low-profile duty won't drive you to insanity, much as you'd like to argue that point.'' Captain MacIntosh informed Luke of related cases, and handed him another list. ''We need to inform the store manager and find out which employees may be involved. Think you can handle that?''

Calli was at the top of the list. He'd handle it.

''You putting a man at the store?''

Mac ignored the question. ''It's just for a few days, Luke. I don't want the streets to become a war zone.''

''Come on, Mac!'' He felt the blood surge to his brain.

His commanders' voice grew louder, while he continued to ignore Luke's protests. ''You might want to suggest that the store offer a few weeks' vacation to the involved employees.'' With a threat of suggestion, the commander added, ''A permanent transfer might not be a bad idea, either.'' The captain stood; a calm sense of authority overcame Luke. He may as well resign himself to the order.

Luke stalked out of the commander's office, mumbling.

''Northrup, be careful out there. Remember, you're on the list, too!''

An hour later, Luke was discussing the situation with the manager of the store.

Luke made note of the conversation on his daily log. His next stop was Calli's. In the lobby he studied the locks then rang the intercom.

''Hello.''

''It's Luke.'' In the lobby, fake ferns hung above the table with a chair on each side. Mailboxes graced one wall and the mirrored walls in the background gave the lobby that seventies feel.

There was a long hesitation before she responded. ''Come on up.''

''I planned on it,'' he mumbled. Luke prayed that, for once, Calli Giovanni wouldn't argue with him. ''God, help me to get through to her.''

She was waiting with the door open when he exited the elevator. When she saw the uniform, Calli's huge eyes doubled in size.

Calli watched Luke approach, his commanding presence evident with each step. Luke created a powerful image. From the navy blue of his uniform, to the belt full of gear and his own dark coloring.

She looked at the uniform again, then into his green eyes, hoping to find comfort from the Luke she had come to love. "Hi. What's up?" She'd been both cautious and lucky since getting her vehicle back from the repair shop. Cautious not to express her pleasure with the *new* color, and lucky to catch herself before inviting Luke to assess the beautiful results. After all these months she'd finally relaxed. There was no way he could have figured out that she was A.C.

"This is official." He followed her into the room, closed the door behind him and motioned to her to have a chair.

"I could tell." Her heart pounded against her chest. "I don't take bad news sitting down. Just spit it out."

The radio squelched and Luke adjusted the volume without a hesitation in his conversation. "Taylor's death wasn't an accident."

She watched the painful play of emotions possess him. "I'm sorry." Calli fought the selfish sense of relief washed through her. Relief that it hadn't been Luke.

"The rear of the store is full of graffiti. We made one arrest and the kid is making threats. Is this why they were harrassing you the other day?"

Calli nodded. "But they have no reason to blame me. I didn't tell anyone."

Merely hearing the gang's name bristled her anger. Taking a deep breath, she hoped he missed her reaction.

"Don't pretend you don't understand, Calli. You're in danger."

Calli walked to the sliding door, looking at the lights of the troubled city. "I'm a realist, Northrup. I've accepted the risks."

"Good. Because reality isn't always pretty."

She leaned her forehead against the cold glass. When would this end? She'd finally found a man with integrity, and every time she turned around, they were being pulled apart. She was trying, really trying to listen to His plans, His instructions, and still felt under attack.

"I love this—a realist and a pessimist. We don't stand a chance."

"We just have to be cautious." Luke's voice was calm and reassuring.

"I know, but I still worry about you."

He stepped behind her and whispered in her ear, "My number-one priority each day is to make it home to Jon. Now I have you, too. Don't worry. I'm always careful. Remember that arrogance we cops have will bring me home at night."

Calli turned and wrapped her arms around him. "Promise me tomorrow, Luke."

He lifted her chin and placed a gentle kiss on her lips. "I promise. Stay home tonight. Don't make me worry about *you*."

A chill went up her spine as Calli looked him in the eye. *Sometimes, I feel like you know all my secrets, Lucas Northrup.* "I didn't have any plans tonight."

"Good. And it goes without saying, don't let just anyone in."

"Is that an order?" Calli smiled.

Luke didn't. "It most certainly is. May I call you when I get home in the morning?"

She realized she didn't mind the order at all. And definitely didn't mind the love that was behind the order. Calli was afraid to admit how much she respected this man, and afraid not to. "You'd better."

He hugged her closer, and she felt the bulky bulletproof vest that was a vital part of him, just as vital, she realized, as his attitude and determination. She watched him walk out the door with tears in her eyes. "Please, God, if you're going to make me fall in love with a cop, give him enough arrogance to keep him alive."

Chapter Seventeen

After his shift ended, Luke went to Calli's apartment again. Warning Calli wasn't enough, he had to make sure she was safe. He approached the lobby of her apartment building and jiggled the locked inner door. After slipping his driver's license into the gap, it opened right up. "Just as I figured."

He rode the elevator to the third floor, then knocked on her door. There was no answer.

A woman with a tiny baby and toddler walked past, the woman eyeing him warily.

After the elevator doors closed behind the trio, he knocked again, louder this time. Fear began to churn in his stomach. *I should have done this last night.* Finally she answered, eyes sleepy and hair disheveled.

"Luke. What are you doing here? How did you get in the lobby doors?"

"Close your door and lock it. I want to check it out."

Calli yawned and brushed the hair from her face. "What?" He held up his license and waited as she followed his instructions. "It won't work. I've already tried," she said as she closed the door.

A minute later, Luke stepped into her apartment without any problems.

Calli stood there, blank, amazed and very shaken. "So what's your point? I can't keep you out of my life, or what?" Her tone turned very chilly for a woman who had just the night before asked him to give her a promise.

"Sit down, Cal. We need to talk."

She hesitated, then threw back her head and placed her hands on her hips. "If you think you can barge into my apartment and start ordering me around, think again. No one has the right to scare me like this."

Luke crossed his arms in front of him and nodded. "You're right. No one has that right."

"What are you talking about?"

"Somebody left a message painted on the store's parking lot."

Calli slowly sat on the sofa. Her body stiffened.

Luke squatted in front of her, resting his rump on his heels. "They've made more threats."

Fear showed in her eyes, though she tried to cover it. "Since last night? What kind of threats? What does that have to do with me?"

"You may have forgotten that scene I interrupted at the store, but I haven't. I want you to pack a few things and disappear for a while."

She sighed. "That was nothing."

He reached up and held her face between his strong hands. "Did you hear what I said? Your life is in danger."

Every nerve in her body fought her attraction to Luke. She twisted out of his hold and stood motionless. "I heard you. Did they threaten *me?*"

"Not by name, but we do have to take precautions."

"I'll be fine, Luke. I know how to take care of myself."

Calli proceeded to rattle off a list of precautions she'd already taken, including the key episode they'd argued over just a few days ago. "I'll be fine right here."

In place of a response, Luke gave her a look of disbelief, which she totally ignored. She then turned her back to him. He had to give her credit—she was holding up just fine. He watched the way she moved. Confident, determined, obstinate. Yet her strength did nothing to lessen her femininity.

"Besides," she added, "even if I do need to take precautions I'm not going to involve you and Jon. I've gotten myself into this...."

He pulled a ratty blue bandanna out of his pocket and tossed it to Calli. "I found this next to your car about four o'clock this morning. Is it yours?"

"They've tagged me? How could they? I'm careful, Luke."

"All it takes is one person sitting in the parking lot watching."

From the look of panic in her eyes, she was beginning to understand.

"Now, will you go pack a few things, please? We'll check your apartment occasionally to see if they press the issue."

Her face turned ashen. "But Luke..."

He lifted her chin and kissed her gently. "Ask questions while you're packing, Calli. You're the cautious one. For once, be cautious when it's necessary."

"Where are you taking me?" He could see ideas racing through her mind at lightning speed.

He shook his head, totally exasperated with Calli's stubbornness. "You can stay with Jon and me. I don't want to endanger your family, or Hanna, or anyone else. I want to keep an eye on you myself."

"Oh, Luke. No."

Luke took hold of her hand. In one fluid motion, he

stood, pulling her up with him. ''Oh, yes, Calli. I have enough to worry about without you arguing with me. Let's boogie. We don't have all day. Be sure to take any valuables you have.''

''I just have a few pieces of my grandmother's jewelry, I'll take it with me.''

She packed a suitcase while Luke made sure the windows were locked. He looked around the cozy apartment with curiosity, trying to picture her dolls and cutesy things in his apartment. He chuckled. Jon would think his father had totally lost his mind. He picked up the rag doll she'd called Bessie, and tucked it in the crook of his arm. ''From the looks of you, Bessie, you must have a lot of stories to tell about Calli.''

Just as he said it, Calli walked up behind him and snatched the doll. ''And she's not telling *you* any of them.''

''Then I guess I'll have to find another way to get answers about you, huh?''

She tossed the doll into the cradle, and headed for the door. Luke again tucked the doll under his arm and followed Calli. She headed toward her car.

''Where are you going?''

''I'll follow you over. I need my own transportation.''

He looked at her, ready to argue, then reconsidered. ''Let me have it checked out first. They'll bring it over later.''

He stepped up next to her, took the suitcase from her hand and firmly escorted her to his car. ''Get in.''

Calli couldn't miss the concern in his voice. He closed the door behind her.

He put her luggage into the trunk and slammed it closed. They drove in silence. As the sun rose, smog blanketed the city in an eerie glow.

''The store manager called after you left last night.'' Though Luke didn't comment, she knew from the smug look on his face that her assumption was correct. ''You must have been very convincing. He tried to put me on mandatory leave until further notice."

"Tried?"

"I agreed to a change of schedule and a week's vacation."

He glanced at her from the corner of his eye. "I must not have been all that convincing then, because I pushed for a transfer."

She was flattered that he was truly worried about her. "He suggested it, but I'm planning to go back to school this fall. No need bothering everyone with a transfer if I'll be quitting anyway. It's time I get that last semester out of the way."

"You quit one semester before graduating?"

Calli swallowed the lump in her throat, praying for the courage to open up to him. "My brother died unexpectedly, and I just couldn't pull myself together in time to study for finals."

He let up on the accelerator. "I'm sorry."

"Me, too."

"That would do it, for sure."

She straightened her shoulders, refusing to let the past continue to pull her down. "I can do all things through Him who strengthens me." *I can do this.* "And now it's time to get on with my life." Calli reached for his hand. "For the first time in three years, I have something to look forward to. So what do you have in mind?"

"Uh," Luke stammered. "Uh, in mind."

"The threats," she said, grinning. Knowing she had flustered him for a change gave her immeasurable satisfaction. "You do have a plan, don't you?"

He nodded, seeming to pull himself back to the business at hand. "When I told the captain about Tiger and his boys harassing you at the store, and me stepping in at the wrong time, he suggested I take a few days off, as well."

Calli was speechless. *Good thing he doesn't know about A.C., or he'd really be worried.*

Pulling up to the red light, Luke handed her a set of keys. "This is for the outer doors. This is to our apartment." He shot her a wary glance. "Ours, as in Jon's and mine, I mean."

Calli lifted her eyebrows. *I don't think I'd better tease him about that one. We're already walking a very fine line. And I'd better find a better solution to my safety—soon.*

"You have to lift the doorknob slightly to turn it."

"Extra security, I suppose."

"No, a royal pain. No one's getting past these locks unless they're authorized." He drove down a long cement ramp and pressed a lever. "Another pain, but under the circumstances, the precaution is necessary."

The garage entry was cold and dingy compared to the rest of the building, yet she had to admit, the place even felt more secure. It was just another reminder of the danger he, too, lived with each day.

They again took the elevator, and Calli remembered the kiss he'd given her right in this elevator. She wondered if he remembered it, too. He opened the apartment door and Calli felt an instantaneous discomfort, carrying a suitcase into a single man's apartment.

"Good morning, Marge. I'd like you to meet Calli Giovanni. There have been some gang-related threats, so she's going to stay with us for a while."

"Hello, Calli. It's nice to meet you, though I wish it had been under better circumstances."

Everything in black and white, down to the detail. He took her suitcase and set it along the wall. "Could we get another set of keys? I gave her my spare set."

"Of course. If you need anything, Calli, our apartment is the first door to the right of the lobby."

"Thank you, but I don't plan to be here very long. Since I'm on vacation now, I'll be glad to stay with Jon."

"If you'd like, Marge, take a few days off, then. I'll get in touch with you when this is over."

"That's fine. Call if you need me," Marge said. After an update on Jon, Mrs. Maloney left.

Luke's low voice was a little awkward as he showed Calli to the extra bedroom. "I'll clear out a couple of drawers for you. We'll have to wash the sheets. Marge sleeps in here when I work swing or graveyards."

"Why are you doing this, Luke? I could find somewhere else. I could..."

"Do you really have to ask?"

She fought the dynamic presence he exuded. She wasn't ready to hear his feelings. Wasn't ready to face her own. His professional instincts seemed to cross that invisible line and read her thoughts.

"I'd like to talk to your parents, let them know you're here, and why."

"No." A sensation of nausea and desolation swept over her. "I don't want to worry them."

"That's why I want to explain the situation. If they call and you're never home, well I don't want them to think anything is going on here. I don't want you to think so, either, Calli. I want you safe, that's it."

There are no shades of gray, are there, Luke? Calli turned away, hoping the emotions he stirred would eventually settle to a dull ache. "I'll explain it to them when I'm ready."

His expression turned grim as he watched her move her suitcase to the bed. "Feel free to make yourself comfortable here. Do what you want with the room. I know you'll want some space to yourself."

"Thank you, but I don't plan to be here that long."

The disappointment she saw in his eyes spoke volumes,

and she was surprised to find her own instincts working on him.

"Yeah. I suppose you're right. I'm going to finish moving this stuff into my room. If you need anything, let me know."

He walked into the next room, and Calli wondered how she was going to survive this. They had the entire day together. Several days together from the sound of things. At least there was only a few more days of school. Then Jon would be here to act as a buffer, or at least a distraction.

She noticed that Luke had carefully set Bessie on the pillow, and she hugged the doll to her chest. "Luke?"

"Yeah?" He came into the room for another load of clothes, then went back to his own while she followed.

Hearing his deep voice so near was comforting, she couldn't deny that. But she couldn't hide forever. Not from her feelings nor her past. And she couldn't inflict them upon Luke and his son. Jon needed his father, now more than ever. She didn't want to distract Luke and certainly didn't want Jon to feel she was here to keep tabs on him.

She rounded the corner to his room and watched Luke arrange his shirts in the oak dresser drawer. "How will Jon feel about all of this? He still seems upset about Nancy. I don't want to add to that. This should be time for you two to be together."

With his back to her, Luke placed his hands in his pockets. "I hope he'll do fine. Besides, I want the two of you to get to know each other."

"Are you going to tell him about the threats?" She narrowed her eyes in speculation.

"I don't lie to him—about anything." He turned to face her. "I won't lie to you, either, Calli. I'm worried. The Eastsiders are ticked off at something, or someone."

"How do you look these kids in the eyes, knowing what they're capable of?"

"They're lost kids who want rules. And they want someone to care enough to enforce them."

"I've noticed, they *love* rules."

"I never said they wouldn't push their limits, just to see if you have the backbone to stand up to them. Once you do, the majority of them will respect that. The rest, well, they get attention however they can." Luke packed the last of his clothes into the drawer and placed an arm around her shoulder, leading her to the living room.

"But they make victims of innocent people. I don't understand how can you overlook that." Frustration and confusion had given her a headache and she rubbed her temples to ease the pain.

He sat on the sofa and pulled her close. "Who said anything about overlooking anything? It's the same as when God disciplines us. We know His laws. Because we're human, we're going to sin, and there are going to be consequences. It would be nice if we learned the first time, but most of us don't." His gentle gaze was full of understanding. "We all make mistakes, but we still have to pay the consequences."

She felt both disturbed and comforted by his tone. Once again, she found herself wondering if he suspected she was A.C. "I know that. I just don't know how to make them right again."

He kissed her, and all of her loneliness and confusion welded into one swell of yearning. "When you're ready, remember, I'm here."

Tears welled in her eyes, and Calli buried her head in the hollow of his neck, absorbing his strength. She had seen too much, witnessed too many painful scenes and lost everyone that had ever meant anything to her.

Yet sharing them with Luke could cost her more than her peace. She could lose the only hope she had.

The deep timbre of Luke's voice vibrated in her ear.

"Father, be with Calli today, help her to fight the invisible battles that wage a very real war within her. King David claims the Lord is close to the brokenhearted and saves those who are crushed in spirit." He paused, running his fingers through her hair. "We know that the battle must be fought, but must rest assured that the victory is already ours. Amen. I love you, Calli."

"I love you, Luke."

Chapter Eighteen

Luke's phone rang and Calli stared at it as if she'd never seen one before. Luke was taking Jon to school. She looked around to see if he had an answering machine, feeling somehow obligated to answer if not. She jumped when the lock rattled on the door behind her.

Luke barrelled through the door and grabbed the receiver. Calli returned to the kitchen and wiped the counters, feeling strangely unlike a guest.

The low tone of Luke's voice made Calli hesitant to pass through the living room to go into hers. It was obviously a private conversation. Trapped, she dried the dishes, found where most of them belonged, then knelt in front of the opened refrigerator to take inventory.

"You hiding?"

She looked up at him leaning over the door, suddenly feeling terribly awkward being alone with him. "I didn't want to interrupt your phone call, so I thought I'd...I could...I was..."

He smiled up, the refrigerator door separating them. "It

was just something to keep me busy. I wouldn't presume to guess what you and Jon like to eat."

"If it's edible, we like it." Luke pushed the door closed, easing her out of the way. He poured himself a cup of coffee. "Would you like some?"

She shook her head. "You just got off work. Won't that keep you awake?"

"Better now than tonight. Since I won't be working for nearly a week, I'd best change my schedule now. If I nap now I'll be up all night. Since we have the day together, why don't we do some shopping? As you can see, the fridge is empty."

The thought of going to her grocery store brought a chill to her today, yet she couldn't admit to Luke that she was afraid of returning. Not after the brave front she'd put up earlier.

"Maybe we could check out the stores on the south side. We can grab a bite to eat and make it home before Jon is out of school. That call was Jon's mother, I could use some advice, from a unbiased party."

"And you think that's me?" She smiled. "You'd better think again."

"From a female perspective, then."

"That, I can handle."

They headed south out of the city. Luke clipped his pager to his belt and set the volume. "Nancy's coming to stay with her parents for the last few weeks of her recuperation. She wants to spend time with Jon."

Calli studied Luke as he stated the facts then waited for her response. Reading his emotions was impossible, his police training was so ingrained into his character. "And you want me to tell you…what?"

He looked at her slyly. "Very clever. What did you say your major was? Psychology?"

"Almost. Education." She looked out the window to the

mountains in the west, then back to Luke. "Why don't you start with the benefits."

He grimaced. "Ouch. You go for the jugular."

"Get the pain over with early."

Luke shared his reluctance to believe Nancy could really stick around, and his relief that she finally wanted to know their son. After a short list of "hopeful" benefits, Luke and Calli discussed the drawbacks, which boiled down to one thing—Luke was afraid Jon would end up hurt if his mother changed her mind again.

"How do you convince a child to give his mother another chance?"

Calli remained quiet. She wasn't the person to ask about second chances. She thought of her own parents and the many times they had asked her forgiveness. The worst part was, she now realized that it wasn't them that should have been asking. It was her that needed to ask their forgiveness.

"Calli?"

"If it helps any, you've already convinced one child—me." Her voice broke as she struggled with the admission. "After my brother's death, my parents grieved and moved on with their lives. Because I couldn't, they had to make a painful choice. And I'm ashamed to admit, I still haven't asked them to forgive me for holding it against them."

He took her hand and apologized. "I just keep saying the wrong thing, don't I?"

"No, not at all. I'd say God brought us together for a lot of reasons. Thank you."

"You're welcome. Let's pray Jon experiences the same change of heart that you have. It would sure make this dad's job a lot easier." He smiled confidently. "Nancy's getting into town late next week. I asked her to let me talk to him this weekend. Jon and I have plans to go to my parent's cabin. You will come with us, won't you?"

Luke turned into a shopping center and parked the car

while Calli struggled with his invitation. ''I've already intruded on you and Jon. I can go to Hanna's for the weekend.''

''Jon's not the only one whose feelings matter here, Calli. While I won't say that I've always let him have his say when it comes to my relationships, well, this time our instincts match pretty well.''

''And I pass the test?''

Luke leaned across the console between their seats. ''With flying colors. I'm crazy about you, and so is Jon.''

Calli laughed. ''I guess we'd better keep the weekend in mind when we're shopping, then, hadn't we?''

The next few days went quickly. Jon finished the school year while Luke spent the time off catching up with odd jobs he'd let slip past. They had Tom and Vanessa over for dinner one evening. Calli let Hanna know where she was staying in case her parents did happen to call. And she and Luke checked her apartment daily. So far, there was no sign of trouble.

Luke was asked to return to work early because of the holiday weekend. After his shift was over Monday morning, they planned to head for the hills.

''Dad, where are my new jeans?'' Jon's voice cracked, and Calli grinned, remembering her brothers' voices changing.

Calli zipped her own suitcase closed. ''Were those the one's in the laundry, Jon?''

There was an uncomfortable silence followed by a sarcastic response. His behavior had progressively worsened in the past week.

She took a deep breath, trying not to let his attitude feed her guilty conscience. ''Check the top of your dresser. Unless I put them in the wrong pile, they should be there.''

There was a long silence followed by Jon's sarcastic response. "Thanks, Calli. I'm not used to having the laundry folded."

Luke stepped around the corner from his room. "You don't have to let her know all of our bad habits, Jon." He winked to Calli and smiled slowly. "I could get very used to this," he said quietly.

"I'll warn you, I'm only this efficient when I'm on vacation."

"That's a relief. These two bachelors might go into shock." He smiled, then called out over his shoulder, purposefully trying to lighten the mood, "My bag is ready. I'll be home around eight in the morning and we'll load up and leave."

"Don't you want to get some sleep first?" Calli stepped into his open arms, becoming increasingly comfortable with their closeness.

"You'd better not be late or Calli and I'll leave without you," Jon warned.

Luke laughed. "Does that answer your question?"

Calli gazed into his eyes and shrugged. "Be careful out there, Luke."

"I'm always careful. You and Jon take it easy. Don't let his attitude bother you. He's just anxious to get away." He kissed her cheek, whispering into her ear. "I love you."

She smiled. "I could get very used to *that.* I love you, too." Calli felt a tug on her heart as he walked out the door. *Take care of him, Father.*

Later that evening Jon answered the phone, then stomped into Calli's bedroom where she was reading. "Did Dad tell you that Nancy's coming to visit?"

Calli swallowed hard, determined to avoid the question. "What did your mother say?"

"She told me she wants to see me. When I told her we were leaving tomorrow, she was in a hurry to get off the phone. Why didn't Dad tell me?"

Nancy must have not realized Luke's weekend wasn't the traditional Saturday and Sunday. "He must have wanted to tell you about it at the cabin."

Jon stared at her, his confusion obviously simmering. He dropped onto the sofa and pouted. "Why does she have to come here now?"

There was an awkward silence between them. "I went for almost a year without talking to my parents once." She set the photo frame back on the shelf and sat in Luke's recliner. "That first visit was really tough. It still isn't easy to talk to them. It's going to take time."

"I don't need her," he snapped.

Calli recognized Jon's anger all too well. "We can't ever have enough people who care about us, even if we don't *need* them."

"She doesn't care about me."

"She obviously does, or she wouldn't be coming." This conversation was supposed to be between Luke and his son, not her. "Why don't you talk to your dad about it in the morning?"

"I can't talk to him about *her*. He has enough to worry about without my mom showing up. Do you really think he knows already?"

He called her "my mom." He's making progress, whether he'll admit it or not. Calli nodded. "Maybe your mother has realized that she made a mistake, and wants to..."

"She can't take me from Dad."

Calli shook her head, trying to calm his unspoken fears. "I'm sure she knows that. After her accident, she may have figured out that time is too short...." Calli felt her own regrets of letting time slip away without telling her parents of her love and regret. "Give it a try, Jon. Your dad wants you to have the chance to know Nancy. To have some relationship with her, whatever that turns out to be. It's really okay."

"She's not cool like you."

Her heart swelled. "You don't know her well enough to say that. She's probably as scared as you are about getting together."

"Then why does she keep calling? Why doesn't she just leave Dad and I alone? We've done fine without her." Jon took an envelope from the end table and started tearing it into bits.

More and more, Jon reminded her of her brother Mike. She hadn't wanted to get into this conversation with him, but now she felt good that he'd confided in her. As she searched for the right response to his anger, she hoped she'd helped him sort things out. She knew talking to him about Nancy had helped her.

"Listen, Jon, have you ever had a friend hurt you, and you just keep thinking that if you keep trying harder, one day he'll like you again and won't hurt you anymore?"

Jon's eyes grew huge as he nodded.

"It isn't easy to keep trying to make amends when someone keeps saying and doing things that hurt. But when they come back again and again, I'd guess your friendship means an awful lot in order for that person to face the constant rejection."

Calli wanted the impossible: to take Jon into her arms and soothe his pain, erase his confusion and tell him everything would be okay.

Chapter Nineteen

No sooner had they finished unloading Calli's SUV than Jon was ready to vacation. "Let's go fishing, Dad. I already got the canoe out."

Jon had ignored Calli all morning. *What in the world is wrong with you, Jon?*

"Later, Jon. I've got to get a little shut-eye. The three of us can go this afternoon." Luke picked up the cooler and took it down the short flight of stairs and began unloading the food into the refrigerator.

Calli was right—he and Jon needed time to let down. Next week he was going to have his evaluation for his promotion, and he and Jon hadn't even talked about Nancy's wish to be part of his life again. Like Calli, Luke had noticed his son's moodiness in recent weeks.

Mumbling, Jon disappeared through the front door, and Luke immediately stepped outside. "Don't leave the property, Jon." He dug three lounge chairs from the shed and opened them on the deck. He took a deep breath of fresh mountain air. "Have a seat, Cal."

"I thought I'd unpack. You go ahead and rest. Where do you want me to put my things?"

He led her up to the second level. "Jon and I'll share the bedroom, if you don't mind. It has a bigger bed. You can have the loft." Luke lifted her bag over the rail and motioned for her to climb up. She expected him to follow, but he stayed below. The room was hot and stuffy.

There were only five rungs on the ladder, and the ceiling in her room was, at its highest point, barely five foot high, causing her to hunch over when she stood. "I doubt you even fit up here, do you?"

"I haven't tried recently. Obviously, no one spends much more time than sleeping up there. You may not want to open the window now. When the afternoon sun hits, it'll be unbearable up here."

"Do you and Jon come to the cabin very often?"

"Every month or so we squeeze in a couple of days. When Mom and Dad bought it, they picked one that was close so all of us could use it as much as possible. Between the five families, it's rarely empty. We're going to add on in the back this summer. All of us kids are paying for the renovation. We'd like everyone to be able to come at the same time."

The concept of an entire family working on one project overwhelmed her. Her own family was scattered now, and barely kept in touch. Of her siblings, she was the nearest in proximity to her parents, and the furthest emotionally.

Calli gazed at Luke, who had folded his hands together, and leaned his arms on the loft floor. Pretty soon, his chin was rested on his hands and his eyelids closed. She knelt down next to him and whispered, "Luke, go to bed."

He jolted up and shook his head. "I'm going to nap on the deck, enjoy this fresh air. Why don't you join me?"

"What about Jon?"

"He'll be okay. He knows there will be consequences if

he doesn't stay close. It isn't your job to keep track of him. You could put your swimsuit on and sunbathe while I nap if you'd like."

Calli laughed. "I didn't bring my swimsuit. You didn't tell me there was a pool."

He grinned mischievously despite his droopy eyelids. "I didn't? Sorry. It's near the entrance to the development. There's a swimming pool, weight room and a clubhouse that we rent when the whole family comes at the same time. We had Christmas here once. If that wasn't crazy!"

She giggled at his sleepy babbling.

He was fighting to keep his eyes open, let alone stay in an upright position. Luke lifted his pointer finger and motioned for her to come closer.

When she did, he patted the carpeted floor for her to sit on the floor of the loft. Luke took hold of her hands and pulled her off. A moment later, she was wrapped in his long arms. She smelled the mingled scents of soap and his spicy aftershave. He locked his hands behind her and leaned back to look her in the eyes.

His gaze searched her face, as if reading into her thoughts.

"Just one more thing, this is supposed to be a relaxing weekend. Time to forget all the trouble at home. That's the one rule to this cabin. It's a retreat. There's *no* discussion of problems or work here."

Calli swallowed. "Nothing?"

"I want us to have fun. And that's an order."

"Yes, sir." *I guess that means no sharing secrets, either.*

He placed one hand on the middle of her back and pulled her toward him. "Have I told you that you're an answer to my prayer, Calli Giovanni?"

"You asked for me?" She lifted her hand to his cheek and admired his green eyes. She saw loneliness and love waiting for the right person to share his pain. Despite her fears she smiled. "Could've fooled me. You didn't even know which name to ask for."

"Calandre or Calli, somehow God knew just who I was missing in my life."

Luke looked at Calli and saw doubt behind her mask of caution. During a recent Bible study, he'd come across a verse in Proverbs. "A good wife who can find? She is far more precious than jewels. The heart of her husband trusts in her, and he will have no lack in gain."

Had he found the woman God had planned just for him? There had been others that he had once believed to be God's choice, but in the end, had been merely a distraction. Calli could certainly be distracting, but more than anything, she was a friend.

Calli lifted her chin and kissed him lightly. "Get some sleep, Luke. Jon's going to be bounding in here ready to go, and you won't have even closed your eyes."

He listened to her soft voice and wanted to ignore the advice, but in the end, he gave in to her words of reason. If he held her much longer, he wouldn't want to let her go. Luke took a deep breath and blew it out. *Why did you have to make her so tempting, God?*

"You know just how to keep me in line. I'll see you later."

"Sweet dreams."

His dreams were far from sweet, and Luke woke crankier than if he'd not slept at all. Luke jumped from the chair and tripped over Calli who was in the chair beside him. His foot caught on her chair and he dumped her next to him.

Luke stared into her dark eyes, panting as if he'd just run for his life. "You must have been having quite a nightmare."

"You're okay?" Luke furrowed his brows.

"Fine, thanks. But I'm not so sure about you." She smiled. "What happened?"

Still sprawled against the railing of the deck, he raised himself on one elbow. "I think I just met your ex-fiancé."

Her face paled and the smile disappeared. She untangled herself from him and the chair and stalked into the cabin, turning briefly. "You don't want to go there, Luke. That subject breaks 'cabin rules.'"

Luke collapsed on the warm wood deck and took a deep breath of the thin mountain air. He closed his eyes. Whatever this man did, he'd left quite a scar to heal. *You sure I'm the right man for this job, God?*

He heard a rustling in the trees and peered through the slats on the railing. Tiptoeing through the woods, Jon was soaked from head to toe and shivering in his boots.

Without a word, Luke went to the back door and waited until Jon slid the door open. "Don't even think of coming in here in that condition."

Jon jumped. "But I'm cold."

"Not half as cold as you're going to be. Weren't you told to stay here?" The voice was that of a cop—stern with no vestige of sympathy.

"You said on the property."

"Have our property lines moved, Jon? It's always meant *our* property, not the development's, and don't pretend that's what you thought."

Jon was quiet and stood with his arms around himself. "Can I come in *now?*"

"You know Mom doesn't let any of us step foot in here when we're dripping wet. Strip down," he said impatiently.

"But *Dad.*"

Luke followed Jon's gaze, surprised to catch a look of reprimand in Calli's dark eyes. "I'll go for a walk." After she'd pushed her way past them and hurried out the door, Luke ran his hand through his hair in frustration.

"I'll be right back with a towel. Guess you won't be going on the lake today, will you?"

"But Dad..." Jon said, removing his wet clothes.

Luke felt like a teakettle ready to boil over. "But Dad nothing, Jon. Every choice you make has consequences. You didn't follow the rules, did you?"

Jon lowered his chin to his chest in a full-grown pout. "No. But you were asleep."

"And so you went into the canoe alone? That's two rules broken, Jon. You could have been at the bottom of the lake, and I'd have been nowhere to be found." When he returned with the towel, Luke lowered his voice. "Jon, rules are rules, whether anyone is around to catch you or not. Vacation hasn't even started yet. It could be a very long summer at this rate."

Jon started to argue and Luke interrupted him. "Go shower and get warmed up." He waved his hand in a gesture of dismissal. "I'm going to catch up with Calli before she walks all the way home." His son's lanky legs shook all the way to the next room.

Luke ran up the mountain, in the same direction Calli started out. He saw her in the distance, sprinted ahead of her and turned around. "Okay, Calli, let's set things straight here. Jon was wrong, and it's my duty to discipline him." His eyes clung to hers, trying to analyze her reaction.

"Everything is black and white with you, isn't it, Luke? You didn't even listen to him. How do you know that he was going out in the canoe?" Calli walked past him without hesitation.

Arms crossed over his chest, Luke stepped in front of her. Not fond of giving the neighbors anything to gossip about, he lowered his voice. "How many thirteen-year-old boys have you raised? The canoe is gone and Jon came home soaked. He didn't fall into a mud puddle."

She deliberately invaded his space, to the point that he

wanted to step back. Calli poked her finger on his sternum, and he was shocked to admit that it actually hurt. "All I'm saying is that you know he's excited for school to get out. He stretched the boundaries a little. Maybe you should listen to him. This was supposed to be a weekend for you two, Luke, and I'm in the way. He wants your attention."

He started to respond, but Calli continued.

"I had brothers, for your information, and let's just say that I gave the term 'tomboy' an all new meaning. You could have let him go. I was here, too." She reeled on, as if short-circuited, as if proving to both of them that she was immune to him. Every curve of her body screamed defiance.

Listening to her, he realized God knew exactly what he was doing, bringing Calli into his and Jon's lives. All around them the ground was turning green and wildflowers were beginning to bloom. Luke bent down and picked one. "I'm not used to sharing that responsibility. When we're with others, he knows he still answers to me. I may have been a little harsh, but thank you for not saying so in front of him. I'm sorry." He handed the yellow blossom to Calli. "I'll talk with Jon. Let's get him and go catch dinner."

She looked stunned. "Why don't you two bring dinner home? I'll make a salad and rice. Maybe you and I can go out on the lake tomorrow."

"Jon and I both need you, Calli. It doesn't bother him that you're here." He slid his arm around her waist and started walking back to the cabin.

"He's been sharing his home with this strange woman for three days, and then she horns in on his weekend with his dad. I just think he'd like time alone with you. He's not used to sharing you, either. Or is he?" Calli stopped suddenly and turned toward him, waiting for an answer.

Luke shook his head and drew Calli close. "No he's not, but he'd better get used to it. Real quick."

Two hours later, Luke and Jon came up the road with a stringer full of trout and smiles across their handsome faces. Calli nervously bit her lip. The argument with Luke that afternoon had renewed old fears and uncertainties. There was no way around it, Luke was *all* cop.

She hurried to the loft, leaving the kitchen so they could clean and prepare the fish. They had agreed to eat around six, so she had an hour to rest. The door opened and Jon called her name.

"I'm upstairs."

"You ought to see these fish! One is sixteen inches long. And it has *pink* meat. Those are the best. Dad caught one and I caught the other three of them."

"Congratulations, Jon, but I'm not good with blood. I'll enjoy eating it though."

"Okay."

Calli turned away from the railing, cherishing the comfort of their laughing voices. The sun was hot on her back and she closed her eyes. It had been years since she had felt such peace. Even at her apartment, guilt ate the comfort away. She'd come to expect herself to take care of everyone. For three years the weight on her shoulders had stripped her of her own life. With Luke around, she felt safe and loved, and at home.

Yet there was Jon. At this critical age was there any hope of the two of them forging a relationship? His mother finally wanted to know her son, and more than ever, he needed one. She knew the pressure on Luke had to be terrible.

Calli felt the tears sting her eyes. *Father, I don't know if I can be a mother to Jon. And I don't know that he can take another person leaving his life if I don't have what it takes to commit myself to them. And I couldn't bear to lose them, either.* She wiped her eyes on the pillowcase.

"In quietness and trust shall be your strength."

She sniffed. *I'm trying, God, really I am.*

"Are you okay, Calli?" Luke's hand rested on her arm.

She jumped. "I didn't hear you come upstairs."

"S.W.A.T training."

Surprised by his retort, Calli turned and looked into his green eyes, her tears turning to laughter. She wiped them away and rolled over to face Luke. He was on his knees next to the bed, a gentle smile on his unshaven face, the face she'd fallen in love with. After removing the baseball cap, his unruly hair stuck up all over. That, too, she'd come to find boyishly endearing about him.

"Why the tears?" Under his steady scrutiny, she found it impossible to sort out her thoughts.

She bit her lip and looked away. "I think it would be best if I go back home, Luke. I'll install a better lock. I'll move. I don't know what I'll do for sure, but I can't stay with you."

He leaned closer and lowered his voice. "Because of Jon?"

She nodded. "He's not ready."

"He's thirteen, Calli. He isn't an easy sale, so to speak." Luke's whisper was so low, she had to read his lips to verify what he was saying. "Don't worry about being a mother. If that's too much right now, just be his friend. He does like you."

She looked away, thinking of Mike, and the sister she hadn't been. Why would this be any different? "I don't want to let either of you down."

"He has nothing to compare a mother to. You can't let him down." Luke smiled.

That was exactly what she was worried about. Jon needed a mother, someone he could count on, someone to be there when his dad wasn't available. She didn't want to interfere with Jon's chance to start a new relationship with his mother.

She was getting attached to Jon. And there were times when she saw hesitation in Jon's expression. Like he wanted to be friends, then, realizing the risk involved, he would back away. They were spending more time together, yet she and Luke had never discussed her role with Jon. She wasn't his guardian, she wasn't his stepmother, and lately, she was beginning to wonder if she was his friend.

"I'm afraid to get close and have things not work out for us. I don't know what's bothering Jon—if it's his mom's accident, or his friends...or us. I'm afraid staying with you, even temporarily, isn't wise."

Luke's brows lifted. "Now, are you referring to Jon, or me?"

"All of us—" she turned away "—could use some space. There's a lot to consider, Luke."

His expression grew serious. "I suppose you're right. We'll talk about it later, okay? Dinner's ready." He took her hand in his and pulled her close. "Get ready for the best catch of the Rockies."

"I thought I already caught the best," she said jokingly.

Luke wore a smug grin. "Lady, that's what I've been trying to tell you for weeks now."

During dinner it was obvious that Luke and Jon hadn't talked about Nancy's impending visit. Jon looked at Calli defiantly. "Nancy called again last night. She's coming next week and wants to see us. Do I have to go with her?"

Luke choked on the French bread. How could Nancy have said anything after agreeing to let him talk to Jon this weekend? Luke looked at Calli, surprised to find her purposefully ignoring both of them.

While he and Calli had talked about Nancy and Jon, they hadn't discussed his determination to help Jon through every step of his mother's return. It was important that he encourage and support Jon throughout this adjustment. Though there was nothing left between him and Nancy, that didn't mean Calli, or Jon for that matter would understand or agree with his desire to make this work. After a long silence, both sets of eyes were fixed on his. "Yes, Jon." He could see the emotion rising in his son, and rushed on to defuse the anger before it got out of hand. "Your mother and I have hashed through a lot of things. I think it's important for both of you to give this a chance."

"You've got to be kidding. You told me..."

"I'm not going to force you. I thought we'd start by having her over for dinner, just to let you two have a chance to talk. I'll be there with you, as long as you want me to stay."

"But why do I have to do this? She's the one who dumped me."

Luke set down his fork and swallowed. "She regrets what she did. Right now, she doesn't even feel she deserves to have survived the accident. It's been a really rough few months for Nancy. She was pregnant and lost the baby. She's trying to pull herself back together."

Jon remained quiet.

Calli wiped tears from her eyes.

"I'm not asking you to do more than you're capable of. None of us are free from error. She's asked our forgiveness. Though it doesn't make up for all we went through, just knowing she wants to know her own son eases some of my pain. This could be a good thing, Jon. For all of us.

"Calli..." He glanced at his son, then into her eyes. "I didn't mean to discuss this with you right here, but now that it's over, I'm glad you heard. You may as well know how I feel. If things work out the way I hope, for all of us, this is a major issue that won't ever go away."

She looked at Jon, then back at Luke. Her gaze was gentle and understanding. "I don't feel our relationship has to change at all because of Nancy. There's room for all of us to learn how to show God's forgiveness. Like I said last night, Jon, your dad wants you to be happy. I'm sure finding out that your mom really cares about you will fill the spot inside that's always wondered."

"It does, kind of...." Jon shrugged.

"And Jon, no matter what happens, no one can take that comfort away from you. You are loved, very much." She looked at Luke and the tears flowed.

She met his smile and accepted the hand he offered. He'd have never had the courage to address such an emotional subject with Jon tonight, yet Calli had barrelled right in and taken on that maternal role of making both of them face their feelings. "Jon, all I've ever wanted is what's best for you. I think it's important for you to know your mother."

Jon looked at Luke. "If it's really okay with you, Dad, I'll give it a try. As long as you two will be there at first. I don't know what to say to her."

Luke looked at Calli as she nodded. "It's more than okay, Jon. I've prayed your mother would want to be a part of your life since the day she walked out. And don't worry, I doubt that she knows what to say to a son, either, so you're not alone. We'll work through it."

After watching a movie, Jon went to bed, leaving Luke and Calli alone. Suddenly Luke felt as awkward as a sixteen-year-old on his first date. The earlier conversation had exposed so many emotions, he didn't quite know how to thank her for supporting him.

Seemingly unaware of the battle going on inside him, Calli gathered the popcorn bowl and glasses and headed for the kitchen. Luke took a deep breath and leaned his head back on the sofa. *Okay, Tom, I'll admit, I have it bad. Now what? I've already dropped enough bombs on her tonight.* When Calli returned, she'd changed from her shorts and T-shirt into jeans and a Colorado State University sweatshirt. Just looking at her warm clothing made him realize how cool the evening had turned.

"You want to watch another movie?" She ran her hand through her glossy dark hair.

How could she stand there and pretend she didn't notice that he was being tormented? Trying to remind himself of the cool air outside, he cleared his throat. "Which one?"

She read the title, and he knew he was in trouble. He wasn't in any mood to watch a romantic movie with her tonight. "I'm not watching some 'chick flick,'" he grumbled.

"It's a comedy."

"It's about weddings. That's a romance. Besides that, true tomboys don't watch chick flicks, either."

"Oh, no?" She raised her eyebrows again, and a look of determination sparkled in her eyes. "Define tomboy."

He was sinking fast. "Well..." His gaze roamed from her head to her painted toenails. "Tomboys aren't beautiful. They aren't feminine."

She motioned to her shirt, then her jeans, and looked at him like he'd lost his mind. He had, and it wasn't coming back any too quickly.

"What is feminine about jeans and a baggy old sweatshirt?"

"I plead the fifth." He forced himself to look away and take a deep breath. He stood up and backed away, hoping to capture some of that cool air on the deck. "Tomorrow, I'll challenge you to the 'tomboy test.'"

Calli laughed. "The tomboy test?" She stepped closer, following him through the screen door and to the railing.

"I'll prove that you've outgrown your tomboy days." Luke pulled her into his embrace and kissed her thoroughly. "So you'd better rest up, Calandre Giovanni."

"Just what exactly is included in your little 'test'?"

"That's for me to know and you to find out."

Chapter Twenty

Calli smelled the coffee early the next morning, and peeked over the loft banister just as Luke carried his mug to the deck and quietly closed the door behind him. Enjoying the wonderful view, Calli watched as he took a long sip, then leaned his elbows on the railing and bowed his head. The muscles in his neck relaxed, and the weight seemed to left from his shoulders.

She turned away, smiling. *God, I can't begin to understand your awesome ways. But I thank you for bringing Luke into my life, for allowing me to grow and find hope again. What a precious gift you have given us. Amen.*

Though she wouldn't admit it, she had lain awake half the night wondering what in the world Luke was going to come up with for his crazy test. She'd already proven she could hold her own in class, for her size, anyway. Surely he wasn't going to put his brute strength against hers.

Calli pulled on her cutoffs and a T-shirt. After she ate a doughnut and drank some orange juice, she went outside to find Luke, and ended up hiking all over the mountain. An hour later, she still hadn't seen any sign of him and headed back. Unexpectedly winded, Calli stopped to rest against a huge boulder. Behind her she heard a rustling in the bushes.

"Luke?" *Trying to scare me, huh?* She waited a few minutes, then turned around to find a black bear sniffing her through the leaves.

Calli screamed. Too frightened to look behind her to see if the bear was following, she ran down the path. She rounded the curve and knocked Luke, Jon and herself to the ground.

Luke grabbed her, trying to calm her down as she kicked and stumbled in her feeble attempt to get back to her feet. "What's wrong?"

Jon jumped to his feet and ran on up the path. "It's just Eunice," he reported.

"Eunice?" Calli gasped. "It's a *bear!*" Calli felt the rumble of Luke's laughter as she pressed against his chest to stand up and brush herself off. She felt the sting of a scrape on her shin. She grimaced and tried to wipe the sand from the wound. "And don't you *dare* try to tell me that it's not!"

Jon returned. "You scared her off."

"Gee, too bad."

Though he tried, Luke failed to wipe the smirk off his face. "Eunice has lived here for as long as we've had the cabin. She rummages through the trash cans every morning, but never hurts anything."

He wrapped his arm around her and led her back to the cabin to clean up her leg. Calli sat on the counter by the kitchen sink, trying to get the courage to touch the washcloth to the cut.

"You want me to do that?" Luke stepped closer, reaching for the towel.

Calli pulled her hand away. "I can do it," she insisted. Thinking all night long about the endless possibilities Luke could conjure up for his ridiculous test, Calli was determined to prove she could handle a little scrape. After all, she had to do something to redeem herself—as she'd already failed miserably with her confrontation with the bear.

"You're turning white, Calli. Let me do it for you."

Refusing again, she took a deep breath and turned her attention away from the injury. Finally she lathered the soap and dabbed it onto the wound, then stuck her leg under the running tap water.

Then his warm hand held her leg still while he dabbed the raw skin with antiseptic. Calli bit down on her lower lip to muffle a groan.

"There, it's done," he said.

He carried her to the deck and set her on the lounge chair, then went back into the cabin. He returned a few minutes later with ointment, gauze and tape and applied the dressing.

"You're a good patient. Very brave," he teased her.

"Thanks. Do I get a lollipop, Doc?"

"How about a kiss?"

Their gazes met right before his lips touched hers.

She felt her cheeks regaining their color. "So far, I'm miserably failing the 'tomboy' test, aren't I?"

Jon ran up the steps to the deck. "The *what?*"

Luke lifted one eyebrow and laughed. "Calli says she's a tomboy."

"Oh." Jon turned into the cabin muttering something about being "The Hulk."

"At least he had the tact not to laugh."

Luke smiled without an ounce of regret. "One day, you'll laugh at this, too."

Calli fixed dinner for Hanna and told her all about the wonderful weekend she'd spent with Jon and Luke. About the romantic sunsets when Jon snapped pictures of her and

Luke laughing in the canoe, all-day hikes and Luke's tomboy test.

"Sounds like it's getting serious. Have you told him yet about being the anonymous caller?" Hanna took another bite of crab salad and cracker.

"Do you always have to bring up the downside of everything, Hanna?" She set her fork on the edge of her ivy dish and took a sip of water.

Hanna lifted her eyebrows. "Reality check, cousin. You *are* the woman he's looking for—personally…and professionally. What do you think he's going to say when he finds out Calandre, a.k.a. Calli Giovanni, is A.C.?"

"I don't think about it anymore," she said, listening to the rumbling thunder outside. "He's not going to find out, at least not from me. I'm not patrolling—end of story." Calli opened the door to let the cool breeze inside. "I've spent months trying to put patrolling and Mike's death behind me. You were the one who talked me out of telling Luke before. Now you've changed your mind?"

"Humph. I never said that, exactly. I did say honesty was the best policy. I give up on you, girl."

After supper, she and Hanna sat down to watch the romantic comedy that Luke had refused to watch with her.

She smiled, thinking of Luke teasing her about true "tomboys" not watching "chick flicks." He claimed she must have outgrown the "tomboy" stage, and she'd spent the rest of the weekend failing to prove him wrong. Her heart swelled when she realized Luke really heard her lecture about listening to Jon. He had made a point to take time away from her to spend with his son. It was reassuring to know that Luke respected her opinion, even if he did grumble about it at first.

In the evenings, Luke and Calli had escaped to the deck to visit after Jon went to bed. They all came home happy. She and Jon had the chance to talk, hike and grow closer.

She found herself wanting more then ever to reach out to kids like Jon, to make a difference.

And she and Luke came home closer than ever before.

Life was looking up. Jon was in a better mood. Calli was less stressed about letting Jon down and less pressured by their relationship. Things seemed to be going great.

After they got home from the mountains that morning, Luke and Jon immediately installed a new door and dead bolt for Calli's apartment while she was at work. The dream he had at the cabins drove him to convince the building owner to make improvements to the security system in the lobby as well.

Before Luke clocked in, he and Tom worked out together. They jogged a few laps around the indoor track then went to the weight room.

"How was the weekend?" Tom asked, as he began to lift.

"Really nice. Started out tense, but ended up great." Luke told Tom about the weekend as they moved on to the shooting range.

He thought of Vic Taylor and the threats that continued to pour into the precinct. Fifteen shots later, Luke dropped the magazine to the ground, reloaded and fired again, running around the barricades, then dropped to the prone position. Then Luke stepped to the background while Tom went through the course.

"Are you joining the racketball league this season?" Tom asked.

Luke shook his head and looked down. "I've got enough at home to keep me busy."

"I know what you mean," Tom said, then added, "Still in knots over Calli, huh?"

"There's something bothering her."

"Her?"

"Yeah, yeah, it's getting to me, too. I asked her about her ex-fiancé at the cabin, and she threw 'house rules' at me. Then I got mad at Jon, and she gave *me* grief for not listening to *him.*"

Tom patted him on the back and laughed. "You'd better marry that lady so you can concentrate, bro." Tom finished and rested on the bench.

"I'm thinking about it." He watched the "I knew it" look spread across Tom's face. "Thinking seriously about it."

Luke wrapped a towel around his neck and headed upstairs to change. Tom followed close behind.

"I know she's a Christian, struggling with trust a bit, but she seems to be rooted on His word. She was upset about her taking time away from Jon and I. No matter what I said, I couldn't convince her that she's not going to let Jon down. What does concern me is that it doesn't sound like she gets along with her parents. When she came to stay with us, she refused to tell them."

Tom wiped his brow and turned into the locker room. "You blame her? Didn't you say her dad was military? She probably saved your hide, Northrup."

"Come on, Tom. It isn't like she 'moved in' with me. I made those boundaries very clear. I just worry about who she would turn to if she needed someone. Hanna's fine, but it bothers me that she can't turn to her parents. What will she be like with Jon? And if her parents were strict, why'd she give me grief for disciplining Jon?"

Tom took a long drink at the water fountain, then slapped Luke's back. "Probably because you *didn't* listen to the kid. Sounds like maternal instincts kicking in."

"Yeah, yeah. Just wait until Jordan and Joseph are thirteen. We'll see how much guff you take off them." Luke laughed, knowing his friend's intentions were noble. Luke showered and dressed for work, ready to head to the lounge to eat his dinner before going on duty.

An ebony hand touched his shoulder. "Luke, give it to God. Hand your relationship with Calli to God."

"I have, again and again." He leaned against a locker, waiting for Tom to finish dressing. "Sometimes I wonder if this frustration isn't Him handing it back."

"So you moved her back home today?" Tom tied his boots and buckled his belt.

"New door and dead bolt are installed and painted to match the others. Jon and I did what we could on the windows and sliding door, though she's on the third floor. I have to admit, I'd still feel better with her at my place."

"I don't think this has anything to do with the Eastsiders. You'd better do some serious planning before you move her in this time."

Luke shot his partner a look of warning. "There was nothing going on. Nothing."

"I know that. And I for one think Calli's just what you need, along with a house, and a dog, and a few more kids." He laughed. "She needs more room than in your place."

Luke thought of the day he'd climbed up to the loft and seen her sobbing. The fear that jolted him was something he'd never forget. He was almost relieved to hear Calli admit she wanted more space from him. The other part of him realized how much he liked her company.

It also made him realize he wanted her with him more, and that installing a sturdier door and lock on her apartment was a long-term solution to a short-term problem. He wanted her back, soon. Tom was right. He'd better start some serious planning.

The thunderstorm arrived with a boom. Luke and Tom ran outside to look at the sky.

"From the look of these clouds, we're in for a big one," Tom said. "That is one cool breeze."

"In the briefing room now! We need to get out there," the drill commander bellowed. By the time they stocked their bags and ran to the squad cars, the rain had turned to hail. The wind whipped the pebbles back into the clouds and spit them out again as stones.

They switched on the radio and listened to the weather warnings, and Tom kept his eyes open for tornadoes. All over the metro area, electricity was out and limbs were ripped from the trees. Streets were flooding. It was going to be another busy night.

Jon was at the amusement park with friends from the Youth Group when the storm hit. The electricity flickered, sending the two miles of riverfront fun into a terrifying hysteria. Rides stopped and started. Hail pounded everyone and everything. Screams of terror took on an all new meaning. Jon gave up trying to follow his scattering group. They were to meet at the entrance at midnight, but that was three hours away, and the gates were flooded with people trying to escape to the shelter of their cars.

After unsuccessfully searching for his group, Jon found a phone. He called Information and asked for Calli Giovanni's phone number, relieved that she answered on the first ring. "Calli, I'm at Riverbend Amusement Park. Everything is a mess here, and I can't find my group. Could you come get me?"

"I'm not sure how long it will take, with the street flooding and downed limbs, but I'll get there as soon as I can. Is there a shelter near the entrance?"

"I'll be okay."

"Stay inside, Jon. There's another storm cell coming our way. See you soon."

He waited, keeping an eye out for his friends. Ten minutes later, they made a dash for their cars. Jon told them he had a ride on the way, and to leave without him. Luckily, none of their group was trapped on the rides. Rescuers were still struggling to free those people stuck on the rides from the threat of lightning and pummeling by golf-ball-size hail.

Calli pulled up and honked the horn. Jon ran, dodging the pounding stones, and jumped into her four-wheel-drive.

"What's going on here? Didn't they see the storm coming?"

"I guess not. I was playing a video game when it hit. Sorry about your car."

She shrugged. "Don't worry about it. I don't have a parking garage, so it was out in the weather anyway. Have you called your dad to tell him you're okay?"

He shook his head. "I'll call when I get home. I'm supposed to stop and get Mrs. Maloney when I get there."

Calli moved her purse out of his way. "There's a cellular phone under the seat. Hand it to me and I'll call him."

"Can I do it?"

She laughed. "Sure. Plug it into the cigarette lighter, then push the power button."

"Will it work in this storm."

"Should. I just used it to call help for the driver of a flooded compact car. Which reminds me, since we have to go out of our way to avoid the low underpasses anyway, I'm going to return these movies at the store. Do you mind coming with me?"

"No problem." The phone rang, and Jon asked to send a message to his father that he was with Calli, and they were both okay.

He told Calli about all the rides and hurt people while she drove to the market. The worst of the storm was over by the time they drove into the parking lot.

"You want to come in with me? We could get you something to eat. Then I'll take you home."

"Sure." Food was always welcome.

They walked into the store and dropped the videos into

the slot, then headed for the frozen pizza since the deli was closed. They checked out and got into the hail-battered vehicle.

As they drove down Columbia Boulevard, Jon noticed some of the storefronts broken. "Did you see that?"

She looked in her rearview mirror and nodded.

"Go around the block."

"I should get you home. Your dad's probably trying to reach you."

"Then we should call on your phone." Just then Jon saw Nate and about ten other Eastsiders bashing in the storefront of an electronics store and begin loading stereos and televisions into cars. He turned as they drove by. "We have to do something."

He looked at her and wondered why she was hesitating.

A block away, Calli turned suddenly and lifted her foot from the gas. She didn't look happy. "Hand me the phone."

Chapter Twenty-One

Three days later, Calli stopped after work and bought groceries to fix dinner for Luke and Jon. Calli saw Jon enter the store, trailing behind several gang members. She looked again at her watch. School wasn't out for another hour. Careful not to draw his attention, Calli watched the group from the corner of her eye. Jon was obviously out of place with the group of hoods. He nudged a Hispanic boy and pulled him aside.

The two appeared to be disagreeing, then Jon backed away.

Calli paid for her groceries, and stalled, trying to find a way to approach him. He walked toward the door. "Hi, Jon."

He turned around, eyes wide. "Oh...um...hi."

She looked at the cart, and back to Jon. "I don't suppose you could do me a favor?"

"A favor?"

"If it wouldn't interrupt you and your friends, I could use some help getting all of these up the stairs to my apartment."

The Hispanic boy nudged Jon. "You don't have an elevator?"

"Broken. But it's okay, I'll manage."

His eyes pled with her to insist. Calli didn't know what was going on, but she didn't like the way Jon looked. "I'll see you for dinner?"

"Yeah. See you later."

The minute she got home, Calli ran to her closet and dug through the box where she'd packed away the wig and glasses she wore while patrolling. Clutching the pouch to her face, she stopped herself, reminded of her vow to commit her way to God.

"Let not your hearts be troubled: believe in God, believe also in me."

But Jon's in trouble. Calli hesitated, struggling with the temptation to handle the situation herself. *I know, God. Trust.* She closed the apartment door and tossed her pouch of makeup and the wig back into the box. *Okay, I can do this.* She walked back to the kitchen and unloaded one sack, then ran down the stairs to get another armful of groceries, determined to make herself leave it in God's hands.

When she reached the top of the stairs with the last load, she collapsed in the chair. Calli pulled out her information from the gang symposium. Flipping through the pages, she puzzled over Jon's choice of company. Reviewing the warning signs of gang involvement, Calli ruled out some signs completely, but couldn't deny there was enough reason to be concerned.

After Calli left, Jon argued with Nate again. "This isn't my scene, Nate. Yours, either. Come on, let's get home." He had to hurry home, before Calli could call his dad.

Nate pushed Jon away. "And what are we going to do, Jon, go home and baby-sit a house full of brats?"

Jon didn't know how to argue with that. He didn't know

what it was like to have a brother or sister. He rarely had anyone but Nate over after school. "We can shoot some hoops or play hockey while your sister and brother play at the playground."

"It's Friday. I just want to kick back with the gang." Nate tied a blue bandanna around his shaved head and pulled it snug.

"You don't need them, and you don't need this trouble."

"If you want to wimp out, Jon, go on home to Daddy. These guys are the only friends I have who really care about me."

Nate strutted away.

"And what am I?" Torn between staying to fight for his best friend or doing what was best for himself, Jon backed out the door and ran home, tears blurring the way. He stopped in their apartment building lobby and pretended to get a drink from the water fountain, hoping to rinse the redness from his eyes.

He didn't want to tell his dad, because he would go straight to Nate's mom, and then Nate would be even madder. He wanted his best friend to trust him, to like him again. But most of all, he wanted Nate to be safe.

While he was walking toward the elevators, Jon heard his dad talking to the manager about renting a second parking place in the security garage. They already had one spot for the motorcycle and its trailer. Why was his dad wanting to pay more to put his old car in the garage now, after it was already dinged up from the hail storm? Jon went to the apartment and waited.

A few minutes later, the phone rang. Expecting Calli, Jon snatched the phone before his dad had a chance. It was Mrs. Maloney calling to tell them she couldn't come tonight because she had the flu. Three more times the phone rang, and not once was it Calli. He began to think she might be different from his father's other girlfriends.

They were going to her house for dinner, and Jon couldn't figure out a way to convince his dad to stay home. And even if he had, what was the use? Calli was going to tell on him sooner or later. May as well get it over with. Jon started thinking about his excuse.

His dad really liked Calli. As far as he was concerned, she was all right. Calli seemed to care about him, too. The past girlfriends were always telling on him right away. But Calli was different.

They had been at her house now for two hours, and she hadn't mentioned seeing him at the store. Was she trying to make him squirm? Did she even know that Nate and the others were part of the Eastside gang? *Maybe she doesn't know who they are.* From out on the balcony, Jon could overhear Calli and his dad talking.

"Mrs. Maloney has the flu, so could you do me a favor and stay with him tonight? I know that's asking a lot...."

She looked at Jon, then his dad. "I'd be glad to, but would either of you mind if we stay here instead? That way you could go home and get some sleep before I need to go to work. I could drop Jon off at home on my way to the market in the morning."

"Is that okay with you, Jon?"

"I guess."

The three of them watched a movie together, then Luke went to work. After he was gone, Calli walked over and sat down at the other end of the sofa. There was an uncomfortable silence.

She changed the channels, then finally turned the television off. "I may be out of line here, Jon, but I would like to know what was going on this afternoon."

He shrugged. "I needed to talk to Nate."

She didn't smile or say anything for so long that he began to wonder if she'd heard him. "Does your dad know you cut classes?"

"No. Aren't you going to tell him?"

"Aren't I?" she repeated. "I guess that depends on you." She crossed her legs and swiveled toward him. "I don't want to see you get hurt. That's my first priority. If I think you're in danger, I'll talk to Luke about it."

Jon realized she knew exactly who he was with, and that coming up with some story probably wouldn't work with Calli any more than it would with his dad.

"So, why were you out of school early?"

"I told you, I needed to talk to my friend," he said, hoping she'd back off.

"How do you plan to keep your father from finding out that you missed part of the day? Did you forge Luke's name on an excuse?"

She wasn't any pushover. He nodded.

"How did you get hooked up with the Eastsiders, Jon?"

He leaned forward in his seat and opened his hands in front of him. "I'm not a member of the gang." He made the mistake of looking at her.

Her voice remained calm. "Then what are you?"

He didn't have to answer to her. She wasn't his mom—yet. "Why do you care?"

She looked sad. "Because the gangs are trouble, and I don't want to see you get hurt."

"What makes you think they'd hurt me? I told you, I'm not a member." He looked at all the dolls she had lying around, figuring someone with that many dolls would never understand guy stuff. *I hope she doesn't bring these to our house when they get married.*

"Because you were arguing with that boy. Was that Nate?"

"Yeah, so? We've been friends forever. He's not going to hurt me." He glanced at her and rolled his eyes.

She nodded. "Then why did you look concerned?"

"You sound like Dad."

Her eyebrows lifted. "I do?"

"He's always asking a hundred and one questions. If I'd known you were going to question me all night, I wouldn't have agreed to stay here. Dad could've taken me to Grammy and Gramps."

She smiled. "I am honored that you chose to stay here, but I won't ignore my concern about the kids you're hanging out with. You know they're trouble, and I hope you decide to keep your distance. I'm willing to listen, if you decide you do want to talk."

Calli told him he could watch television while she did some stuff, so he turned to the basketball game. She went to the kitchen and washed the plates and forks from the apple pie she'd made for dessert, then went down the hall to the bedroom area. Pretty soon she came back in, wearing pajamas and a housecoat. Calli reached into a basket and started stitching some towels. They talked about sports, and he was surprised that she liked to ski and play volleyball.

"Wait a minute."

Calli set the sewing in her lap and looked at him. "What?"

"You're the girl Dad met skiing, aren't you?"

She tried not to laugh. "Well, I don't know. How many times has your dad gone skiing this year?"

"Once. I gave him a ski pass for Christmas."

"Then I guess I'm guilty."

"You're the one who was hanging off the chair?"

"Guilty."

He started laughing. "Did you know Dad's afraid of heights? You're lucky to be alive." She seemed happy to be talking about his dad, as happy as his dad was when they talked about Calli.

"Your dad makes a difference in people's lives every

day. I'd like to know that I made a difference in someone's life."

"Have you been married before?"

Calli shook her head. "Thankfully it broke up before that. Why?"

He shrugged. He'd be in big trouble if he told her about the ring he and his dad picked out for her just before they came over. "Just curious."

"It's nearly midnight. We'd better get some sleep. I work at eleven in the morning, so we'll need to get you home around ten. I left some extra towels in the bathroom, and if you'll move, we can put the sheets on the sofa. It pulls out to a bed." She put her needlework away and walked down the hall.

When she returned, she had an armful of pillows and blankets.

"Calli."

"Yes, Jon."

He looked at the floor. "Thanks."

Chapter Twenty-Two

Luke called the next morning when he got home from patrolling and updated her about the gang activity. Calli felt a pull to join the battle, but snuggled in her bed instead, remembering the commitment she was making—to God, to Luke and to Jon.

As Luke talked, she remembered her conversation with Jon the night before. She and Luke really needed to find a time when they could discuss parenting, and what role, if any, she should take with Jon. As Luke had admitted, he wasn't used to sharing that responsibility. For whatever reason, maybe he wanted things to stay as they were. Parenting a teenager was like walking a fine line anyway, without starting on the defensive. Yet she desperately needed reassurance that she was doing the right thing.

"You busy tomorrow night?"

Calli rolled over and curled into a ball, a smile on her face. "That depends, Officer."

"I'm only suggesting dinner. I thought I'd see if my folks could have Jon stay with them. That way we wouldn't have to worry about time. I think we're going to have a lot to talk about.''

''You think so, do you?'' She felt her face turn pink. ''What're you up to, Northrup? I thought we were going to take some time to think about all of this.''

''I guess you'd better be thinking then, because I'm ready to talk.'' His voice was low and husky.

She sighed. ''Where are we going? How about that new café on the corner?''

''I'm talking about *dining,* Calli. As in a dress and tie.''

Calli tried to moisten her rasping voice. ''Luke, I think we'd better *talk* first.''

''Isn't that what I just said?''

Her breathing was shallow and fast. She wasn't ready for his proposal. ''Luke,'' she pleaded. ''You didn't...''

He hesitated, and uncertainty crept into his voice. ''I guess you'll just have to wait and find out.''

She could tell he was tired, and she needed to fix breakfast for Jon and get ready for work. All night long, she'd wondered if Luke had learned she was the anonymous caller. If she told Luke about her patrolling now, he'd be awake and furious all day, and in no shape for work tonight. Fatigue could put his life in danger. By the time she got off work this evening, it would be time for him to report for duty.

Luke interrupted her thoughts. ''Can you go to church with us in the morning?''

''Sorry, I work the early shift again tomorrow.'' By the time she got off, there would be no time to talk before dinner tomorrow night. She would just have to talk first.

Calli heard Jon get up and go into the bathroom. He turned on the shower and started singing. ''Does Jon always sing in the shower, or is it just around me?''

''Always, but it's louder when you're around.''

''I'd better get moving. What time tomorrow night?''

"Mom's fixing dinner for the family at two, so I suppose about seven. If you happen to get off early, everyone would love to meet you."

"Thanks, but I don't want to barge into your family dinner in the middle, especially the first time I'm invited. I'll talk to you at seven."

Calli hung up the phone, then let out a groan of frustration. *I have thirty-six hours to figure out how I am going to tell him.*

At the breakfast table, Calli couldn't relieve the pressure she felt sitting across from her prospective stepson. Luke said tension with the Eastsiders was stretching thin. What she did now would set the boundaries of their entire relationship.

"Jon—" Calli sighed "—I really think it would be wise for you to visit with your dad about Nate today."

The teenager shook his head. "No way. Nate would…be really mad."

She stared at him. "I know that, Jon. I also know what the Eastsiders are capable of doing. And so do you. You need to talk to someone who can help."

"I'm talking to you."

Jon looked at her with total confidence. He actually meant it. Calli swallowed. She was it. "Jon, I don't know Nate. Luke does. Nate might listen to your dad." *Welcome to parenting, Cal.*

"They already think I snitch on them. I can't, Calli."

"You know who's involved and what they're doing. You know way too much. Not to mention that your dad's a cop. Did you ever think they could be using you?"

He stared at his food. "I only went with them once. And yesterday at the store, Nate told me it was just going to be us. That's why I was mad at him. I thought we could be like we used to be, that maybe we could talk."

Calli smiled wanly, feeling sympathy for the boy. "I

know it hurts to see him make poor decisions, Jon, but you could end up in trouble just trying to help him. Your dad works with gangs. He understands them, why they do what they do. He'll know how to help you and Nate without repercussions."

He didn't answer.

"It's admirable to want to help someone you care about. But the problem is bigger than you are." Calli realized she could very well have given herself this lecture any time during the past three years, and she would have listened just about as well as Jon.

"I can handle it. I'm not going to stop until Nate's out!"

Calli saw reflections of her own stubbornness in Jon. "Why won't you tell your dad?"

"He has enough to think about."

Jon's compassion was inspiring. She could hardly believe he was only thirteen. Calli decided that there was no way around it—she had to be the one to try to reach Nate. "Okay, Jon, tell me what you know about gangs."

He thought. "They cause trouble."

After a long silence and deciding he didn't know more, or didn't want to elaborate, Calli responded.

"That's it in a nutshell." She tried to see this through Jon's eyes and saw Mike. She saw herself, in charge. Could she change the outcome this time? She had to; there was no choice. "Do you know why kids get into gangs?"

"I used to think it was because they were bad kids, but Nate wasn't, until he started hanging out with these guys."

"When did Nate get involved with them? Was there something stressful going on in his life?"

"I don't know."

These Northrup men were impossible. "Jon, I want to help. In order to do that, we have to know what might have made Nate turn to them. Kids that get pulled into gangs can be rich or poor, come from loving families and broken families, but the one thing that's most common is that they are hurting inside over something and they don't have anyone to turn to. The gang welcomes them, makes them feel loved. And then..."

"He's not bad!"

"I believe you. I do." *Neither was Mike.* Calli took a deep breath, groping for the words to help Jon, and Nate. *God, help me.* Calli struggled with memories, and unshed tears. She couldn't cry now, Jon needed someone to look up to as much as Nate did.

"And he has me to talk to, so that can't be it."

She knew how Jon felt. She, too, would have done anything for Mike. For three years she wondered why he had never tried to tell her what was wrong, or worse, that he had, and she didn't hear him. *Psychology 101—listen.* She waited, silently struggling with wanting to talk to Luke, to someone who could ease this pressure and guilt.

"I know what he's feeling, because my mom walked out on me when I was a baby!"

"Did that happen to Nate recently?"

"His dad left. Now he's supposed to be taking care of his little sister and brother after school while his mom works. Dad and I keep inviting Nate to do stuff, but he refuses."

"What does Nate's mom say?"

"He doesn't listen to her."

Calli felt the situation pulling her into a direction she wasn't prepared to handle.

"What about 'putting in work'? Do they drag you and Nate along?"

"I went once, because I was afraid to back away. They didn't do much, spray painted a few fences and walls. Now I don't stick around that long."

"Good. You have to leave Nate to make his own choices, Jon. If you want to talk to him here, or at home, that's different. But outside of that, steer clear. I don't know how to reach Nate. We aren't professionals. There's a local ministry we could talk to."

"You'd go with me?"

"Sure. I don't want to see anyone hurt. Maybe they can give us some ideas to help Nate."

"Us? You don't know him. Why do you care?"

"Because I don't like people hurting other people. It isn't right. If we hurry, we can go this morning." Calli made a quick phone call to the mission, then rushed through her shower and called the store to tell them she might be late.

They walked into the converted warehouse. The church looked less than spiritual. Posters of teens lined the walls. There were televisions and vending machines.

They walked past a room of young women, pregnant or holding tiny babies, apparently learning parenting skills. The kitchen was filled with teenagers studying stoves and poring over recipe books.

Hanna had told her about Pastor Ortiz, a dignified-looking man with dark hair and a friendly face. He greeted them warmly, and led them to his office, talking as they walked.

"You know as well as I do that every day we fight battles. For some it's everyday survival. Some are invisible battles that we fight with invisible weapons."

"Invisible weapons?"

"God's word. This battle you are fighting is very real, Jon. Indeed, it must be fought, but know that you already have the victory." Pastor Ortiz pulled out two chairs and sat down behind his desk.

Calli looked at the muscular man. "I admire your efforts, but how do you work with these kids? Do you ever really 'reach' them?"

"It means digging pretty deep inside. Deeper some days than others. And I make them search, too. They need to find the desire to change before I can help them. All these kids are making that choice."

Looking through the glass walls, Calli saw the kids' enthusiasm in the activities and knew there was still hope.

"What happens when they make the wrong choice?"

"The same that happens when the rest of us make the wrong choice—they pay the consequences. Maybe it would help you to understand if I told you that I see members of gangs as victims."

Calli shook her head, fighting the temptation to understand. "No, I don't think that helps." These were the kids that she'd spent years supposedly "helping." But she hadn't helped them. Stopped them, maybe, but the mission was meeting these kids' needs. *This* was making a difference.

"Look at it this way. These kids are looking for love. For friends. They may be from broken homes, victims of physical or emotional abuse or neglect."

Calli wanted to see the minister's point. Wanted to understand the flip side. "I know the statistics."

"Don't get me wrong, Miss Giovanni, I'm not approving of the negative behavior. That's why I opened these doors, to get kids off the streets and into a place where someone cares for them. Where they can try to overcome their problems."

She wanted to believe him. Envied his generosity. Fighting the battle her way not only held no rewards, but was making no headway in the rash of gang involvement. She knew that, but it was all she could do to focus on the innocent victims. "That's admirable."

"And sometimes we succeed. So what can I help you with?"

"My friend's dad left, and his mom is so busy trying to

work and make sure the little kids are okay, she doesn't know what Nate's really doing."

Calli looked at the pastor, then at Jon. "She knows he's not home. What does she think he's doing?"

"She thinks he's at my house."

Calli touched his arm. "Have you been covering for him?"

He looked away. "Not since I found out how often he's with the gang, but his mom doesn't even bother to check. She believes him."

The pastor took Jon's hand. "You can't take responsibility, Jon. You're going to end up in the middle of a huge problem. We need to let his mother know what's going on."

Jon shook his head. "Nate won't listen to her. It's too late."

"It's never too late," Calli said, praying that it would be true. For Jon, and Nate. For her and Luke. "Jon, Nate knows you'll stay with him anyway. It's his parent's attention he needs. And if they don't know, they can't change."

"I'm not going to be the snitch. I've seen what they do to snitches." The fear in his eyes was very real.

The pastor interrupted the duel between Calli and Jon. "I'll be glad to make a call on his mother. No one will have to know it was you that sent me."

Jon looked to her and then to the pastor and nodded. Jon wrote down the address and he and Calli went to Luke's.

When they arrived, Calli went up with Jon, just in case Luke would be awake and asking why they were late. There was a note on the table.

> Mrs. Maloney's still sick. Calli, can you pick Jon up after work today? If not, Jon, call Grammy and Gramps ASAP.
> Love you both.

"I'll see you after work. Go on in and make sure your dad's asleep." Calli waited for Jon to confirm that Luke was sleeping, then turned to leave. "And, Jon, please talk to your dad. He'll understand."

Luke leaned back in his chair, making notes on his pocket notepad while waiting for the commander to join them for the briefing. Tom repeated an address he overheard was related to one of their cases. "You think A.C. was the caller?"

Tom shrugged. "We'll check the address, make sure everything's quiet. Remind me to see if they got a trace on that cell number before we leave."

Luke closed his eyes and said a prayer.

"Hey, Fife," one of the officers bellowed, imitating Andy Griffith. Everyone looked at the sergeant entering the room. "You drop something, 'Barney'?" Bill's partner held up a shell. "Found this on the ground next to the car last night. Was that the clanging sound I heard when you cocked your shotgun last night?" Muted laughter spread across the room. Bill turned red all the way to his necktie.

Soon everyone was poking fun.

Patricia asked if they'd had any follow-up reports on the alleged "pool cue holdup." Across the room, the new recruit mumbled, "Gimme a break. In the dark, it looked like a sawed-off shotgun."

Luke chuckled, amazed that something so simple could relieve such insurmountable levels of stress.

The white-haired captain strolled into the room shaking his head. "Children, children."

Luke wiped the grin off his face, ready for the ugly side of his job to begin. Until they were home safe again, laughter wouldn't be nearly so easy to come by.

Mac continued. "I hear love is in the air."

Luke grinned. "Northrup."

He dropped the chair to all four legs. "Yeah, Captain."

"You have some earth-shattering news for us?"

He looked at Tom, who had a "not me" grin on his face.

"You'll be the second to know."

"Keep us up-to-date on the progress of that case." Laughter filled the room.

Luke nodded. "This place is worse than Aunt Nellie's gossip chain," he mumbled.

"*Now,* we can get on to business." Mac turned the page. "There was more vandalism at the market on Columbia. Some windows busted, too."

Luke looked up. Mac was staring right at him. "That's right, Northrup. I should take you and Davis off the streets for a few more days."

Calli was working this afternoon. "Anyone hurt?"

"No injuries reported. We're not sure if it's related to the threats or not."

Luke lowered his voice. "With all due respect, Captain..."

"As I was saying, we're already shorthanded out there. So let's be careful. I don't want another officer down."

The room hushed in respect for Vic Taylor.

Tom put his hand on Luke's shoulder. "I'm sure she would have called if she needed you."

That was the real question. Did she need him? He listened in silence as the latest cases were discussed, and pushed his way through the door after roll call was over. "Let's get out there."

He made short order of inspecting the squad car and loading his gear, then got behind the wheel.

Tom closed the trunk and buckled himself in. "Guess I don't need to ask where you're headed, do I?"

Chapter Twenty-Three

Calli rushed to Luke and Jon's after work, lugging three bags of groceries and a bucket of fried chicken down the hall. She rang the buzzer and waited for Jon to open the lobby door. There was no answer. Stuffing her key ring into her pants pocket, she dug out the keys that Jon gave her that morning and searched to match the right key to the right lock. *I hope he just fell asleep, that he didn't go out with Nate.*

The elevator's slow climb gave her a chance to take a deep breath. It was a busy day complicated with the drive-by shooting at the store, a shortage of checkers and knowing she and Jon would be spending another evening together. So much seemed to ride on these first few days with him.

If she and Luke did decide to get married, her commitment would be doubled; she'd be a wife *and* a mother. Kids had always been a part of her dreams, but starting out with a teenager was far more than she expected.

More important to her at this point was earning Jon's respect. Everything with teens seemed to hinge on that.

According to her friends, kids that age rarely admitted to liking their parents' decisions, but if they listened, a parent could feel somewhat confident that they had the child's respect. She really needed to know how Luke would handle *this.*

She picked up her bags and balanced the load so she could get both locks opened.

"Jon!" She stepped into the apartment. "Jon, are you here?"

The silence grabbed her. She dropped the bags on the table. Calli ran from room to room calling his name.

He wasn't there. Remembering the police department's nonemergency number from her days patrolling, Calli dialed the precinct. "Luke Northrup. It's urgent."

"If it's an emergency, call 911."

She took a deep breath, trying to hold her patience. "No, I need to talk to Luke." She turned, frantically searching for a message from either Jon or Luke.

"Let me check his status."

Rushing through the apartment for any signs of where Jon could have gone, Calli waited for the answer on the other end. *Maybe Nancy had arrived sooner than expected…? No, she wouldn't have left with Jon without telling someone.*

"I'm sorry, miss, Officer Northrup isn't available at this time."

Without responding, she dropped the receiver onto the base and sprinted up the stairs to Nate's apartment. His mother answered her knock immediately, and seemed unconcerned that Nate hadn't told her where he and Jon were going.

Before Nate's mother could even close the door, she was gone. Calli paused at the elevator, then decided the stairs would be quicker.

"He is a shield for all those who take refuge in Him."

Please God, be with Jon and Nate. It can't happen again. I know I promised, but I have to go. I have to find them. Please. She prayed all the way to the parking garage. In the SUV, Calli dug the cellular phone from under the seat and plugged it into the car's lighter.

She tried to call Luke again, but the phone went dead. Jamming the plug into the socket, she tried again. It rang, then disconnected. She tossed the phone into the seat and pounded the steering wheel in frustration. Calli had no choice but to continue into the shadows of the city without the security of a connection to the police. Or a way to call the apartment to see if Jon had returned.

Fear consumed her, worse than ever before. She had spent three years wishing she could turn back the clock, change the outcome for Mike. All that time she'd been preparing for battle. She had a chance to make a difference.

"What would you do if you were here, Luke?" *This is no time for natural consequences. The stakes are too high already.*

She tried to remember the verse Luke and her father kept in their hearts. "'Be merciful, O God, for in thee my soul takes refuge; In the shadow of thy wings I will take refuge, till the storms of destruction pass.'" *Forgive me if I don't have it down perfect, Father.*

Calli started the truck and backed out, then stopped. She put the brake on, then jumped out and called Jon's name, hoping she was wrong. Hoping he'd just brought the trash downstairs, gone to the store...anything, except followed Nate tonight. She had to find them before either of them got hurt.

Luke's only been gone an hour. Unless someone had given them a ride, they had to be close. Getting back in the vehicle and zigzagging her way to the south, Calli checked the convenience store.

Then the sleazy café two blocks away.

Her heart raced, making the slow pursuit that much more difficult. She didn't have time to take it slow. Couldn't bear to consider the chances of missing him.

"Not Jon, too. Please God, not Jon. I can't let him down."

"He who began a good work in you will see it through to completion."

This time, there could be no peace from God's reassurance until she knew Jon was home safe. Anger welled within Calli, and she felt the pang of guilt for wishing harm to come to Tiger and the others who continued to make victims of the innocent. *They may be victims in their own way, but that doesn't give them permission to hurt others.*

"Trust me."

A group of kids congregated on the corner. After a careful search, she drove on. She checked the time. Another hour had passed. Calli quickly checked her apartment, then drove past the nearest gang hangouts. When nothing turned up, she went back to Luke's, through the puzzle of matching the right key to the right lock and finally into the apartment to see if Jon had returned yet.

There was no sign of him. She scratched a note on an envelope and not knowing where they kept the tape, set it on the table. Calli dialed the station again.

"Officer Northrup is still busy. May I take a message?"

"Yes, tell him to call Calli at 555-7995. It's an *emergency.*"

Running down the stairs, she wove the keys between her fingers. She pushed through the lobby door and turned straight into Jon, and the rest of the gang.

"This her, Jonny?" Tiger asked, yanking on Jon's arm.

Calli tried to hide her shock at seeing Jon already looking like he'd been used as a punching bag. Counting Jon, there were five of them. She presumed the other battered kid was Nate.

"No! I don't know her." Nate was silent.

Calli's gaze darted between the teens, her other hand clutching the canister of Mace.

"This is the same lady we met behind the store, isn't it, Pete? She was with you the night of the storm, too. Right, Jonny?"

"What do you want?" Calli moved her thumb to the trigger.

"We're after a snitch. And when we find her, she's dead."

She looked at Tiger. His hair was slicked back into a ponytail at the nape of his neck. Another kid wore torn jeans and a white undershirt with the sleeves rolled up.

Her heart raced, and her throat constricted. "Looks like you've already made your point. Let them go. This is between us."

"No." Jon started to protest, but Tiger pushed him to the ground.

A tough-looking gangster with a shaved head grabbed Jon by the collar, then dropped him again. "Shut up, kid."

Calli sprang forward. "He has nothing to do with this. I'm the one you're looking for."

Tiger nodded, and one of his punks shoved Calli away, but she quickly regained her balance. *A woman's best defense may be the element of surprise.* "You won't get away with this!" Her voice was already raspy, yet Luke's advice spurred her on. Calli lunged at Tiger, using her entire body to slam him into the brick wall and jabbed the keys into his side.

"Get her off me!" he yelled.

Somebody picked her up from behind. Screaming for help, she broke her captor's hold with a kick to the knee and he dropped her to the ground.

"Stop!" Jon turned to his friend. "Nate, do something."

Calli tried to stand, but it hurt to breathe and her legs

would barely support her. She pointed the canister at Tiger and sprayed him and another kid with Mace. They both hit the ground, knocking her against something hard as they landed....

She heard voices. "Calli, wake up."

Calli realized she had passed out. Her head hurt. She opened her eyes.

"Jon? Where is he?" She rolled to her side and tried to blink away the blurry picture. "Jon?"

"Jon's right here. Lay still. Calli. George called the police."

She looked up to the silver-haired woman staring at her. "Mrs. Maloney. Is he okay?"

Luke heard the call to a gang fight over the radio and recognized his address. He hit the light switch, flipped a U-turn and stepped on the gas.

"We were just there! How did we miss them?"

Tom picked up the mike. "Officers 1097 and 1120, E.T.A. four minutes."

"Make that two."

"Slow it down, Luke. It may not be them."

Luke ignored him. It was Jon and Calli they were talking about. No way was he going to slow down. "If it is Jon and Calli, Father, take care of them."

"Amen," Tom added.

Swerving through and around traffic, Luke made it in just over two minutes. Calli's vehicle was parked right in front of the doors, as if she'd arrived in a hurry, as well.

He slammed on the brakes, and both men were out before the car stopped bouncing.

Mrs. Maloney waved her arms.

The ambulance sirens warbled to a halt. Backup officers followed.

Dodging oncoming traffic, Luke ran across the street.

Nate and Mrs. Maloney told Tom what had happened while Luke examined his son. The paramedics pushed Tom aside. Another pair of medics were treating Calli.

Luke felt the tears sting his eyes as he stood looking at Jon.

His partner touched his shoulder. "I'm sorry, Luke."

"Jon." His son was immobilized. Splints surrounded one arm, and an IV was already taped to the inside of Jon's other elbow.

Luke took a deep breath. "Jon, it's Dad. I'm here." With only a glance, he questioned the paramedic.

"Hi, Luke. This is *your* son?"

Luke nodded.

"He woke up for a few minutes. Looks like he has a broken arm, but my guess is it looks a lot worse than it is. Cuts and bruises will heal."

"I love you, Jon. We'll pull through this together." The paramedics lifted the cart into the ambulance. "I'll be right back. I want to check on Calli."

"She's about ready to go with us," the medic added.

"Good." Beads of perspiration blended with tears and dripped from his lip.

He went to the second group of paramedics. Calli's face was already swollen and bruised. "Oh, Calli. No."

"Is Jon okay?" Tears streamed down her face and she gasped for air. "I tried, Luke. There were too many of them."

Nodding, he patted her arm, and her eyes closed. He squeezed his own eyes shut and gulped air, trying to block out reality. "Thank you for trying. I love you."

The EMTs lifted the gurney and nudged Luke. "We're ready."

Luke followed them into the ambulance and offered to help. The paramedic handed him saline solution and gauze, and Luke gently washed his son's face. He spoke with barely checked anger. ''Who did this, Calli?''

She answered in a suffocated whisper. ''Eastsiders. And this time, Tiger isn't going free.''

Chapter Twenty-Four

Luke walked into Calli's hospital room, his usually tan skin now pale, dark shadows under his eyes, his unshaven jaw tight with stress. "Jon's going to be okay. The surgery on his arm went well. It wasn't as bad as they originally thought."

"Good. The nurses kept me updated during the surgery, but I haven't heard anything since." She noted that he didn't make any effort to come closer. Try as she may, she couldn't stop the pain.

"Haven't you called Hanna?"

Calli shrugged. "She left a while ago. I didn't want her to be up all night." *And I hoped you'd be here with me.*

All along she'd been lying to herself, convincing herself that it was going to be different this time. Jon was going to make it. Her parents would finally understand. And this time, the cop would stand beside her.

She tried not to notice that Luke hadn't looked at her. Yet when he walked to the window, she couldn't ignore it. She felt that everything they had become was gone. "Go ahead, Luke. Tell me I should have minded my own business.'' She refused to be intimidated. Yes, she regretted that Jon was hurt, but she knew from experience the outcome could have been so much worse. ''You won't be the first.''

Luke seemed to be studying the sunrise. The firm outline of his shoulders strained against his uniform and served as a painful reminder of the pressure Luke was feeling. ''Why didn't you tell me?'' A nerve along his jaw flinched.

Calli paused to wonder what he was asking, then decided it didn't matter anymore. It was long past time for her to tell him everything. ''I tried. There wasn't time.''

He turned and sat on the marbled windowsill. ''How long have you known Jon was involved with the gang, Calli? One hour, two, twenty-four?'' He turned his head, his gaze meeting hers. The anger in his voice turned to a tomblike silence. ''And you didn't have time to tell me?''

She'd gone through everything regarding Jon a hundred times in the last few hours, and decided she couldn't have done anything differently. Except that she should have told Luke weeks ago about being the anonymous caller. She did regret that. She expected to hear Luke tell her, ''It's time to face the consequences.'' But he just stood there in deafening silence.

Now there would be no more chances.

No more tomorrows.

''I tried to help. Jon wasn't joining, but he wouldn't give up on trying to get Nate out.'' She couldn't tell Luke that his son asked her *not* to tell him.

''So you put yourself right in the middle.'' His words were unforgiving. ''Why didn't you let me handle it?'' Luke's raw voice lowered, his pain excruciatingly evident with each word he spoke. ''I'm his father, not to mention a cop.''

''Everything happened too fast, Luke. I tried to convince him to talk to you, but Jon was afraid of the gang. I took him to the Mission to talk to Pastor Ortiz.''

Luke picked up the straw from her tray and twirled it from finger to finger, pacing the room.

"I tried to call tonight, but you were on patrol. The dispatcher obviously didn't believe me when I told them it was an emergency. There wasn't time to explain."

"And look where that got you," Luke snapped.

"You can't hurt me, Officer Northrup. Three years of hearing Brad's insults reverberating in my mind have taken care of that. I knew the risks of what I was doing. I accepted them long ago."

"We're back to the jerk, huh?"

Calli swallowed the fear, denying that Luke would react like her ex-fiancé, blaming her, playing the perfect role of macho man. With quiet determination, she took a deep breath and recited her statement again. This time for Luke.

"When Jon wasn't home, I just knew he'd gone after Nate." Her mouth grew dry, her voice weakened as she now realized, she should have done more. "I had to find them, before they got hurt. As it was, I barely got there in time. With all the stress you've been under lately…I'm sorry, Luke, but I'd do it the same way in a minute."

"Who do you think you are, a psychologist?"

"It didn't take a degree to see Jon was upset. I only tried to—"

Luke pounded a fist into the foot of the mattress. "Save him? And what about Tiger? You trying to save that worthless punk, too?"

Bile rose in her throat. "Hardly."

"Oh, you *do* realize your limits, huh, tough girl?"

There was no use trying to hide her anger. "I'm not the only reason Jon was hurt. But if it wasn't for me, he could have died tonight."

He didn't argue. Luke just stood there in his filthy uniform, perspiration dotting his forehead.

Calli pulled herself to her feet and stepped closer. Luke

took a step back. She followed, her blatant stare challenging him. ''There *are* no limits when it comes to Tiger or any of the Eastsiders. And this time, finally, I have enough to put Tiger away. I'm the woman you've been looking for.''

For a brief moment, there was an almost hopeful glint in his eyes.

She stepped past the IV pole and picked up her journal from the bedside table and held it in the air. ''Three years, Luke. I've waited three years for this day.''

''What are you talking about?'' The lines on his forehead grew deeper. His eyes narrowed.

''Mike Giovanni. My kid brother.'' She swallowed the tears, and turned away from his angry stare. The words had a bite of their own. ''I've spent three years trying to prove that my brother wasn't a gang member, and didn't want to be. That he was the victim. Maybe *now* someone will listen.''

''Y-you,'' he stammered, staring at her with a look of utter disbelief, ''are claiming to be the anonymous caller?''

She nodded. ''Hanna brought me my journal. I finished my last entry this morning. Enter the book into your evidence, Officer Northrup. Every call is there, every step I've taken in the name of justice.''

He stepped closer and closer, backing her against the wall, the words grinding from his mouth. ''It's bad enough that you used me! But you used Jon?''

Calli pushed him away. ''You're the one who fell into that chairlift, Luke. I didn't even know you were a cop! And when I found out, I ran. Again and again. How many times did I tell you this wouldn't work? Did either of us have any control over falling in love?'' She stared him in the eye. ''I didn't tell you because I had nothing that would help.''

''How do you know that?''

"Fine, Luke. Interrogate me. Ask me why there are no entries after you came to see me in the hospital, Luke."

Silence.

"I gave up my mission. For you. For Jon. For us."

Luke stepped closer, stopping just out of reach.

He shook his head. "All this time, you've been after Tiger? Why didn't you let the authorities handle it?"

"The authorities had their chance. Does the name Brad Burns tell you anything?"

Calli saw the connection being made. Luke's shoulders sagged. "That crooked cop was your fiancé?"

Calli looked away, unable to face the anger in his eyes.

"Brad determined that Mike wanted in, and the case was closed. Said there wasn't enough evidence. For three years, I've vowed not only to find my brother's killer, but to protect other innocent victims like him. Like Jon. I can't prove it, thanks to Brad discarding evidence, but I'm convinced that Tiger is responsible for my brother's death."

Luke lifted her chin and stared at her, his deep-set eyes filled with disbelief. "Why, Calli? Why didn't you tell me?"

"You showed me how to hope again…how to forgive and move on." She bit her lower lip and swallowed the lump of regret in her throat before continuing. "I was afraid I'd lose you."

Luke turned around and took several deep breaths.

"Tiger was with Jon tonight. But Jon didn't want in. I saw it in his eyes. Jon was the victim as much as I was. And if it kills me, I'll prove it. You can't stop me. I won't let Jon down, too. I've come to terms with the risks. That's something you should understand."

"I've had years of training. A few self-defense classes and seminars hardly prepare you for what's on these streets."

"Don't, Luke. I've made a difference and you've said

so. Only, you didn't know it was me. But of course that alone changes everything, doesn't it?''

''It sure does. Everything.''

''Check your records, Luke. I stopped patrolling the night of my accident—the night we met.'' Derision and sympathy mingled in his glare. He didn't seem in the mood to test her. Probably for the best, she decided. It had been a long night, and she was out of strength to fight anyone.

What she wanted, she couldn't have. Support. Luke and Jon. A family.

Tears fought for release—finally. After years of none, all she wanted tonight was to cry, to let it all out in Luke's embrace. To be held and comforted. Yet she had to remain strong for a while longer. She couldn't break down now.

Disappointment consumed her. She'd thought Luke was different. That he'd support her efforts. That he'd understand her need to protect her brother's reputation, her family name, as well as other innocent victims.

Calli walked to the window and heard Luke leave the room and the door close slowly behind him.

Chapter Twenty-Five

"Luke, you've been up all night. Go home. We'll stay here with Jon. You have to get some rest." Luke gazed at his parents. His father's eyes looked tired. He had called them right after signing the waiver for his son's surgery.

"I can't go until Jon wakes up. I have to see that he's okay." Hunched over in the chair, Luke rested his head in his hands, noting the bloodstains on his uniform. Calli's blood.

"You're going to fall out of the chair, Luke. Don't they have someplace you can lie down? We'll call you when Jon wakes up." His mother rubbed his back, and he thought of the night he heard about Vic Taylor and Calli had been the one to ease his tension.

He hadn't been able to tell his parents the role that she played in all of this. Tonight he didn't have the energy.

He fought to understand Calli's reasoning. And soon the entire precinct would know, would think that he knew all along. *How could she have kept it a secret for five months?*

His father cleared his throat. "Is Calli doing okay?"

Luke nodded, too choked up to speak. He didn't know

how to feel: betrayed, grateful or angry. Today he'd been planning to propose. They were going to have talked, and he'd hoped she would agree to be his wife. Now he couldn't help but wonder if she would have ever told him.

The nurse walked in, carrying the journal Calli had offered. "Miss Giovanni asked me to give this to you." She shrugged her shoulders and handed it to Luke.

"What's that?" Joan Northrup's brown hair still looked elegant, even after spending the night in the hospital waiting room.

He set it aside and ran his hand through his hair. "I'll look at it later."

"Luke? What's going on?" His father's voice held the same depth and authority that Luke had learned to rely on and respect.

He looked into his father's steely eyes. If anyone would understand Luke's struggle, it was him. "Mom, could Dad and I talk alone for a while?"

"I'd like to hear this, too."

Knowing there were no secrets between his parents, he almost felt asking her to leave was useless. "It's work related. And I don't think I'm ready to hear the emotional side of it quite yet, but I'm sure after Dad fills you in, you'll get your say."

"Just so I do. I think I'll go check on Calli. What room is she in?" His mother raised her eyebrows, waiting for him to protest. Luke didn't have the energy.

"Room 382." Once his mother was gone, Luke inhaled deep. He was sick of this antiseptic stench. He leaned back in the chair and folded his arms across his chest. "She didn't just happen upon the fight, Dad. Calli is the anonymous caller."

There was a moment of silence. "Your Calli has been cleaning up our streets? She's the superwoman we read about in the papers? Why didn't you tell me?'' His father was acting like she was a national hero.

"I just found out tonight. They were waiting for her, Dad. They used Jon.'' Luke explained everything. He voiced his pain, and his doubts, and the love that felt like it had just been stabbed to death. Without trust, was there anything to build on? He longed for a relationship like his parents, where there were no such things as secrets.

"I'm not excusing what she did, but after being betrayed by Burns, it's no less than a miracle she's on the law's side at all.''

"I know that. And I am grateful that she saved Jon's life. I'm just not so sure...''

"Marriage is forever, Luke. Good, bad and ugly times all go together. And I can guarantee you, a cop's marriage will suffer more than the average share of hard times. You'd better be more than sure this time.''

Luke nodded.

"There will come a time, Luke, when you'll be ready to work through this. A marriage can't survive without forgiveness.''

"It can't survive without trust and honesty, either,'' he said bitterly.

"Trust is built when we can face one another with forgiveness in our hearts. It's easier to be honest when you've built a foundation on trust and forgiveness. None of us could forgive if He had not first forgiven us.''

"But you and Mom don't keep secrets. I don't know if I can deal with that. How can I be sure there aren't others?''

His father chuckled. "That has to be worked through together. When I worked undercover, there were plenty of secrets. It wore on our marriage. But our love was stronger than our differences.''

Luke said nothing. His father offered again to let him go home, but he refused.

His parents went home to get some rest so they could stay later when Luke would consent to take a break.

Jon stirred but didn't wake. There was barely an inch of his face that wasn't battered and bruised. Mesmerized by the rhythm of the IV, Luke watched the liquid drip to the tubing and into his son's arm.

You've seen me through thirteen years of parenting, Lord. I could use another dose of reassurance right now. I know You're here, that You were with Calli and Jon last night. Help all of us to work through this.

While Jon slept, Luke read from the journal.

Two hours later, Luke put it down. Reading it had left him emotionally exhausted and mad enough to spit nails. There were several times Calli had taken on situations that were much too risky for a civilian.

In one entry, she'd written that when the police didn't arrive in time, she chased a thief away, preventing him from driving off in an expensive sports car.

Reading accounts of her state of emotions that first year after her brother's death, Luke had to admit he was touched at the tenacity she possessed. Included were details of her spiritual battle and her determination to protect the innocent. He closed his eyes, wiping the moisture from them.

"How's it going, partner?"

Luke jumped. "Do you really have to ask?" He filled Tom in on the surgery, his recovery and Calli's announcement.

Tom looked at Luke, yet remained quiet.

Luke looked Tom in the eye, reading the turmoil reflected in his eyes. "You know?"

"She told me when I took her statement last night. She asked me to let her tell you. I had to tell Mac, but no one else knows. For her protection, I'm not sure anyone else should know." Tom looked him in the eyes. "How are you doing with this?"

Luke started pacing. "Not good." He looked at his partner and motioned to the table. "Have you read any of the journal?"

His partner shook his head. "She wasn't finished. I told her I'd pick it up today."

"It's right there. Take it. It's frightening to see the risks she took. We were this close to catching her—" Luke held up his hand, measuring an inch with his thumb and finger "— dozens of times."

"You've read all of it?"

Luke nodded, struggling to keep the anger from his voice. "I can't believe it. The blonde I ran off the road, the voice I memorized, her determination. It was all right in front of me the whole time! Talk about love being blind. She played me for the perfect fool. But what really makes me mad is that she used Jon."

"You don't really believe that, do you? Come on, Luke."

Luke sat and crossed his ankle over the opposite knee. "Stay on the case, Tom. I want it handled right. I don't want Tiger to walk this time."

"It's by the book, so you'd best stay as far away as you can. Calli's pressing charges."

He nodded. "I never doubted that."

There was a groan from the bed. Luke looked at Jon, who was fighting to wake up. "Jon. How are you doing? Tom, go get a nurse."

Jon mumbled, then ran his tongue along his lip. "Drink." As Luke helped him get a sip of water, he remembered the first time he and Calli met. Thought of the way her helplessness had lured him back to her again and again in the last five months. *Helpless? What a joke!*

Jon squirmed, then mumbled, "Dad, this isn't Calli's fault. How is she?"

Luke hated to admit that he hadn't been to see her in

hours. "Not much better off than you. No broken bones, otherwise, you could be twins."

Jon twitched as the nurse checked his pulse and eyes, then jotted notes on his chart.

"You're doing fine," she told him.

Ignoring the nurse, Jon concentrated on his dad and Tom. "And Nate? Is he okay?"

Tom nodded dubiously. "He's at the juvenile center. A little beaten up, but nothing like you two. He's the one that ran into the apartment building to call for help. We arrested Tiger and two others in the park. All three are in jail."

Luke looked to Tom. "You sure they're the ones?"

"As sure as we can be until the blood tests are in. Calli marked them up pretty well. Can you believe she carries that triple-action Mace that dyes the suspect? I'd hate to surprise that lady in a dark alley." Luke heard the respect in his partner's voice.

"I'm sorry, Dad. This is my fault. I should have listened to Calli. I'm so sorry."

He kissed his son and straightened the sheets. "I am, too, Jon. I should have paid more attention."

"Luke, do you mind if I take Jon's statement now, while it's fresh on his mind?"

With a nod of permission, Tom pulled his recorder from his pocket and set it on the table, then pulled a form from his clipboard.

After Luke heard his son's version, the struggle was even worse. He knew he shouldn't be so angry, that he should be grateful, that he should thank Calli again for risking her own life for his son. He couldn't.

His partner told Jon to get better. He then put his supplies away and turned to leave. Luke followed him into the hall and handed him the journal. Just thinking of what she'd been through in the last three years, his eyes misted over.

"Here's everything you ever wanted to know about the Eastsiders."

Without hesitation, Tom gave Luke a quick embrace. "Let us take care of this, Luke. You have other places to put your energy right now."

As the morning progressed, his fellow officers stopped by to give their support and assure Luke and Jon that nothing would slip through the judicial cracks on this case. Everyone was behind him.

Jon was asleep again, and this time when his parents offered to stay so he could go home and sleep, Luke accepted.

Unable to face the front doors where the attack had taken place, Luke entered through the parking garage and dragged himself into the apartment. First thing he found was the note she'd left on the table. The groceries she'd dumped on the kitchen floor greeted him, as well as a bucket of fried chicken for her and Jon's dinner.

He ignored all of it and went straight to the shower hoping the steaming water would pound the tension from his muscles and wash away the tears. Afterward, he called Nancy to update her on Jon's condition.

Despite the seemingly overwhelming support for Calli's courage, Luke could only concentrate on her betrayal and the five months that she hadn't told him the truth. Her comments came back to haunt him over and again as he tried to sleep. *"I'm attracted to men who are completely wrong for me… Keep it platonic… We have nothing in common."*

He recalled his prayers to find A.C. "Well, I've got to hand it to You, God, You led me right to her. Now what am I supposed to do?"

He slept, then woke, feeling rested, but still bothered by the pressing need to deal with this new list of problems. He wanted to be with Calli, to pretend this had never happened. The pain was too fresh. How could he trust her again?

Luke knew he should talk to Nate's mother, then decided he couldn't face her yet. Right now he was too angry. Because of Nate, Jon and Calli were in the hospital and lucky to be alive. He couldn't place all of the blame on her or Nate, he realized. If he had been paying more attention to *his* son, he may have noticed what Calli obviously saw happening. Then again, if Calli had told him what was happening, he may have been able to avoid the entire situation.

Luke went into the kitchen and put the groceries away, then took the chicken to the trash dump down the hall. He walked in the kitchen and again saw Calli's name on the scrap of paper. He thought back, trying to remember the exact time he and Tom left the station to look for her. Looking at the time she put on her note, he realized they must have just missed each other.

She had tried to call right away. Had wasted no time in looking for Jon. Put her own safety last. Which was exactly what he would have done. With startling clarity, Luke recalled the nightmare he had at the cabin a few days earlier, and closed his eyes. "It's over."

Luke pulled a black T-shirt over his head and thought of Calli. *"You see everything in black and white, I see life in shades of gray..."* How could he turn his back on her now, after all she'd been through?

After straightening the apartment, he stopped at Teddy's restaurant for a burrito and went to spend the evening with Jon.

Luke walked into his son's room, glad to see him sitting up.

An honest attempt at a smile appeared on his son's face. "Hi, Dad. Calli came to see me this afternoon. She was on her way home. She said she's staying with Hanna for a few days."

Luke bit his lip to stifle his disappointment at missing her. "Was her cousin with her?"

"No, I think it was her parents. Her dad's even bigger than Gramps. Grammy says you didn't go see Calli today." From his son's animated conversation, Luke guessed Jon was feeling much better.

As his son again repeated every minute detail, trying to work through the trauma, Luke was unable to put Calli's courage out of his mind. Jon had fought for his friend and Calli had fought for them both.

Though Jon was still peaked and dozed off and on, he was talking constantly when he was awake. Much more like Jon's true nature than the quiet, troubled teen who had been lurking in their home recently.

"Dad? Why didn't you go see Calli?"

"I went to see her first thing after your surgery."

"But not later. Calli says you're pretty mad at her, that she should have told you something sooner."

"She tell you what that was?"

"No."

He switched the television to a baseball game, then turned the TV off and leaned his head against the back of the chair. "Yeah, she should have told me sooner. And she should have told me about you and the gang. Calli is the anonynous caller we've been trying to find."

"I said I'm sorry. And I know Calli is, too. I apologized to her this afternoon."

He held his son's hand. "I hope you've learned from this mistake."

Jon nodded.

Luke longed to hold Calli, to reassure her as he did the first night he learned about the threats. Her words still pulled at his heart. *"Promise me tomorrow, Luke,"* she'd said. *"I just don't know, Calli."*

Luke shook the memory away and looked at his son.

"We all make mistakes, Dad. You say that all the time. You're still going to give her the ring, aren't you?"

Chapter Twenty-Six

Calli's parents had arrived just in time to take her home from the hospital. Driving through the familiar neighborhood, she realized she couldn't return to her place. The memories of her painful journey would always haunt her there.

The time had come to start over. No more working at the grocery store. No more patrolling. Her mission was over. Successful or not, she had done all she could.

Hanna insisted Calli stay with her until she decided what she was going to do. Her parents immediately moved her few belongings into the empty basement of her cousin's new house.

What now, God? There's a whole world of possibilities, but You know my heart's desire. You obviously brought me through last night when I couldn't have stood alone. I'll trust You to show me Your plan.

Calli found Hanna's Bible the next afternoon while Hanna and her parents were cleaning her apartment. She hesitated, then picked it up. *I really blew it this time, God.*

As Calli studied His word, she realized that He had tried

to prepare her for this. Warned her all along of the trials that would test her faith. Right now, she felt she had failed. Succumbed to temptation. *What other choice did I have? I couldn't turn my back on Jon.*

Calli fell asleep on the sofa, and woke to her parents' laughing. *What is there to laugh about?* Pulling an extra pillow over her head, she admitted that she wasn't even sure she wanted them here. They'd been very polite, but the closeness was gone. She didn't feel she had or she ever could live up to their expectations.

"We have some dinner ready, sweetheart. Do you feel like joining us?" Calli's mother was the same after all these years—quiet and strong. Her mother's emotions were never exposed. *The perfect military wife. Strong and silent.*

Rolling over was still a struggle, and pain throbbed in her lower back. Every part of her body ached. Her face was purple. She didn't want *anyone* to see her like this.

"No, thanks, Mom."

"I'll bring it in here then. We can eat together."

"Is everything out of the apartment?"

"Everything." There was a pause, and her mother returned. "I thought this might help."

Calli opened her eye and felt a tear form. Then another, until she couldn't see. It didn't matter now. It was long past time to have a good cleansing cry.

"Bessie," Calli said, straightening the handmade overalls her mother had sewn twenty years ago for her "tomboy" doll. Her mother placed the doll beside Calli and kissed her cheek before she left the room.

She remembered Luke talking to her lifetime friend, then tucking Bessie in his arm, caring enough to make Calli comfortable. "I'm so sorry, Luke." The tears overflowed like a creek in the spring.

The next day her father helped Calli up and insisted she get some sunshine. After helping her into the chaise longue, he took hold of her hand. "I haven't told you how proud I am that you stood up for Jon, Calli."

Despite his words, she felt empty. "Anyone would have done that."

"You'd be very disappointed to know how many people turn their heads and walk away. For three years I've been telling you to do just that. I'm sorry, Calli. I just wish you'd have gone to the academy and joined the force. It's not too late, you know."

"I *don't* want to be a cop, Daddy. I felt guilty. I was mad. By the end of those three years, I wanted vengeance. Patrolling was my cowardly way to get even with the criminals, gangs, the Brads of the world. They hurt others, I wanted them to pay. Whether or not it did any good, who knows? I don't even know if justice was served. Standing up for Jon is the only thing I've done worth remembering in three years."

"That's not so, Calli." He reached to the table and picked up his well-worn Bible. "God uses each of us in so many ways. You faced your fears each time you went out there. What may have been a gentle reminder to one person may have saved another person's life. Like that boy who was hurt at the apartments. Because you got there when you did, he's okay today."

Calli didn't look at it that way any longer. Seeing the price Jon had paid, she realized her reasons were no longer justifiable. She closed her eyes to the bright sunshine and warmth, regretting her stubbornness, and that it had brought pain to Luke, and also his son.

"And there were countless others. Your motives may have started as vengeance, or justice—it doesn't really matter. In your heart, you were doing it to protect others. There's nothing to be ashamed of."

"You really think so?"

"I do." He leaned over and gave Calli a hug.

My daddy is proud of me. Thank you for renewing our relationship, God.

Seemingly oblivious to her momentary escape, her father read, "'And after you have suffered a little while, the God of all grace, who has called you to His eternal glory in Christ will Himself restore, establish, and strengthen you.' Calandre, a warrior's battle is never won, and trust me, the way isn't easy. We're tested each day. And I'm very thankful you're okay."

"If you call this okay." She grinned, longingly remembering the night Luke walked into her hospital room and asked if she was okay. "You and Luke would have gotten along great. You're so much alike."

"Don't give up on him yet, honey. Ask your mother. Our type can be pretty bull-headed. Sometimes takes a two-by-four to open our eyes."

"And once in a while, it takes the whole tree trunk," Catherine Giovanni said as she carried three glasses of lemonade into the yard. "But once he gets the idea, it's there to stay."

"I'm not like you, Mom. I'm not patient, and quiet and...silent."

"Well, sweetie, this is one time you'd better practice a bit of all of them. Because if Luke is like your father, it could take him a while to realize what he's lost."

Calli unpacked a few of her necessities, wary of completely "moving in" until she'd found another job. She and Hanna were getting along fine, her bruises were going away and she was doing everything she could around the house to take her mind off Luke.

She'd hurt him, and there was nothing that could erase that pain. For him, or herself. The emptiness spread like the stifling smog along the Rockies, leaving her in a bleak existence. Tom had called earlier in the day to ask her a few more questions, and reported that Jon was getting better every day. Apparently, Luke felt the same way as she did about leaving the city and had started to look for a house in the suburbs where he and Jon could start over.

Before Luke went to the hospital to take Jon home, he stopped at the station. The commander confirmed that Luke could have whatever time he needed to take care of Jon. He suggested Luke consider a desk position when he completed his requirements for lieutenant, which would be as soon as Luke felt up to the evaluation.

"I probably blew all hopes of a promotion last night. I heard my address, and knew. I should have taken my badge off."

"You did just what any of us would have under similar circumstances. I'm just glad you stayed with Jon instead of going out there looking for the suspects." The commander raised his glasses to his forehead and rubbed his eyes.

"I'm sure you're right, Mac."

"Don't worry, Luke, no one's going to question your integrity on this." With a fatherly look of warning, Mac added, "Just don't give in to the temptation to stick your nose into this case. You want to know anything, you ask me. As for A.C.—Calli—we both know she didn't do anything illegal. And thanks to her, we may have broken up the Eastsiders. No leaders, no gang. We have our work cut out for us to keep it from gaining power again."

"What are the charges?"

"I think the list would be shorter to say what can't we charge them with. For starters, since Calli's come forward, we can also hit them with intimidating a witness."

"She's quite the hero, isn't she?" Luke said cynically.

Mac patted Luke's back. "I know it hurts." He stepped closer and rested his hand on Luke's shoulder. "Father God, provide Luke with the discernment to know the plans You have for his future with Calli. Give him the strength to help his family to recover from this tragedy. Help him to be an understanding father and have the integrity to be a forgiving husband. Amen.'' He lifted his head and winked to Luke.

''You think we have what it takes do you?''

''Any woman who'd go though that for my kid, I'd be a fool to walk away from, Northrup. Think about it.''

After Jon was home and asleep in bed, Luke thumbed through the pictures that Jon had taken of him and Calli in the canoe. He understood her pain, her fears, her drive to find her brother's killer.

If he took himself out of the picture, he could even understand why she'd been afraid to tell him. Everyone else she'd known and loved had left when they could no longer deal with her obsession to find the person responsible.

And now he knew firsthand the anger that had driven her. It was the same emotion that consumed him after Jon and Calli's beatings. Right after it happened, his professional oath could have easily been set aside. The cop in him had wanted nothing more than to take this matter into his own hands. To solve this case himself. He'd wanted justice, without the judge, jury or anyone else. Just himself and Tiger, face-to-face.

He couldn't begin to understand the depth of his anger and pain those first few hours. He was extremely grateful that the greater fear was Jon's health, that God held him at his son's side where he was forced to deal with his emotions face-to-face.

Those two days in the hospital he'd prayed more than he thought was possible. Prayers of thanks. Prayers for Jon, and Calli, and the wisdom to make the right decisions.

Nancy arrived and came directly from the airport to see Jon. After a successful dinner, Nancy asked Jon if he would like to spend a few days with her family. Jon's answer was an immediate "Yes!"

The anger had forced him to come to terms with his own mortality. Coming home to an empty apartment made him face what his life would be without Jon. Without Calli.

He realized that he could turn his back on his love, like Nancy had Jon, but everything he believed said to forgive. "Seventy times seven times. Forever."

Jon agreed to look for a new school to attend the coming fall. They decided to find a house away from the hub of the city. After Jon's recovery would be complete, Luke's convictions would take him back to the precinct. He was a cop.

Luke was faced with the woman he loved, and how to win her back. How to ask her forgiveness. How to offer his own. The world was no longer black and white, but a million shades of gray.

The phone rang. He answered.

"Dad?"

"Yeah, Jon. How are you doing?"

"Okay. Nan...Mom and I had a talk about what happened. And I don't know..." The silence reverberated through the wires.

"You don't know what, Jon? Whatever it is, we'll work through it." He and Jon were working hard to establish trust in each other again. Luke knew the next few months were going to be challenging, with moving and making new friends.

"I don't think I ever told you how great I think Calli is. I mean..."

Luke smiled. He knew Jon and Calli were right together from the start. And for a while, he began to worry that Jon was his main reason for wanting her so much. Thankfully, that fear quickly subsided as they'd become better friends. "Are you trying to tell me how stupid I am to let her go?"

"She fought for me, Dad."

"I know, Jon. And for the record, I agree with you. If she'll give me another chance, I plan to ask for her forgiveness."

"Is that all?"

Luke chuckled. "Is that from your mouth, or your grandmother's?"

"Gee, Dad, you think I'm blind? I'm sorry I messed things up for you guys." Luke stared at the photo of them canoeing. He'd had a copy framed for each of them.

"Don't even think that, Jon. You said it yourself. You and Calli have settled things between you."

"Thanks, Dad. And thanks for letting me come here."

"You have a good time. Just remember, lots of rest. Okay?" His son had a lot of adjusting to do this summer. They all did.

"Dad, I'm fine," Jon moaned. "Anyway, are you going to go see Calli? Maybe ask her to dinner at the apartment so you can talk. You should fix her your barbecued ribs and coleslaw."

"Ribs?"

"Sure, you know, kinda symbolic, like God taking one of Adam's ribs to create Eve."

"Enough, Jon. I'll handle the details."

His son laughed. "G'night, Dad."

"Night, Jon. I love you." Luke hung up the phone, torn between missing his smart-mouthed son and laughing at the accuracy of his analogy.

Yeah, he'd blown it with Calli. He hadn't talked to her since that night in the hospital, but offering himself to her on a platter seemed a bit much. Then again…

Chapter Twenty-Seven

"Dress casual," Luke had said. "Just in case dinner gets messy." *Forever the pessimist, Luke.* Calli's heart hadn't slowed down since she got the phone call.

She checked her watch again, having to hold her hand still, it was shaking so much. Never had she been so nervous to go out to dinner with anyone.

"Settle down, Calli. I'm not going to yell at him," her father said, sounding stern instead of comforting.

"Easy for you to say." Never had she had so much riding on one night, she realized. Never had she felt for anyone the way she did Luke. Never had ten days gone so slowly.

The doorbell rang, and Calli swallowed hard. Luke had never picked her up for a date before. Come to think of it, they'd never had an "official" date before. She wasn't sure this would qualify, either, since she refused to go to a restaurant or movie. Her bruises were uglier than they had been that first day, minus the swelling. Green and yellow and brown weren't her favorite colors, especially now.

Though the makeup helped in one way, in others it made her look even worse.

She opened the door and struggled to get words from her mouth. Trouble was, it wasn't emotion choking her up. Luke stood in the doorway looking taller and more rugged than ever. His beard was a day or two old, just like the day they'd met at the ski slope. His black jeans and buffalo plaid shirt were boldly telling her she was about to be courted as never before.

"Hi," she gasped. She remembered the first time he'd worn the shirt. She'd teased him about the black and white checks being his true nature. He'd argued that there was no gray in his line of work. She'd said there were gray shadows all around them. He'd missed the point.

"That's it? I was hoping for this wildly romantic reunion, and you whisper, 'Hi.'"

She managed a small, tentative smile. "You flustered me." Luke laughed, just as she hoped he would. Calli stepped back to let him in.

"I know the feeling." His smile broadened and Calli felt herself relax.

She turned to her father and made introductions. While the two men visited, Calli called her mother to come meet him. After a few minutes of conversation, her father excused them. "I'm sure you two have plenty to talk about. We can visit later."

Calli gave him a quick hug. "Thank you, Daddy, for everything." She hugged her mother and turned to Luke. "I'm ready."

Luke turned to her parents. "Thank you for being here for Calli this week. I won't keep her out too late tonight."

"Luke, there are no hard feelings about this. You had your son to care for, and we were here for Calli. I'd have been more upset if you'd have rushed right back without taking the time to think everything through."

"Thank you, sir. I'll take good care of her."

"Have a nice evening."

Luke helped Calli into the car and closed the door for her. He climbed in and leaned over to kiss her.

"I'm truly sorry for everything, Luke."

His finger lifted her mouth to his lips. "You're forgiven," he whispered before kissing her again.

Calli asked about Jon. After answering, Luke told her they were going to his apartment for dinner and maybe a movie. "I don't know that I can go back there, Luke."

"We'll go in through the garage, but I think you need to face your fears. I just thought we could talk easier here. If you get tired, you can go lie down." He reached over and took her hand in his. "I'll be right here for you."

They walked into the elevator and Luke wrapped his arms tenderly around her waist. "Does this hurt your back?"

"No." Calli closed her eyes then dropped her head against his chest and ran her fingers along the squares of his shirt, not feeling anything except his warm embrace.

He placed a gentle kiss on her forehead and released his hold and she backed away. "I found those gray areas." One by one, he pointed to the gray checks on his shirt, then stepped closer.

Tears filled her eyes.

"You were right, Cal, they were there all along. I never noticed. There are probably some more that I haven't found yet. Maybe you could point them out."

"I'm not chasing shadows anymore."

"Even if you were, that's okay by me. We can use all the help we can get out there."

She shook her head. "I'm breaking out of that trap. I'll leave the bad guys up to the pros."

"We all have to face our fears."

"Don't worry, Northrup. I'm still facing my fears. Right now." She wanted Luke to take her in his arms again. Even with the pain, she longed for the security of his embrace.

"I'm sorry I didn't come back to see you, Calli. There's no other way to say it besides I was a coward. You were so independent and brave to go out there alone, night after night, fighting back. I didn't want to understand, but I do now. I see your shadows, and I want to share them. I don't want you chasing them alone."

Luke wanted to heal the hurts that kept Calli from him, though he knew he didn't have that power. But he sure wasn't going to walk away. That was just what she expected him to do, because everyone else in her life had given up on her.

They went into his apartment and sat down. Luke brought out some chips and dip and sodas. "Are you comfortable?"

She nodded unconvincingly.

"Calli?"

She nibbled her lip, avoiding his gaze. Luke knelt next to her and lifted her chin. She closed her eyes. A single tear escaped, yet she refused to give in and let herself cry.

"Let it go. Let your tears wash away the pain. Don't let the guilt crush you any longer."

She gasped for breath. "I can't." She shook her head. "I have to be strong."

"God gave you tears, and He gave you me. Trust me, Calli." He brushed the wisp of hair from her eyes. "You don't have to take care of everyone and everything all by yourself. Let me share your pain." His hand gingerly touched her face and wiped the tear from her eye.

"I should have told you..."

"You were right where God needed you, all along." Luke smiled. "I love you, Calli. I need you. Jon needs you.'' He looked deep into her eyes, his gaze soothing her soul. ''Don't you see?''

Tears flowed freely, and Luke sat next to her, then wrapped her in his arms. ''I don't know what I'd do without you, Luke.'' He felt her body relax and tears drip on his shoulder. ''I was so afraid you wouldn't call.''

''I did, though. You'd do just fine, honey, but I don't want you to have to face anything alone again.''

''No, I wouldn't. I'd quit praying, Luke. I didn't think He was listening anymore. Nothing was going right.'' She inhaled quickly, then babbled on and on. He couldn't understand her words anymore.

Luke closed his eyes, sending a silent prayer upward before speaking. ''Being submissive is the *real* challenge.''

Calli pushed herself away.

Luke had a grin on his face. ''Don't go getting all riled up here, Calli.''

''Then I think you'd better start explaining yourself, Lucas Northrup. That sounds a bit domineering.''

''We need to give control to Him. We're told not to worry, to give our troubles to Him. That goes against our instinct. Submission is trusting.''

''I've tried. Really, I have.''

Luke found his fingers in her hair. ''I'm not criticizing you. I'm the same way. It wasn't until I came to terms with being a single father and quit trying to make a relationship where there was none that He gave me you. And I'll admit, it's going to take some time to learn to submit myself and my responsibility for Jon to anyone else.''

She gazed at him with admiration. ''Then you get two women to deal with at the same time. I take it Jon and his mother are getting along since he's staying with her family.''

Luke filled her in on their meeting and Jon's eagerness to visit with Nancy's family.

"Dinner should be ready in about an hour. Why don't you lie down for a few minutes, while I get everything ready?"

She furrowed her brows at him. "Wait a minute, Northrup. One minute you're telling me to be submissive, then you start telling me what to do. Get back here. You aren't going to tease me like that, then go fix dinner."

He knelt on one leg in front of her and placed his arms on the supporting knee. "I also promised your parents that I'd take care of you, and I have every intention on spending the rest of my life doing it. Starting right now. I don't want your back to get sore and tired."

"Really? The rest of our lives?" The sparkle returned to her eyes. "It's that easy for you to forgive me, after all I did wrong?"

"Well, you still have a problem with dating a cop?"

"No."

"Still think we should keep it platonic?"

She was silent.

"Just give me your honest feelings, Cal," Luke continued.

"No," she said in the whisper he'd come to recognize as A.C.'s raspy voice.

"Please don't be afraid, Calli. I was mad and hurt. I won't deny that. But my love for you is stronger than anything the enemy can throw in our way. You are a gift from God for Jon and me." Luke pulled something from his shirt pocket and held it firmly in his hand. He looked into her eyes. They were filled with a curious and deep longing. He moved forward and kissed her, in hopes of answering her unspoken request.

"Each time I tried to refuel the anger, God had erased more and more of it, until it sunk in how many times He's forgiven me." Luke let his gaze roam, lovingly taking in the way Calli had dressed to cover her injuries. He realized she must be suffering on a hot summer day like today.

"I promise there will be no more secrets, Luke." She stared into his eyes and blushed at his loving appraisal. "What?"

"Calli, I love you. Will you be my wife?" He opened his hand, revealing a diamond surrounded by rubies. "'A good wife who can find? She is far more precious than jewels. The heart of her husband trusts in her, and he will have no lack in gain.' I'm in no position to argue with the wisdom of God."

She lowered her thick black lashes, another tear escaping from the corner of her eye. "Oh, Luke, I want nothing more than to be your wife and the mother of your children. This ring is so…awesome."

He took her hand in his and placed the ring on her finger. "Now will you lie down and rest for a few minutes? Jon planned this wonderful dinner for us, and he won't let us forget it if I chicken out."

"Chicken out?"

An hour later, Luke led Calli to the table and turned the lights out, leaving the room in candlelight shadows. Luke pulled the chair out for Calli and helped her into the cushioned seat. "I think a promise of tomorrow should start with a symbolic gesture." He turned to the kitchen counter and set a plate in front of Calli with a single barbecued rib on it. "I'd give anything for you, Calli."

The corner of her lips turned up as she held the rib in the air. "This looks like something Jon would come up with." She pulled the meat from the bone and smiled. "I didn't think your ribs were this meaty."

"I guess you'll just have to set a wedding date so you can find out." Luke's chuckle was deep and tormenting.

Calli leaned over and whispered in his ear.

"Tomorrow?" Luke said, managing no more than a hoarse whisper.

"My parents are here, your parents already have plans to take Jon to the cabin for a few days. I'm not working yet, and you have a few more days off. That way we can look for a house together. Promise me tomorrow, Luke."

"You can have all my tomorrows, Calli. I promise."

Epilogue

Jon braked to a stop by the emergency room entrance. Calli had called Luke at the precinct from her cellular phone and he was already waiting at the hospital. After two years of marriage, the sight of him in uniform still did make her heart beat faster. His smile was welcome reassurance. "If I'd known you were having contractions when I left for work, I wouldn't have gone."

Calli slid out of the SUV and waddled to the wheelchair. "I wasn't. My water broke a block from Jon's school. Contractions are already coming five minutes apart. Glad I wasn't the one driving through this traffic." She took a deep breath. "It's not supposed to happen this fast with a first baby."

He turned the chair around and started to close the truck door. "Jon, go ahead and move it to a parking place. I don't want to leave Calli. Be careful. We'll be on the third floor, labor rooms." His voice was amazingly calm.

"Wait, don't forget the labor bag. It's in the tr..." Calli gasped, arched her back and took a cleansing breath, clutching the arms of the chair so tightly that her knuckles turned white.

"Jon'll bring it in. I admitted you already. They're ready for us." Luke closed the door and pushed the chair up the ramp, then took the elevator to the third floor. Before they reached the labor room, Calli's breathing had become more shallow and rapid. "Slow down, honey."

"I'd love to, but I don't think the baby is crazy about the idea."

They both laughed. "I hear impatience is inherited." The irony of the statement hit him as they rushed down the hall.

The nurse helped Calli move to the bed and into a gown. "Your doctor has been called, Mrs. Northrup. How are you doing?" After all the formalities and making sure Calli was as comfortable as could be expected, she reminded them to do their breathing.

Luke held her hand. "Come on, honey, breathe slow. In, out." Luke dabbed a cool washcloth on Calli's face, and gave her a kiss, hoping to distract her for a minute. "Want some ice chips?"

Calli squeezed his hand. When the contraction was over, she relaxed and stared into her husband's green eyes, feeling less anxious already.

"Did either of you call the Youth Outreach Center to tell Pastor Ortiz that you wouldn't be able to keep your appointments today?"

She nodded. "Shelly started covering my counseling schedule a week ago. I was just taking drop-ins."

Jon peeked his head into the room. "Can I come in?"

Calli smiled, motioning for him to join them.

"Hand me the T-shirt from the bag, son. I need to change."

The almost sixteen-year-old tossed the shirt to his dad. "Here you go."

Calli had a serious look on her face.

Almost ready to change, Luke paused and leaned close. "What's wrong, honey?"

"I can't decide if I want to kiss you for giving me a baby, or kick you out of the room...forever." Luke laughed, not feeling a bit threatened.

"Isn't transition wonderful?" Suddenly she grabbed his hand and squeezed as an intense contraction began.

Luke struggled one-handed with the last button, and the remainder of the navy shirt dangled between them. "Honey, you've got to let go of my hand for *just* a minute so I can take this thing off." When she didn't let go, he tugged the bulky shirt back to his own wrist until the contraction ended, then tossed it into an empty chair and quickly pulled the other shirt on.

"What brought this on so suddenly?"

Jon stepped forward. "She let me drive to school."

Luke nudged his son with an elbow. "Well, that explains everything. Give me a break, Cal. I'd think you'd have better sense than to take a fifteen-year-old driving two days past your due date."

Calli's smile was cut short by the intensity of the contraction. She squeezed his hand tighter. He grimaced. She let go, then immediately grabbed his shirt and pulled him closer. "Ou-uee."

"This is happening so fast I'm not even going to need that goody bag full of candy bars, am I?" She was beyond distraction. "Breathe, Calli." Luke bumped into the bed and held her face between his hands. "In, two, three. Out, two, three."

Jon continued the story, unaware that the baby's birth was imminent. "All of a sudden, Calli was laughing, and said something about her water breaking. I didn't..."

"Jon, go get the doctor. Come on sweetie, breathe with me. Pant, Calli. Hee, hee, hee, haw." His heart swelled with love as he watched her pained expressions.

"C...a...aaan't," she gasped, then held her breath.

"*No,* Calli don't push yet. You've got to wait a minute, honey. Just a few more minutes, sweetie. Jon... The doctor."

The teenager's eyes grew wide. "Y-you mean?"

"Pant, Callie. Jon, go get the doctor, *now!*"

"I'm out of here."

"Luke..." She gasped when the contraction ended. "Is it supposed to happen this fast?"

"You're doing great, Calli. Have I mentioned how much I love you?" He touched her round belly and smiled, then wiped her forehead again. "Looks like Jon's going to get that baby he's been asking for, and just in time for his birthday."

Tears filled her eyes, and she made no attempt to stop them.

"You okay, honey?"

"Do I *look* okay? I'm having a baby."

"You look beautiful." He kissed her forehead, half expecting her to push him away.

The doctor rushed into the room with the nurse following. "Have a little one in a hurry to get here, huh?"

Luke nodded. "She wasn't even having contractions three hours ago when I left for work."

The nurse scurried to get everything ready. "Your son changed his mind about watching. He's going to wait in the hall."

Luke nodded, peering past the woman to see what the doctor was doing, and chuckled. "He lasted longer than I thought he would."

Everything started happening all at once, and soon Calli delivered a beautiful baby girl.

Two hours later, Calli closed her eyes, knowing little Cara Michelle was in her daddy's expert hands. "Luke, don't forget to call Mom and Dad.'' He spooned some ice chips into Calli's mouth and leaned over to kiss her.

''Already done. Grandma and Grandpa Giovanni are en route as we speak. And by now, all the aunts and uncles should have heard the news, too.''

Calli was exhausted, but couldn't stand to fall asleep and miss all this excitement. ''She's beautiful, isn't she?''

''Cara's as beautiful as her mother. Get some sleep, honey. Your daughter's going to need to eat before too long.''

Luke sat on the edge of the hospital bed, the tiny infant wrapped securely in her daddy's strong hands with Grammy Northrup standing nearby watching.

''Who would have thought when you walked into Calli's hospital room that night that you'd wind up back here married and having a baby?'' his mother reminisced, admiring her granddaughter.

Luke lifted his eyebrows. ''I did.'' Luke leaned across the bed and pressed his lips to Calli's. She quivered at the sweet tenderness of his kiss. ''You looked so helpless, I wanted to protect you even then. Little did I know…''

Calli blushed. ''Yeah, yeah, enough already. Could you hand me my ice, Lieutenant Northrup?''

Luke chuckled as they both seemed to remember their awkward first meeting. ''Here, let me help,'' he teased.

Luke's father wrapped an arm around each—his son and grandson. ''What do you think, Jon?''

''She's okay, for a girl.'' The teenager beamed proudly, despite his nonchalant attitude. ''It's a great birthday present. About time Dad remembered. Now, who's going to take me to get my driver's license tomorrow?''

Luke and Calli looked at each other and laughed. ''Maybe your mother would like that honor.''

''Mom and Jack are coming for my birthday? Cool.'' He

slapped Luke a high-five, then froze. ''Hey, wait. When's their baby due?''

''Not *that* soon,'' Calli interrupted, thrilled with Jon's adjustment to having not only one mother, but two.

Cara opened her eyes and looked at Luke. ''Hi there, my little sweetheart,'' he cooed, gently rocking his tiny daughter.

Jon washed his hands in the sink and rushed to have a turn holding his little sister. ''Come on, Dad, it's my turn.'' Luke carefully placed the infant in Jon's arms. His smile grew wider. ''Good thing you weren't an October baby, or Dad would probably call you pumpkin!''

Calli smiled at her family. She hadn't a clue what she'd done for excitement before these two came into her life. And something told her, this was just the beginning.

* * * * *

Dear Reader,

My father was a law enforcement officer for twenty-five years, so I have always held a high esteem for those men and women who every day face risks that many of us take for granted. I felt this was a perfect story to combine the tough and tender sides of a police officer hero who lives his Christian faith in spite of the overwhelming challenges of his career. Throw in a teenager and a heroine who has yet to overcome a painful past, and we see what it takes to turn ordinary people into our everyday heroes.

As Christians, we often hear individuals ask, "Why does God allow bad things to happen to good people?" That's not only hard to answer, but hard to comprehend. Moving on after something bad happens is often a sheer act of faith. It takes courage and trust in His almighty power. When we look back on difficult times and challenges, we frequently wonder how we ever made it through. It is during these times that we learn to cling to His truths and promises.

This past year, I've come to understand the promises made in *Thessalonians.* A few weeks after I lost a brother-in-law to leukemia, my father had a heart attack, and a few months later, my mother had a stroke.

God never promised an easy road, for believers or nonbelievers alike. We're all His children. For those who trust in Him, comfort comes in knowing that though we must struggle here on earth, the celebration of our victory is already being prepared.

I hope you enjoy Luke and Calli's challenging walk to forgiveness and love.

Feel free to write to me at: P.O. Box 5021, Greeley, CO 80631-0021.

Carol Steward